Also by Greg Greene

Newton's Law – The Twelfth Imam

Alain LeDoux

NEWTON'S LAW

SOMEONE'S CHILD

BOOK ONE
OF
The Newton's Law Series

by
GREG GREENE

Our Hill Publishing
A division of
GGA

This novel is a work of fiction. The characters, names, incidents, dialogue, and plot are the products of the author's imagination or are used fictitiously. Any resemblance to actual persons, companies or events is purely coincidental.

ISBN: **978-0-9810742-0-7**

For All my Children
And Eva

CHAPTER ONE

Her lips were a slash of red. One of those bright glitzy colors sold at the local five-and-dime. Around her eyes the remains of eyeliner clashed with the mascara. The eyes were blue, maybe green in the right light. But this was not the right light. She was at that age of timelessness that comes too soon to some women, and never to others. With the awkwardness of adolescence replaced by innate grace and flowing motion. This was the time she would be remembered for most, it was for her the only time, it was the end of time; she was dead.

Her body staked out its place on the beach. Around her the tide-packed sand formed like a bier, garnished with seaweed and framed by driftwood. The stars, if they could have shone through the clouds, would have reflected with the moonlight off the sea. The sand would appear light in color, with the larger logs casting dark holes in the landscape. She was not alone as she waited for the dawn, and the first of the day's visitors to arrive. Already she was joined by the creatures of the night. Small crabs skittered nervously under the lowering clouds. Bats circled in the air above, sending blasts of sound waves out to navigate and seek out their prey. At another time, she might have played with them on the beach, throwing up small stones to reflect the bat-radar. They would join in the game, suddenly changing course and swooping toward the stones until their steady downward course revealed that they were just objects and not prey. Not alive at all, dead, just as she was.

She might have sat on a log that had broken loose by a long forgotten storm, from a mill destined boom, and wondered at the kiss of the wind and rain on her cheek. It might have been summer, and warm, or winter and brisk, with the wind rising from the sea and carrying her golden tresses behind her. It might have been a lot of things, and perhaps where she now was, if you believed in such things, it might yet be still. But here, in this world, the time of What might be had gone, and the time of never was upon her. Such kisses that had come in her life were now the memories of others. Relatives, friends, perhaps a lover who waited still for her return.

At the horizon, the rising sun cast its glow on the underside of the still threatening clouds. The rain abated, leaving her body glistening and the air hung with humidity. If you believed in fairy princesses, she might be taken for one, but Newton had long ago given up such thoughts. Fairy princesses did not exist in the world Newton knew, but the same could not be said for the great evil that good was supposed to overcome. It was that evil, which brought him to this place. An early morning jogger, his footprints etching the still firm sand, had discovered her, made the call to the police, and started the next step in the young girl's journey.

 The phone on the nightstand barked and Newton had shaken the sleep out of his head prior to answering. As he got older, the process had taken more time to accomplish, and he had adjusted the number of rings before the answering machine kicked in upwards with his age. A glance at the phone confirmed the call came from the station; that always meant trouble.
 "Good morning Newton," the voice of the dispatcher, Charley Reddings, welcomed him to the new day.
 "It's never a good morning when you call this early, Charley, what do you have for me?"
 "A body on the beach, up off Parker Avenue, last public lot, no obvious signs, reported by a jogger."
Newton cradled the wireless receiver to his ear as he shifted out of bed. "Who's on the way?"
 "Regular district car—one man unit, new guy named... here it is, William George Fitzgibbons."
Newton cycled through his memory and came up empty "Never worked with him, better have the sergeant head out there ASAP."
 "Already on the way, Alfred," Charley responded.
 "OK, I'll be there soon as I can."
 "The car should be there as we speak." Charley said, hanging up.

 The police arrived in thei usual fashion for a small department. First the patrol officers arrived in a speeding car garnished with lights, its passage accentuated by the threatening voice of the siren.
'Move it buddy, I'm coming through'!
Luck would dictate the particular officer driving, and as luck would have it, it was a young officer. Possessing just enough time on the job to be let out upon the public alone, while still impressed with the lessons of the academy. William Fitzgibbons had the cruiser moving as fast as he dared heading down the public road that ran along the top of the bench. Houses, old and new crowded both sides of the road. Beach front property was at a premium, and the lots were narrow. To his right, the beams of the headlights reflected off the sign marking the location of the parking lot. He arrived in a flurry of gravel and a cloud of dust that caught up to and enveloped his cruiser. The siren died away, the flashing lights remained a beacon for those cars to

follow. Meeting the jogger at the top of the stairs Fitzgibbons adjusted his hat and took out his notebook.

"Are you the one who called?"
"Yes I am, Johnson, Mark Leslie, 837 West Thetis Drive, 555-4532."
Fitzgibbons wrote fast to keep up, the excitement changing his normally neat handwriting into the scribble that would probably follow him throughout his career.
"OK, slow down a little, no one is going anywhere, tell me what you found."
"It's the body of a girl, young, late teens, fully clothed. She is lying below the high tide mark, the sand is packed, no footprints other than mine, appears to be washed ashore. The tide turned at 03:47 and is now flooding. I saw no external trauma or obvious marks."
"Who do you work for?" Fitzgibbons asked, intrigued by the clipped, accurate description.
"Department of Defence, I'm an accident investigator for the Air Force."

The interview was completed and together they went down far enough that his light could illuminate the scene. Other patrol cars arrived, along with the sergeant and inspector in charge of the shift. A quick look confirmed the jogger's account, and the appropriate calls were made for an identification team and a response by homicide.

Homicide was a small unit in a small department. In this case led by Alfred Newton, a twenty-year veteran who had once stood in the same shoes as the young constable now guarding the stairway. He was a tall man in his youth, over six feet tall with a lineman's build. The long hair of his twenties now returned to the brush cut of his childhood. Ease of maintenance had taken precedence over the need to impress the ladies. He was a quiet man, thoughtful and loved to read. Like his namesake, he preferred to swim in the scientific stream of life and was the child who loved to take things apart, find out the how and why of it, and then rebuild it.

Objects were easy to figure out, people were more difficult and life was the most difficult of all. He had been married, once, but that had slipped away like so many things in his life, and the mystery of it still eluded him. He had a daughter, but she too had slipped away. Gone on a quiet summer night when he was off "fighting crime and/or evil" as those in his line of work put it. Of the two, he had wound up spending most of his time fighting evil.

Every life encounters evil in some fashion. For those unlucky few, it comes with the force of a freezing wind in January. But for most of us, it swirls on the periphery of our vision, we know it is there, but are unwilling or unable to confront it. For this girl, it had come with the force of a run-away train. Even with a path marked out and all the warning signs and lights, collision was unavoidable. Newton's job was to determine if it had come from within or without, and in either case, to track down when and where it had spawned.

Newton was a seasoned detective; his profession entailed the asking of questions, both of others and within himself. His days and nights were filled with the finding of how, and when, and why. To Newton, the reason WHY was the most important item on the list. WHY explained When and Who, the How and Where were mostly a matter of circumstance. They mattered only to lead to the answer of WHY, and WHY answered all.

This was Newton's law.

Alfred Newton had long ago garnered the nickname of Sir Isaac. It was of course a natural consequence of his seemingly single-minded pursuit of WHY. Others who practiced this trade sought different truths, for Newton there was only one sure truth, knowing WHY made the rest, if not irrelevant, then certainly much less important.

WHY, he thought, WHY here, WHY now, and perhaps more importantly WHY her?

He would try to place himself in the shoes of others, and imagine how their lives had been. What situations would have led them to where he found them, or where he sought them?

Yes, she would have asked why in those final moments, those brief seconds of measured time in which one's life is said to pass before their eyes. He imagined it a brief book in her case.

Would there be an announcer? An angel who sat turning the pages, pointing at passages outlined in burning flames where one transgressed?
But what transgressions could come with one so young, not yet fully formed in mind or body?
Would the passages of good be accompanied by a choir's song? With words on pages writ large, with the heavenly congregation nodding in approval—Amazing Grace echoing in the background.

WHY ME?

When those precious moments of her time had slipped away—was her question answered?

Could he answer it now?

Time would tell, he thought as he made his way to the scene.
In his world, time was real, and the clock had started.

When Newton hung up, the phone rang in another house across town. Alice Haggerty murmured a 'hello' into the phone and then jostled her husband Gary awake.
"Hello?"
"Sorry to wake you, Gary," Charley's voice rang with a tinny echo on the phone line, "We need you to respond to a call on Parker."
"Who's the lead?"
"Newton."
"On my way." Gary said and hung the phone up.
"Sorry, babe, gotta go," Gary said to his wife who had already drifted back to sleep.
Once in his car, Gary switched on the police radio and contacted the other members of his team. He knew that if Newton was involved, it was a body; nothing else could get that much attention at this time of the day. All this call out of personnel was expensive and only the most serious of circumstances would warrant it.

Charley had also contacted the weather service, rain was the enemy of a possible crime scene out in the open, and the forecast was not good. It was always a race with the forces of nature to record the scene and recover the evidence.

Right now the race was with the morning tide, which had turned in the same age-old fashion that was repeated daily on all the beaches that bordered all the seas ever since the Earth had captured the moon in its orbit and held it hostage there. It was making its way back up to the tide line, back to reclaim all which it had revealed a few hours ago, like a magician, hiding the elusive pea back under a shell in a timeless game.

Alfred Newton was an expert at finding the pea and exposing the con. Logical in his thinking and methodical in his methods, the detective investigated each case as his noted ancestor had pursued scientific truth. All detectives looked at the evidence that was available to them, but Newton took it a step further. He visualized not only the crime scene, but used the evidence to construct a picture of the life that was, or might have been. Life, he found, is always a series of small steps punctuated by a few large ones. People tended to remember the large ones, the births, deaths, funerals, and weddings. There were many more photos in the albums of the world of new cars, houses, and jobs than the everyday shopping trip. Having worked with him before, Gary knew what Newton would want in the way of photographs and was meticulous in his setup. He had set his camera equipment on the tripod he always carried. Unlike others in his trade, he disliked the freehand method of taking pictures, and the tripod provided a much more stable platform and really took no longer to set up. Newton would use the photos to set the scene in his mind. The photographs would show the scene ahead of the tide, recording in digital and film media the positions of all the objects on the beach that were of interest. Others would continue the search for what they already knew they would not find. An object out of place, an unexplained footprint, an article of clothing perhaps. Here the sand around her already told them what they needed to know, the sea had delivered her to this place, and now they would take her away from it.

But before the sea had delivered her, where had she been?

"All done Alfred," Gary said, packing up the equipment.
"Not that much here that I can see." Newton was staring out over the black water, beyond the circle of artificial light. His fingers idly running through the stubble of his hair, and massaging the scar on his temple, a souvenir of a time long ago when Newton had been forced to take a life. The photographs would repeat what he had seen for the rest of the investigators, posted on a white board, examined by all and sundry. No obvious signs of trauma, no obvious signs of having been dumped on the spot, no obvious reason WHY.

At the top of the stairs carved into the edge of the bank and framed with wood and rock, another junior constable, his boots still retaining the academy shine, stood alone with notebook in hand. On the pages, line by line, he recorded the comings and goings of the investigators drawn to the scene. Names, times in, times out, and who they represented, read like refrains from a prayer book.

"What do you have so far Eddie?"
Eddie Hurlman, a small energetic man, looked up from his notebook at Fitzgibbons, and read out the list. His clipped speech and precise

enunciation reminded Fitzgibbons of a lawyer questioning a witness; just the facts, pure and simple with no embellishments. Newton was there of course, as the lead investigator, dressed in his usual slacks and shirt, no tie, black loafers with black socks. At this hour he wore an oiled cotton jacket that made no sound when the material rubbed together. Not like the modern nylon shells the front line officers wore. The forensic team followed, with their equipment packed in metal cases and nylon bags. Some reporters, drawn by the movement of the detectives, waited in the parking lot drinking coffee. Their cameras panned the parking lot, recording background, some took shots of the beach—what little they could see of it in the dark, and the reporters themselves were practicing their lines for the 15-second clips.

"This is Jason Goddard reporting for CHEK TV news, coming to you live from a beach parking lot on Parker Avenue where the body of a young woman has just been discovered." His voice was somber, just above a whisper, tinged with sadness—the universal announcement of a death.

"How's that?"
The cameraman checked his equipment, rewinding the tape a short distance and playing it back through his earphones.
"Scratchy." the camera operator announced after a moment, "Better try it again."
"I told them these old tapes needed replacing," the reporter complained, "but no one ever listens."

Fitzgibbons and Hurlman nodded their heads in agreement; some things are universal amongst corporations.

The lights on the camera flashed on again and the reporter ran through another take for his announcement. This would be followed by an interview of one of the detectives if possible. "You know this guy?" The reporter had asked Fitzgibbons, "I don't think I know him, what's his name—Newton? Will he talk to us?"
"How long have you been doing the crime beat?"
"Two and a half years now."
"How many interviews has he given you?"
"Well—none actually."
"So what do you think of your chances when the lead detective has never given you an interview in all that time?"
The reporter nodded his head in understanding.
Fitzgibbons turned to the rookie and motioned to the receding back of the reporter, "And that, Eddie, is what we in police work call 'a clue'."

The next to arrive were the personnel from coroner's office. Their dark hearse drew up in the public parking lot; curtains on the windows and the company logo on the doors, in small gold print. It was just enough to inform, but not so much as to alarm. They waited, drinking coffee from Styrofoam cups and talking in hushed voices—all the better not to wake the dead.

Below them on the beach, the camera flashes that had filled the air like nightclub strobes, died out, and the identification team started filing up the stairway. As the last one to climb the 47 stairs, Gary nodded to the coroner's people, and they unloaded the gurney and began the trip down.

On the beach, the detectives waited with her. Newton stood alone, to the side, as he often did, the damp sand still sticking to his shoes. He had the handwritten preliminary report in his hand from the initial investigation. It said more about what was not found than what was. No obvious signs of foul play, no marks, no bruises, no broken bones. The cause of death was a mystery now for the pathologist to solve.

He looked down at the young girl.

Who are you, he asked to himself; and what brought you to this place, this time, this oh so premature death, and WHY, why are you here?

To the east, the sun broke over the horizon. A new day was dawning, and life went on. Soon the city would begin to stir, the roads would fill with traffic, and folks would bustle off to their jobs. Somewhere, he thought, there is a bed not slept in. Is there a mother or father checking the room of their daughter? Were they just now finding her gone? Perhaps she was a roommate who did not come home last night, maybe somewhere a partner who left after a fight.

Somewhere, someone has a hole in their heart.

The coroner's group descended the last of the steps and stretched the gurney out to full length from its sitting position. The wind rose off the sea, tugging at the blankets. Even now, the sea reached for her again. It was as if, since all life came from its waters, it was only fitting that it should return there to complete the cycle. Especially woman, the wellspring returning to the well, wheels in wheels.

The gurney wheels did not roll well on the sand, and so they ended up carrying it anyway. Once beside her, they drew back the blanket and removed a large black rubber bag.

The wind died away, the sun briefly broke through the clouds, and the warm morning light shone down on her blonde hair. Its oblique rays lit her face as if it was a photographer's light, placed off to the side. The shadows played at the corners of her mouth, giving a smile to her slightly parted lips. The world around her fell silent. The birds stilled their songs, the waves grew calm upon the sea, and unconsciously on the part of some, deliberate for many, there was a measurable pause in the beat of life.

One of the attendants bent forward and slowly zipped the bag shut.

The sun slipped again behind the clouds and the rain beat against the earth.

The two funeral home attendants found that the gurney wheels refused to roll at all with the new weight upon them. As they grasped the sides, four of the investigators fell in beside them. Grasping the chrome rails of the gurney, they snapped the wheels up and proceeded in step along the beach and up the stairs.

The reporter's cameras clicked away, recording the event for their respective papers, radio, and TV stations. No one paused in the rain to give an interview, and no one asked. Time enough for that later.

The hearse pulled away slowly from the parking lot, escorted by the same constable who had been marking down names. Traffic was heavy as it built up for the morning rush hour. The rain continued, beating on the roof and flowing like tears across the windshield. The steady beat of the wipers supplying the drum beat of a funeral dirge.

Newton followed in his car, eyes on the hearse, with his mind on other things—organizing the immediate investigation for today, and for the days to follow. The first 48 hours were crucial. Manpower was always in short supply with the number of available detectives few and so far the clues were fewer. He ran through the obvious avenues of inquiry in his mind; like scenes from a movie, the questions played on the screen of his mind.

Was there a car sitting empty somewhere?
A passenger who had not arrived?

An office missing a worker?

He knew the normal reporting period for a missing co-worker was hours at best and days at worse. She was too young to likely have a record of perfect attendance. People in her age group typically missed a few days due to partying, and so being absent for a day or two would not seem out of place.

Newton thought it unlikely that she had her own car, it would be better if she had been a member of a car pool. The others in her group would notice her absence right off, after waiting at the appointed spot for her to show up. Likely, they would not wait long, perhaps one of them would check on her...banging on the door, maybe calling her later after they got to work.

If she did own a car, where was it? There were many parking lots in the area, they would be checked by the parking patrol, and most were jealously guarded by the surrounding residents. If there was an unoccupied vehicle in the area, they would know about it before noon—especially after the word went out to the day shift to look specifically for one.

Newton picked up the radio and punched in a series of numbers on its keypad. This connected him to a recorder in his office. The dayshift would automatically check it for instructions when they arrived later in the morning.

"This is Newton," he began, "check on the following." The message laying out the plan for the team to follow in crisp logical sequences, tinged with intuition.

If the car was at a marina, she was likely to have been on a boat of some sort, unless she swum out from shore, then it probably would be parked in a common area of some sort. He would have a phone call made to all the marinas within 50 miles and have them check for a vehicle that appeared out of place.

Details, so many details. Somewhere there existed the evidence of her passing through the sea of life, as would a boat that leaves a fluorescent trail when it churns up the water at night. Like that surreal light, it can only be seen for a short time before it dims and is swallowed by the currents around it.

The journey continued. The suspension system of the hearse specifically designed to absorb the bumps in the road, torsion bars took the lean out of the corners. In the back, there was no swaying on the gurney.

Was it odd to have so gentle a journey for those who could not notice? Was it compassion that compelled the custom? A way providing what life did not—a smooth passage? Or was it collective guilt from doing, or not doing, enough for them in life?

A funeral procession is by tradition, marked by lights, from the torches of ages long ago, to lanterns and the modern equivalent, the lights of the mourner's automobiles. The acknowledged reason was to light the way for the dead. The truth is it was to light the way for the living. Funerals are not for those who have passed, but for those who remain. It is the living who fear the dark; the dead have no fears.

With its lights on, the hearse made its way through the morning traffic. By habit or design, those already on the road deferred to its passage. Making room for it where they would not for others.

Better you than me?

Was this the road that led her here?

Did she travel it alone? Or did she have company, A friend, a lover—if so, where were they?

No buses ran by here—would there have been a taxi perhaps?

Another detail to check.

Stopped at a light, Newton looked over to a corner playground.

Children were playing in the manner that children do. Some made use of the playground equipment, others formed teams and played tag, hide and seek, and other games.

Did she play there or somewhere similar as a child?

Would she have been one of the group on the slide, laughing in fear or delight as they slid down the polished metal?

Look Mom—I DID IT! All by myself!!

Did she fall, scrape a knee, and run to...........who?

A parent? A sibling? A nanny?

Did she play on the merry-go-round? Holding on with white fingers while those boys spun it faster and faster? She would show them she was just as brave as they were, no matter how she felt inside. Dumb boys anyway—why did they always wreck everything—why couldn't they just play nice?

And why did she care about what they thought anyway?

Maybe she was a loner, sitting on a swing or bench, rocking gently, lost in her own thoughts, trying to find meaning in her own world.

Too scared to go home? If so, WHY? Where was the greater danger, without or within?

The light changed and the hearse and the world moved on.

Another road, another path. This one led through a neighborhood, long ago consumed by the greater need to move traffic in the city. The quiet residential street had been widened over time. The schools, all in a row were built in different times. Large substantial sandstone buildings built at a time when labour costs were cheap enough to make them economically possible. Their playgrounds and sports fields now wore skirts of chain-link fencing, to protect the kids from the world.

But the world came in anyway.

Elementary, Junior High and Senior High schools or if you like, regular, middle, and senior, same school different names. Different kids—or just different times?

Had she gone to one of these schools?

Newton would check. Her picture now pale and wan would be compared against the hundreds that papered the walls.

Miss Rose's Class of '92 Grade 6. Mr.Peabody's graduating class 1967 and on they went. The school debating class—winners of the city championships 1989, the sports teams and science classes.

Bright scrubbed faces, the future in miniature. Where are they now?

Was she there, a face staring back?

Did she attend one of these schools? Did her spirit now roam for a moment reliving those playground and high school moments?

"Miss Smith! Bobby Carlson is throwing things again—MISS SMITH!"

"Well, really, Sally Robertson, I NEVER said any such thing about you."

"Beverly, did you see those boys playing football? That Jimmy West is sooo cute!"

"The prom? No, not yet, no one's asked me, mom, no one ever asks me to dance anyway—I'M SO UGLY!"

Giggles in hallways, furtive looks in the parking lot, whispers between friends, notes given and received, mementoes of moments now forever gone.

Those first days in September, when school started up again, new clothes, new friends, new classes. Over the years "What did you do?" would be replaced with "Who did you meet?" as the number one question. There was always an answer to the first, not always the second.

What thoughts then—when there were no new friendships, no summer romances, no dreams to carry you forward into the next year of your life. The biggest anticipation was the start of another year at school—and when there were no more of those to look forward to, what did one see on the horizon of life?

The hearse moved on.

The road led through neighbourhoods long gone, replaced by shopping malls and retail outlets.

Had she once walked these streets too?

A group of girls waited on the corner, chatting amongst themselves. Only one turned to look at the hearse, did she feel some connection? Had she been a friend?

Did she feel some invisible tug reach out to her, a tiny voice that whispered loud unheard words?

"LOOK AT ME!"

"I'M HERE!"

"I EXISTED!"

"I matter—don't I? Didn't I?"

The connection faded and the voices ceased, replaced with the noises of here and now.

Was there a time when they had been to the mall together? Wandering in and out of the clothing shops trying on the current fashions? Checking out the cosmetic counters, trying things there that they would not, or could not, at home?

The food courts would be filled with kids, all sizes, groups, and ages. Her picture would be shown to the staff and posted on the bulletin boards.

"Do you know this girl?"
"Have you seen her?"

One never knew where leads would come from.

The tags on her clothing were common to the big box stores, millions made in some far off factory on a foreign shore. Nothing special about the size or colour; they would be checked of course. There was always the chance that the dye lot was a special run to accommodate a store's special opening or celebration.

"That's right, Miss, only this store sells that shade of blue."

The city featured many attractions for families beyond those of the malls and schools and neighbourhood parks. It was, after all, a tourist destination. The harbour boats regularly plied the waters showing those who were interested in the views available only from the sea. Some of the larger boats took folks out to the straits where killer whales, 'orcas', made regular visits throughout the year. There was scuba diving for those inclined to endure the claustrophobia of the dark and cold waters in order to visit the sites of long ago tragedies.

The grand hotels that lined the waterfront offered a glimpse into a more genteel age for all who wished to take a step back in time.

If she could take a step back now, would she?

Would she try to change the course of events?

Was it despair or desperation that flooded her senses at the end?

Did her spirit walk even now amongst the glass-walled rooms of the conservatory, or the paneled rooms of the grand foyer where tea was served at 4 PM in the custom of the old country?

"Yes, dear, you look lovely."
"Do I?" She asked dressed in a light coloured cotton dress, short sleeved with ruffles, gloves and a wide brimmed hat completed the outfit. She stared at her reflection in the full length mirror. What did she see?
Apart from the superficial reflection of images thrown back from the silvered glass, what else presented itself to her mind's eye?

Did she see herself as a young lady, sweeping through a room filled with young men dressed in formal suits of black and shirts of white with ruffles tied at their throats?

Would some be dressed in formal military attire, bright red and blues and shades of green? Medals pinned to their jackets, swords at their sides ready to defend her against the world.

If she did—they didn't—did they?

Or did she feel awkward, playing a role in a scene directed by a mother whose vision of what might have been and might yet be was out of step with what was and would likely be.

Did the reflection of the clothing in the mirror give way to jeans and a shirt tucked in at the waist with sleeves rolled up? The hat disappeared, replaced by long blonde hair tied up in a pony tail, the gloves gave way to slender fingers holding the reins of a stallion, snorting at the ready, impatient with being held back, wanting, like her, to get on with life.

Perhaps the vision in her mind was much blacker. The room transferred into a small apartment with locks and chains on the door. A tiny kitchen, a living room filled with a TV, stereo, and books, with a small bedroom that had few visitors other than herself, a lonely place with a lonelier spirit.

The hearse moved steadily through traffic, with the police car trailing it, and Newton following. Constable Hurlman would be occupied with taking notes, talking into a portable recorder, noting the time and places of this journey.

"8:05 AM: vehicle stopped at corner of Douglas and Government waiting for light to change."

These notes would be transcribed and the tape made available for any who needed to hear. The purpose was to document the minutiae of the trip to show the courts that no one had an opportunity to alter any evidence. This may, after all, be a homicide, perhaps the most important case the young officer would see in his career. Homicides, despite all the TV shows, were not that common, and in this city scarcer still. His teachers at the academy had been explicit, and he had been thoroughly drilled in the documentation of the chain of custody. In due time the notes he had made at the scene, and those he was making now, would form part of the official record of the young girl's last days. He gave it his full attention, keeping the language structure within that prescribed by the legal community as being acceptable.

Newton knew well the questions the lawyers would ask, having himself been in court many times.
"And what did you mean, Constable, when you stated in your notes that you were waiting for the lights? Were they operating correctly? Or was there a problem with them? Did you take your attention away from the vehicle for any length of time?"
Hurlman and Fitzgibbons would both be subject to this examination, routine in its nature, important in its context. A check and balance in the system that evolved to ensure no shortcuts were taken and nothing was overlooked that would prove to be important in hindsight.

Only later, perhaps years later, would they come to feel the impact of their words. Life, any and all life, is worth so much more than words on paper could ever describe.

The hearse pulled into its accustomed spot. The "Coroner's Parking Only" sign in lettering larger than that on the hearse's doors. Backing up to the loading dock, it came to a gentle stop. The staff got out and went around to the back. Unlocking the doors, they pulled the gurney loose and snapped the legs down into position. The hallway led down a long corridor, the top of which was lit with fluorescent lights. Their light flashed down in patterns of light and dark, like the sun that had marked the days of her life.

One that was too brief, too short.

At the end of it, they moved her from the gurney and placed her on a cold metal slab. On the toe of her right foot they put a tag, with the name Doe, Jane, followed by the date.

The slab rolled silently on rollers, the door closed.

Hours passed, neither long nor short, for they marked a time for her that had no measure. Only the living knew time. In due course she was removed from the metal drawer and moved to a table. A microphone hung from a cord suspended above the table. Its purpose to record the findings of a pathologist whose job it was to determine the cause of death. In time, the words on tape would become words on paper. They were words that for many were the last official markers of life's road.

For some, there would be more, an obituary, a funeral, a memorial service, words of condolences or sympathy, feelings shared amongst friends, the last public sharing of tears.

Who would write such words?
Who would read them?
Who would weep for her now?

The words on paper would become the official findings of the coroner, and due to the nature of the case, they would be communicated to Newton. They would not be long in coming, less than 24 hours in Newton's world, the old world, the world that had been for her. The words spelled out the how, but not the why. The why was Newton's job to find out. Fingerprints had been taken and sent to the appropriate authorities. The initial results would be the same as the final results—no match found. Similarly, DNA taken had also returned no matches. All the modern equipment of law enforcement when bent to the task could not find what was not there. That would form part of the record, her record, no previous contact with the authorities. At least, none serious enough to afford the taking of fingerprints or other markers. So then, what did that mean? Someone who was never the ring leader? Or someone who was never in trouble? If never in trouble, then how did she come to such and end? There are always hangers-on in the periphery of any group. Those who wanted to be more than they were, but were unable for some reason to take the next step into a leadership role, content to be a follower.

There were dental impressions of course, and radiology scans to search for any broken bones that had healed. Everyone makes an impact as they travel on the journey of life. Medical records of some mishap suffered on a piece of playground equipment perhaps, or an accident graduating from a tricycle to a two wheeler.

Look Mom! No hands! Oh that, that's OK, I just skinned my knee, sorry about the jeans though, Mom, you can patch them can't you? I rode my bike all the way down the driveway, all by myself! Aren't you proud of me, Mom? Mom? Are you listening, Mom?

CHAPTER TWO

Starbuck's coffee on Douglas was the coffee destination of choice not only for the regular citizens of the city, but also for the beat constables who patrolled the downtown area. Newton regularly stopped in and chatted with them on his way into the office. His workday officially started at 8 AM, and the night shift ended at about that time. From 7 AM to 8 the tired beats would find a spot to finish paperwork and talk about the events of the night.

"Morning, Smith," Newton called as he took a seat in a corner booth.
"Hey, Alfred," Andy Smith replied. "You're up early."
"Too early for an old guy," came the spirited response. "Are you still working the night shift?"
"Yep, I figure I'm the city's oldest beat cop. At age 52 I'm probably the oldest in the country."
"When are you going to retire and let the next generation take over?"
Andy could have retired years ago, but he loved his job, and as he had said many times—everyone has to do something.
"I'm holding out for a better offer." Andy laughed; his beat was one of the oldest in the country, let alone the city. "But no one has come up with one yet."
"That's not what I hear; you could have a place on my team, just say the word."
"Maybe later, when I get too old to walk these venerated streets."
Andy raised the cup of steaming coffee to his lips.
"So what are these streets telling you these days?" Newton asked.

Victoria, British Columbia is a provincial capital, and as such entitled to a certain amount of government largesse that is not found in other areas of the province. Save those which had the good luck to be the home of a Premier or powerful minister. This was a consequence of the importance of being a capital city. Along with the title came certain public buildings and services. Provincial governments did not pay a land or business tax to the city whose lands they occupied. Instead, they built tourist attractions, and provided a steady payroll, the recipients of which did pay taxes. All in all, it was an equitable trade off. One of those attractions was the provincial museum. In the case of Victoria, it was a large multistoried building of modern design set on the south side of the Inner Harbour. Together with a variety of private and public enterprises they formed an attraction that brought in thousands of visitors and millions of dollars in revenue.

Andy's beat incorporated all the government buildings. Over the years he had gotten to know most of the security guards and regular employees that worked at them. Almost all of the security personnel were part of the Canadian Corps of Commissionaires, a government organization. The only building using a private source on Andy's beat was the most popular amongst the many tourists that visited each year.

"Strange things going on at the museum," Andy responded. "Nothing definite, but I think they got some trouble headed their way."

The museum had gained a much deserved reputation of being a leader in the creation of public displays. These had attracted many artifacts, and the safekeeping of those artifacts meant there was an elaborate security system.

"Oh, and what would be the cause of that," Newton asked, ordering another cup of coffee.

"What else, it's the wannabes that cause the problems. Ever since they changed over to a private security company, things have been going downhill in a big way."

Newton had heard that from other beat cops, some, but not all of which, could be dismissed as the normal friction between the professional police service and the private firms.

"As you know, the turnover there is rapid, so they have a large portion of inexperienced guards and the training is not up to college standards." Newton nodded, all police personnel were trained at the provincial police college while private firms had more "elastic" standards.

"One of the contacts I check in with regularly is the head of security at the museum. I give him a call every now and then to find out about any shift changes I should know about—any new people coming on stream, things like that. Seems like they got a new guy, one of many, I might add, by the name of Reginald Johnson. Like all the new guards he was required to do shift work for which he was frequently late. This brought him to my attention more than once. He drives a bright red convertible which is hard to miss when it's in the parking lot. Now I know what those guys make and when he moved up from a rusted out wreck to a shiny new sports model, well, that gets my attention."

Newton smiled to himself, beat cops like Andy were amongst the best sources of information he had.

"Something is going on there, Alfred." Andy was saying. "Maybe the kid got an inheritance, but I don't think so."
"Did you talk to any of the management people about this?"
"Not yet, no real evidence, just a feeling. You know how that goes."
"Yep, not enough to put in a report about, but enough to keep your eye on to see what develops, and something usually does develop."
"You should have stayed a beat cop Al; you were one of the good ones."
"I'm too old now Andy, I'll have to leave that to you young guys."
"Young—don't give me that, Newton. I'm only a year or two younger than you, although most days I feel older."

 As they were talking, the subject of their conversation was having a very bad day. He was expected in at 8:00 AM sharp to relieve the night guard. The night guard, one Homer Baker, a young man of 23 years and who was trying to broaden his horizons and income by peddling drugs, was pissed off. He had worked diligently to insert himself into the local drug scene by first pushing a little weed, then a small amount of crack to his former school buddies. As it happened, one of his dealers had met with an unplanned "accident." The word was that he had come up short in a payment to his suppliers in Seattle. They had escorted him onto the Seattle-Victoria ferry and somewhere during the journey he had been encouraged to take up whale watching—from the bottom—so to speak. Nature, it is said, abhors a vacuum, and into that particular vacuum Homer had eagerly stepped, along with some of those same school friends who had been his customers. Why buy it when you can make it, they thought, and so they were about to embark on a new career path as the proud owners of their very own crystal meth lab. That is, they would as soon as that slug Johnson showed up to relieve him. Johnson was, in addition to being his relief, a customer. A small amount of meth given to him at a party had hooked him solid. It had also had the unintended side effect of making him unreliable, sloppy and, like today, often late for work. Homer did not see the irony of one of his customers standing in the way of his own upward financial success. Instead he waited with increasing impatience until some 45 minutes later Johnson showed up. Homer waited for him in the locker room. After a quick look around he grabbed his shirt collar and threw him up against the wall.

"You fucking asshole, you're late again."
"Sorry, man. I promise it won't happen again," Reggie replied with alarm, looking down at his feet.

"Fucking right it won't. You know why? Because you'll be dead, that's why. I miss my meeting this morning and someone else gets that property, I'll kill you myself. Now you owe me two large and I need it by the end of the week."

"Sure thing, Homer, I'm good for it, no problem man, I got it covered."

"See that you do," said Homer and he left the room

Reggie shrugged his shoulders, straightened his shirt, and checked around the room. Seeing no one had come in, he reached into his locker and took out a cell phone. His eyes grew hard and his voice changed as he dialed a number with a long distance area code. The phone was answered on the second ring.

"Vinnie," he said, "I got a job for you."

CHAPTER THREE

Newton made his assignments, and the initial round of inquiries began. There was a plan of course, his years of experience had formed the plan, and as times changed, it changed too. In times past the number of areas to search would have been dictated by many factors.

Every detective on the team knew from experience that other than the crime scene, one of the most important investigations would be in the areas where the victim would have been in the hours before her death. Where did she grow up, what was her economic status and so on? In simpler times, the physical area to search was smaller as people had traveled less, their circle of friends closer to home. Folks knew each other then, and a strange face was cause for someone to take interest and remember. Now though, people traveled from one end of the country to the other in hours, and cheaply. So cheaply that no one noticed at all. New faces were now the norm, and you only took interest in the ones you saw repeatedly. The team of detectives worked hard those following hours, starting with the marinas, however distant.

"Have you seen this girl?" They asked.

"No," came the response.

"Are you sure? How about strange cars that didn't belong?"

"Take a look in the parking lot, officer, we got everything from 25 years old to brand new, all makes and models, nothing looks strange anymore."

"What about any visiting boats? Or someone who left in the middle of the night?"

"Yes and yes, it's fishing season, lots of people leave in the middle of the night, and arrive also, boats move according to the tide, not the hour."

"How about surveillance video?" The detective asked, "Do you have cameras installed to watch the docks?"

"Sure, but the tapes only record about eight hours' worth of video before they loop, still you're welcome to them. Camera three out on the end of the dock hasn't been working so well lately and we have been trying to get a guy to fix it, but they are all too busy it seems."

"What's the problem with it?"

"Great big pelican sat on it a month ago, busted the gears on the panning mechanism, so now it points pretty much straight down, instead of sweeping the entire dock. When you review this," the owner said reaching into a metal box and withdrawing a much used video cassette, "it will be marked as 'Dock east', and good luck with it."

"How many of these folks sleep on their boats this time of year?"

"Well now, that depends, during the week we got maybe thirty or so, but on the weekend it can be as many as seventy—if the weather is nice."

"I see you have gates on the gangways, is that a combination lock, or are keys required?"

"Electric combination lock, used to be keys, but I could never keep up with folks losing them."

"We will want to canvas the owners, see if they noticed anything, what is the code for the locks?"

"1-2-3, got to keep it simple for everyone, you wouldn't believe the problem some folks have trying to remember something different."

"Sure I would," the detective responded. "Sure I would."

"How about a movement log? When a boat leaves or docks, does the owner have to let you know?"

"Only the transient ones, the rest pay moorage by the month, so they could leave and return a dozen times a day and I wouldn't really know."

"Fuel records, pump logs, that sort of thing, do you keep those?"

"Only for the large ones, the small boats generally bring their own fuel, here is the log from the fuel pumps," the owner said handing over a dog-eared book.

The detective recorded the names of the boats from the last week, only seven entries.

"You mind if I put this picture up in your window, someone might have seen her recently."

"Not at all, what is she anyway, a run away, drug mule, skip bail?"

"Dead." came the reply. "She's dead."

Newton reviewed the information he had gathered so far along with his observations from the beach. The time she spent in the water was an issue. The coroner could provide some information about that. Her skin was intact with no signs that she had been in the water long enough to arouse the interest of any of the creatures who lived there. Her clothing showed no signs of deterioration, and the time of death was within hours of her being discovered on the beach.

These facts suggested three things to Newton.

One, she had been on a boat for an indeterminate time and entered the water close to shore by falling off the boat. If so, where was the boat? If she was not alone, why had her companions not reported her missing?

Two, she had been alone on a boat and fallen overboard and the boat had drifted away. If so, where had it gone? The currents in the area would not have moved it far, and the coast region was well traveled. If there was a boat drifting it would soon be spotted. If it had sunk, there should be some wreckage, lifejackets, gas cans, an oar; something should turn up before the day was out. But it was very unusual for a young woman to go to sea alone in the day, let alone at night.

Three, the boat and its occupant(s) had already returned to its moorings, and her leaving the boat was not by choice.

There was one other possibility Newton knew of. There was no boat to find, and there were no companions to report anything. She had chosen to swim out from shore to a point where she would seek the solace of the sea without a struggle, rather than continue with the struggle of life.

Would he ever know for sure, Newton mused. Without definitive proof, these things were classed as "death by misadventure" at the coroner's inquests.

Humans were always reluctant to admit failure.

And so it went. There would be the occasional leads of course. There always were.

"I think I saw her."
"That could be..."
"She looks like..."

All of the leads might fail to materialize in anything substantive. The search would then be widened. Missing person's lists expanded into neighboring areas and even neighboring countries.

The pervasive and ever increasing network of surveillance camera tapes would be searched.

Malls, nearby convenience stores, and even bank tapes would be reviewed for the two days previous to her discovery. This all took time, and time took manpower, and manpower was always an issue for a small department.

On arriving back at the office Newton found the night shift still working. Off duty members "forgot" to go home, save to shower and return. They all had children of their own and most of their children were the same age as the Jane Doe on the beach.

They knew, as did Newton, that the first 48 hours were the most important. After that, other events took hold and assumed increasing importance, demanding time and manpower.

Still, Newton kept at it. His list was long and the only way to get it done was to start at the top and work through it. Starting at the top was to write a list of the things they knew and the things they didn't. The things they knew occupied a very small corner of the white board, the things they did not filled the rest. The theory was that you considered the things you knew and used them to find out the things you needed to know. When all the things you needed to know were gone, then the case was likely solved. If not, then it would likely never be.

In addition to the physical evidence present at every scene, crime or not, was the moment in time that formed the starting point of the investigation. To that, Newton and his team would add those details that were derived from that evidence or found during additional inquiries. This information would of course be chiefly concerned with the movements and activities of the deceased. If any suspects or "persons of interest" came to light, then their activities and movements, past and present, would also be scrutinized. Thus, the investigation moved at first into the past, then possibly into the present depending upon developments. Most cases quickly assumed a life of their own; the investigators went along for the ride.

They gathered the information, sorted, and catalogued it, followed the leads and asked the questions.

The next major piece of information Newton would receive would be the coroner's report. The coroner, or medical examiner, played a pivotal role in any investigation of a sudden death.

When is death not sudden?

Birth at least provided an anticipated starting point—nine months give or take a couple of weeks. Birth was usually a joyous and celebrated event, the continuation of the species. People looked at a newborn and saw hope for the future, a new mind, endless possibilities, and the promise of a better life. But death, well death was seldom welcomed;

mankind has yet to make that leap of faith, faith being a declining commodity. Yet death is as natural as birth and the only sure thing about living is that no one gets out alive.

It was the timeliness of death that disturbed people. For this girl, life had yet been a road that led in many directions. Like a superhighway, it had many branches which were unexplored. Careers, motherhood, wife, so many side roads to take, so many sights unseen. Why had she taken the one marked "exit?"

It was not a homicide unless the coroner said it was. Until then it was known as a suspicious death. It was the law in most countries that every sudden death is subject to examination. The purpose, of course, was to determine the circumstances of each death. The evidence gathered at the autopsy would form one of the building blocks of the investigation.

Newton picked up the phone and made a call. "Quincy," he said, "how are things going?"
"No shortage of work Alfred," Johanus DeGriebe answered. Johanus was the chief coroner, born of the same generation as Newton and over time they had become friends. Just as Newton had garnered the nickname of "Sir Isaac", Johanus had been baptized with "Quincy>" His appearance and mannerisms had matched those of the main character in the television series. Besides he still retained his thick Dutch accent and "Quincy" was easier to pronounce and spell.

"I hate to rush you, Quince," Newton began.
"No problem, Al, I know this is important to you and I can tell you a few things."
The coroner cleared his throat.
"The cause of death was drowning, water in the lungs, unmistakably sea water. No signs of a struggle, no signs of trauma, just death by drowning. Sorry, I can't give you more than that for a cause."
"Anything that struck you as unusual about her general condition?" Newton asked.
"Yes and no, she was in good shape, no needle marks, no stomach contents either, so she hadn't eaten in the hours before death, but no signs of malnutrition or other health problems."
"So she wasn't run down?"
"No sign of that, her teeth were in good shape so she had to have had regular checkups and one other thing—her eyes had received laser surgery—probably within the last three years."
"Now that is interesting, can you tell what kind of laser was used?"

"No, sorry about that, but the eyes deteriorate very quickly, and I can't tell."

"OK, Quince, I owe you one, thanks for taking a look."

"No problem, Al, I'll let you know if I find anything else, this was just a quick look."

Newton hung up the phone. On the white board he wrote down the findings. The team could now make inquiries with laser eye clinics, a long shot to be sure, but everything helped.

One question answered, more brought forward. The how was clearer—but not completely. How had she come to be upon the sea, and what had taken her out on its waters.

Newton's next important task would be to identify the girl. So far that had drawn a blank. Every avenue was pursued but it was as if she had dropped out of nowhere. The teams canvassing the marinas, malls, schools, and neighbourhoods had so far drawn a blank.

CHAPTER FOUR

Every city of substantial size has a homeless community, young and old, some trapped by circumstance, some by choice. By nature, these communities are made up by smaller groups of people in similar circumstances. The working homeless were in one group, the runaways in another. The older folks who long ago surrendered their lives to the abuse of drugs of alcohol formed the largest of the groups. Their addictions demanded that they be forever on the move, searching for sources of money with which they could feed their habits. These folks were the eyes and ears of any detective with the smarts to use them. They saw what others had no time to see, they saw the day to day ebb and flow of life on the streets. If a new member showed up in the community they would likely know it first. Every arrival and departure would be assessed to determine if it posed a threat or provided an asset to their lives. A strong person was a challenge to the established order of things; a weaker one was a potential worker who could be exploited. Runaways were the hardest to category and thus the most scrutinized. A young man or woman represented a potential source of revenue, either as a prostitute, drug consumer, beggar, or thief. One of the marketable commodities from the street was information, and someone who took note of the activities on the street was in a position to benefit by providing such information—for a fee.

The occupation of "snitch," or "rat," or any of the other euphemisms that described such behaviour was a risky one indeed. Their presence was known and tolerated by the groups they associated with, for they offered a way to control the activities of the competition, and the information they gleaned was as useful to them as it was to the authorities.

Too much information given too freely was discouraged, sometimes with extreme prejudice if it threatened the survival of a group. Thus the police and their informants dealt on a quid pro quo basis. The occasional low level bust of a drug dealer was exchanged for the allowing of a group to pursue activities basic to its survival. An understanding existed with the police that they would insist on when the welfare of children was involved. Any information divulged under such circumstances would carry only a relatively mild penalty for the informant.

Newton and his detectives had canvassed their street sources with no success. Then, as often happened, came a phone call. It came early in the morning to Newton's answering machine—regular hours for most of the city's homeless.

"This is Rusty."
Most street people had only one name. "I think I seen her last week—that girl you're looking for." The voice was raspy and weak. "They didn't say—but I want a reward. I gotta leave town."

The voice paused, as if the speaker was thinking hard about his next words. "OK, then, I'll meet you later today—at the duck pond in the park—9:00 AM—I'll be wearing a red toque."

Newton arrived at work early as was his custom. He had found over the years that he could accomplish much more in the silent hours before the rest of the morning crew arrived, than after the phones started ringing and the social chit chat began.

The message from Rusty was the seventh on his machine.

Newton looked at his watch; it was 7:35 AM.

He went through the other messages, making notes and updating files. A couple of the callers merited a return call, arranging interviews and clarifying points that arose from previous investigations. Two calls were from compatriots in other agencies, long time friends who had worked with Newton on other cases and whom he could trust. They both requested more information about the Jane Doe from the beach. Most agencies, swamped with cases of their own, had little time to spare for others. Newton was heartened that at least two other investigators would make the time to assist. But then, he had expected it, he knew why they would help.

At 8:00 AM the rest of the morning shift arrived. Newton had added the coming meeting with Rusty to the information posted on the whiteboard. Automatically each member of the shift would glance at the board as they came in. If they had anything to add, they would let Newton know.

"Hey, I know a Rusty." One of the older members, Jack Strong, said.
"Yeah, ain't he the dude with the red toque?" another chimed in.
"That's right. He usually works with the narcs, belongs to Fast Freddie's little group."

"And 'Fast Freddy' would be?" asked Newton.

Jack Strong came over and sat on the edge of Newton's desk. "Freddy is the head of the Esquimalt meth boys, got pretty high up in the food chain 'til one of his boys sold a pack to the son of one of the Navy lads."

"I remember that," said Willy Jackson, a junior member of the crew. "Turned out the Navy guy was one of those special ops guys, a seal or something."

"Yep, and that weekend, he and his buddies went and had a 'talk' with Freddy, took him and his group off the street for a two-month stay in the hospital."

"Oh, right. We ought to 'solve' Freddy's assault complaint one of these days."

"You bet, it's on the list right after all the barking dog beefs."

"And Rusty was one of his crew?" asked Newton

"He's a new player, came on board when Freddy tried to rebuild his power base, seems most of the old guys scattered to the winds after being released from the hospital."

"Yeah, he's not a dealer, he's a source."

"OK," said Newton. "Is his information reliable?"

"Usually, if he needs something he'll be pretty straight with you," Jack said, heading back to his own desk and the pile of folders that sat in the middle of it. "All those guys would sell out their own mother for the right price."

"Thanks," Newton wrote a few lines in his notebook. Not the one that he kept the results of his daily investigations in, for if he did, he could be called upon to produce that notebook in court, where it would be subject to examination by the defence's legal team. It wasn't that Newton objected to the rule of full disclosure, where the Crown was required to put its entire case on the table for perusal prior to the trial; he thought that was a good thing. For example, detectives were human and it was possible for them to read something into the evidence that was not there. For example, a fingerprint only shows someone HAD contact with something, it can't say WHEN it occurred.

You needed other evidence to establish a reliable time line.

Sometimes an investigator, particularly the young ones, would miss that, or another important point. Disclosure helped to reinforce the requirement to cover all the bases, Disclosure could also persuade an accused that he was caught pure and simple, and the best way out was to plead guilty—saving everyone time and the taxpayer a chunk of money.

Some defence lawyers had taken the opportunity to go beyond the scope of the case at hand, searching through a police officer's notebook when it was produced in court and getting the names of confidential informants or details of other cases. On the express orders, it was believed by many in the police community, of their clients. For this reason, Newton kept all his confidential information in a separate notebook which he never took to court, and therefore could never be forced to produce.

Rusty's name went into the second notebook.

CHAPTER FIVE

Newton left the office at 8:30. The ride to the park would be short, but he liked the walk, which would take longer and provide more thinking time. As he made his way along the scenic pathway overlooking the strait of Juan d'Fuca, the day was brightening. There was a freshening breeze coming off the water, teasing the leaves of the dogwoods lining the bank. Out on the sea the sailboats were already testing the strength of the winds. Giant ships laden with goods from a hundred foreign ports made their way along the coast to the ports of Vancouver and Seattle.

Newton entered the park from the south end, and headed down one of the many walking paths. This route would allow him a full view of the duck pond, and who would be there, from a distance. It wasn't long before he noticed a lanky figure cross the street west of the park and walk quickly into the pond area. Taking a bag of bread crumbs from the pocket of a dirty coat, he sat on a bench and began to toss them to the expectant flock of ducks gathering at his feet.

Newton smiled and shook his head. The red toque marked the visitor as his contact "Rusty," but the attempt to look inconspicuous was having the opposite effect. The ducks were making a racket as they loudly quacked and waddled up to the bench. This attracted the ever present sea gulls, whose raucous cries added to the cacophony. All that noise and the increasing amount of ducks and gulls attracted the attention of every kid within hearing distance, and it all centered on Rusty's bench. By the time Newton reached the pond, even Rusty's impaired mental faculties had finally realized that these efforts at being incognito were perhaps not having the desired results. Newton walked up to Rusty, and with a mutual nod of recognition took the bag of bread crumbs from his hands and gave them to what appeared to be the oldest kid in the increasing crowd surrounding the bench.

The youngster, pleased at suddenly being the centre of attention of both the birds and the other kids, lead the whole group around to the other side of the pond. Newton motioned Rusty to sit on the bench. When the last duck had waddled away, Newton turned to Rusty and taking an envelope from his pocket removed three pictures. These he spread out on the bench.

"You said you may have some information about one of these girls."

Rusty bent over the pictures and ran his fingers over first one, then a second.

"Yeah, man, I seen this one last week on Robson and Cook," indicating an artist's rendition of the girl from the beach. She was portrayed as if in a school picture, three quarter view and smiling. "But this one," he said, "I ain't seen in a couple of years, last time was in Bellingham."

Newton froze; no one had ever identified that picture before.

"How do you know them?" Newton asked; his voice even but his heart racing.
"This girl here, she's been around a while, maybe a month, not a hooker or anything like that. I seen her get into a cab a few times so like, she's got some bread, man." Rusty continued, "I told Freddy about her, but she don't look like the type to get into the business."
"When you saw her, was she wearing the same outfit all the time? Did she dress upscale or street?"
"Just regular clothes man, nothing special, not always the same clothes, but still a Wal-Mart kid. You know what I mean?"

Newton did know what he meant, a change of clothes meant she had a wardrobe, a place to keep it and a place to change. The fact that she took cabs meant she had money, but not likely a car. So she was probably not a resident but a visitor. Visitor from where, and who did she visit?

Newton would step up the inquiries to the cab companies.

"Did she ever have someone with her?"
"Nah, always alone when I saw her. Say, man, is there a reward for this? I gotta blow town, ya know? Freddy ain't doin' so good business like and I gotta look out for myself."

"I can get you a bus ticket, but not right now, right now I need you around in case I have more questions." Newton replied.

Rusty nodded with a look of resignation; he was used to things not working out in his favour.

"Freddy cool with this? I don't want you to suddenly disappear on me."
"Yeah, Freddy don't care—he's got his own problems."
"OK, then, let's go to the station, we'll get you some breakfast on the

way and we can go over what you saw."

 Newton and Rusty headed off to the station, where over a breakfast from a fast food establishment, mostly consumed by Rusty, Newton led him carefully through the reported sightings.

 "You say you saw her in a cab," Newton began, "what time of day?"
"What was she wearing?"
"Were her clothes in order?"
"Was she alone?"
"Was she in a hurry?"
"Did you ever see her in the company of anyone else?"
"Where else did you see her?"
"Why did you notice her?"
"Did she always take the same cab company or whichever was available?"
"Did you see where she came from?"
"Did you ever see her go into a hotel, restaurant, or store?"

 From Rusty, Newton learned that the girl had been in the neighbourhood for a good two weeks. He remembered her because she was of the age that working girls were, and Freddy and others paid for leads on girls—and boys—who might wish to work the street in return for a place to stay.

 "Like that girl in Bellingham." Rusty had said.

CHAPTER SIX

Back in his office, Newton grabbed yet another coffee. He was trying to cut down like everyone else, but still needed the jolt it gave him to keep going. At least that's what he told himself. Deep down, he recognized it was just a habit. The walk to the coffee machine and the ritual of dropping in a few coins and waiting for the machine to deliver the hot liquid provided a change of scenery, albeit a small one. With his body occupied with the familiar, his brain was free to concentrate on the day's problems. This would be such things as mapping out a new strategy, considering a new line of inquiry or, as in this case, going over the questions and answers from an informant. Sometimes something new popped up between the fall of the coins and the first sip.

Rusty had the tone of an honest informant. Not someone eager to help the police for the good of society, but willing to tell what he knew in the hope of a reward of some sort. Newton's impression was that Rusty was the sort who didn't have the imagination to make up a story. He just told what he knew and hoped for the best. Flipping out his notes, the detective began to review the responses.

She had been alone every time Rusty had seen her, which was unusual, but not unheard off. Most girls quickly aligned themselves with a partner or group for protection. Life on the streets was not easy. This meant she either had a place to stay, and thus no need for group protection, or she was a true loner.

Newton wrote some points on the large whiteboard that provided a place to diagram an investigation.

Check hotels and motels—again.
Check cab companies, including independents.
Check all stores in the area, recheck the video security tapes. Look for her getting into a cab?

This was the best lead they had. Rusty had been particularly attentive and even making allowances for his less than acute faculties, he had come up with some solid information. Newton also quizzed him on the girl in the other picture, the one whom no one had ever identified before. But other than some being sure of Bellingham as the place he had spotted her, everything else was fuzzy and dim and unsure. Rusty was not even sure which month it was and would probably got the city wrong if not for the fact that he had run out of money and sought help from the local drop in center. There he had got into a fight and spent three days begging enough money to move on. Bellingham had made an impression on Rusty.

Newton began the methodical process of checking out Rusty's information.

First thing on the list was to check the records of the large cab companies. People in a strange town usually stay with the nationally known names in cabs, names like Yellow or Checker. These companies kept good records because the cabs were company owned and leased to the drivers. Rides were assigned by a central dispatcher and recorded on computer logs. Mileage driven was cross checked with the logs to ensure that the occurrences of a driver running a trip for cash and not reporting it were kept to a minimum. The companies kept a watchful eye on their share of the revenue. Private companies were sometimes less circumspect in their record keeping. Their only "partner" might be the tax man. Cash only trips at less than the going rate were not unknown in that sector. The last consideration would be those drivers whose interest in a passenger went beyond providing straight transportation. Rusty was not the only person who might turn a dollar by alerting an interested party to the presence of a newly arrived young woman, or young man for that matter, who appeared to be in the need of work.

Rusty had stated the times he saw her were between 6:00 and 7:00 PM Tuesday and Wednesday past. He was sure of the time period because the supper hour at the drop in ended at 6:00 PM and he had to wait until the Sally-Anne opened at 7:00 to try and get a room for the night. Unlike many of his compatriots, Rusty did not prefer the open but often rain-soaked bushes of the surrounding countryside to the crowded, but dry and warm sleeping rooms of the Salvation Army building.

One of the cabs was a Yellow Cab. Newton made his way over to their dispatch office. It was a trip he had made before and he was familiar with their staff and processes.

The office was run by an elderly lady named Martha. She had joined the company as a driver decades ago, long before it became vogue to challenge male dominated occupations. She did not do it because of some feminist instinct or to make a point, she did it to provide for three kids. Her husband, who had also been a hack, had been killed by a drunk driver one night coming home after shift. The company had allowed her to take her husband's place on the roster, driving while the kids were in school, and the rest of the cabbies made sure they always knew where her trips would take her. Eventually the kids left home and went on with their lives, the daily grind of driving was getting too much for her and Martha took a job in the dispatch office. A sharp mind got her promoted to manager and she had held that position for the last ten years.

Newton had been a young constable at the time of the accident and it had been one of his first investigations. They had kept in touch over the years and more than once as a patrol cop he had stretched his area to cover a trip he knew she was on.

When Newton walked into the office he was greeted with a cup of strong coffee and his choice of the ever present supply of home cooked muffins and cookies that Martha and rest of the crew kept on a side table. The office felt more like a good friend's kitchen than a place of business and that was one of the secrets to the company's ability to attract and retain good staff.

He and Martha made small talk while sipping coffee and waiting for the morning stream of pickups and drop offs to abate somewhat.
"So, Alfred, how are things with you?" she began.
"It's the same as always, Martha, too long on work and too short on time."
"You need a woman in your life, Alfred, I have a friend who …."
Newton held up his hand and smiled "I had that once, Martha, besides I'm too old now and set in my ways."
"Humph, I've heard that before."
"And you should listen!"
They both chuckled and Martha started to look over the logs. Many of the trips were regulars, people who had pre-arranged to be picked up at specific times.
"Mostly these were folks who no longer wished to drive, or who found it easier to take a cab than fight the traffic and parking problems." Martha explained, although it was not necessary. In such circumstances, a preferred rate could be negotiated with the cab company. It was unlikely that Newton would find the girl on that list, but it was worth a try. Martha pulled up the specific trip logs and together they poured over the dates and times that matched those Rusty had mentioned. As expected, nothing popped out at first glance, no entry reading "Missing girl picked up at this time" or any such thing. Newton would get a printed copy from this and the other major cab companies. He would take it back to the office and begin the

process of interviewing the drivers. First of all they would be starting with those who had indicated a pickup in the target area at the right time and date. If that didn't pan out then they would expand the questioning to include all the independent cabbies. When the team added up all the entries from all the cab companies, it was a long list, and time was not on their side.

On the second day they got lucky. One of the Yellow Cab drivers who was on duty the week before the body was found, identified the girl when shown a lineup of pictures. His trip sheet showed a fare from Robson and Douglas to the Inner Harbour. Questioned further he indicated that he had picked up the same fare twice before, always in the area of Robson and Douglas at around the same time, and in all three cases delivered her to the Inner Harbour area.

Newton pulled out a map of the city. He circled the downtown area and marked out a block square area around the pickup point and the Inner Harbour. The team had been augmented by holding over the night shift of beat cops. He singled out Andy and they went over the map. The drawings had been made by some cartographer years before and Andy would know of all the changes that happened since. Buildings get put up and taken down; the hole in the ground from last month is tomorrow's new high rise.

"Where would like me to start Al?" Andy asked, his red rimmed eyes staring down at the map.
"You probably know better than I do, but I think that it was unlikely that she would walk more than two blocks only to be picked up by a cab, and also it was unlikely that she would want to be dropped off more than that distance from her destination. So the initial point should be where the cabbie remembers her being picked up at." Andy focused on the marked map. "I know that area. The pickup point area consists of a mix of commercial and residential housing."

"It's likely that she either had a job or lived in that area, or knew someone who did." Newton said. "Has to be close by, see here? The drop off area is centered on the Inner Harbour; the Empress Hotel is the dominant feature that would have public access at that time of night. The government buildings would all be closed, as well as the museum. Now the harbour itself has restaurants of all types, a ferry service to Seattle, Washington, air service to the mainland, and any number of boats, large and small. The area is also served by all the major bus companies. There are condos and apartments all around, within easy walking distance, even some heritage housing in the area."

"Right. So the area was perfect for someone who wanted to cover their tracks, either intentionally or not." Newton looked up from the map, "What do think our chances are?"

"Mostly a matter of luck, but police work is like that sometimes, hard work will only take you so far, and without the occasional break things can dead end just short of making a case."

Newton nodded in agreement, this was one of the unwritten laws of police work, but unlike Andy, he believed that hard work could make its own kind of "luck."

"I'm thinking that with at least three confirmed trips to the area by the young woman, the chances are just over slim. Finding anyone who would remember her will be more difficult. Perhaps there could be employees of one of the businesses that remembered her, but there are hundreds of tourists passing through the same establishments on any given day. She might have met another tourist, now gone, or a traveler passing through. Still, you never know till you try."

"OK then, you take the area on the west side from, say, Douglas Street over to the water, I'll start on the east side by Beacon Hill Park, and we'll see where it leads."

"Works for me," Andy said. "I'll give you a call at noon and we'll compare notes."

With that, they left the office and headed downtown.

Newton would concentrate on the area where she was picked up, the number of businesses were smaller, with long-term employees more likely to notice a change in their clientele and the more upscale apartment blocks had regular doormen. They may not recognize her, but that was good news too since it would eliminate the apartment from the search. The preferred technique was to start with the buildings in the area closest to the corner where the cabby had picked her up and expand from there.

The search was troublesome from the start. The first two apartments were locked and Newton could not raise anyone on the intercoms. Both were older three story buildings, renovated sometime in the last real estate boom with an eye to having them go condo. The renovations took longer than the boom lasted and they reverted back to rentals. Newton took a business card out of his pocket and left it in the mail slot marked manager. He hoped that the residents had not left on vacation and farmed out the job to a replacement. The regulars noticed so much more.

Moving along the streets Newton checked each building in turn. Most of the residences, older buildings occupying land far more valuable than the structures on them, provided no response to his knocking. All appeared to have been converted to rooming houses and the tenants were away at work. Two had resident managers at home. Both were elderly couples, folks whose retirement income had long since been outstripped by the economy and expenses of living downtown.

"A young woman you say?" The elderly lady at the door asked.
"Yes, that's right, ma'am."
"Well, perhaps I can help you, young man. I'm Mrs. Theodore J. Todd, please come in. We'll have some tea."

Newton took the extra moments to respond to the invitations for coffee or tea even though time was short enough as it was. He knew that people remembered more after they had a chance to relax and talk a bit.
"If you wouldn't mind looking at this picture for me please?" Newton said passing it to both of them.
Neither identified the young woman as a tenant but Mrs. Theodore J. Todd was a schoolteacher and had been in the habit of noticing things since, well, young man, a VERY long time. She sat bolt upright, in a Victorian style chair that matched the décor of her house. The living room, where she served Newton with tea was neat and tidy with everything in its proper place, just like a school room ought to be. Mr. Todd nodded in agreement with a practiced toss of his head and smiled at his wife. While the picture was not of a tenant of hers, she looked a lot like a young lady who knocked on her door not more than a month ago asking if another young woman had lived there.

"Well, of course she wasn't here," Mrs. Theodore J. Todd tsked to herself. "In my day a young woman would not be living alone under such circumstances. That's what relatives were for," she went on, "to provide a safe place for young ladies to live when they ventured out into the world, until they could marry and settle down that is."
Mr. Todd nodded in agreement, sipping his tea in practiced silence.
"The world had changed so much since those days," and not, Mrs. Theodore J. Todd was sure, for the better.
"I quite agree in that respect," Newton said. He brought out his notebook and gently asked some questions.
"If you can remember the exact time of day, and what the young lady was wearing it would be most helpful," he asked.

The answers were punctuated with reminiscences of times gone by and quick lectures about the way the world was going to, well, a lady simply wouldn't say THAT word, but she was sure Newton would get the idea.

He did.

 After concluding the interview and refusing a last cup of tea and a taste of homemade shortbread, an old Scottish recipe from her mother's side of the family, Newton stood by the front door and said goodbye, thanking them both for their help.
"May I ask you a question, Constable?"
"Of course."
"This young lady—she's dead isn't she?"
"Yes, I'm afraid she is."
With a look of sadness hung heavily on her face, the schoolteacher suddenly appeared very old and tired.
"Thank you for telling me," she said and closed the door.

 He returned to his office to review what he had learned. His detective's eye recorded the condition of the rest of the rooming house; everything was neat and tidy, well painted and maintained. The Todds' little apartment was clean as a whistle and in perfect order that spoke of an attention to detail. Mrs. Todd had a schoolteacher's way that brooked no violation of the house rules, and she would be used to having the rules obeyed. Newton had not met any of the residents but he was sure that they would have to meet Mrs. Todd's standards of behaviour and exhibit old school decorum. He very much doubted he would find anyone under the age of 25 there, and certainly single ladies, wild parties, spiked hair or multiple piercing would not find refuge within her house.

 Newton was sure of a few other things, Mrs. Theodore J. Todd was in the habit of noticing things, and Mrs. Theodore J. Todd was seldom, if ever, in error. She would notice if someone was "out of place" in appearance and more important she would be tuned, by long experience, to the unspoken messages of hope and despair that people often broadcast without knowing it. With her schoolteacher's demeanour kids automatically reverted back to the way they behaved in their final school years. Newton trusted her observations and was now sure that he now had another person to look for.

 Who was the girl his Jane Doe was searching for? A sister? Friend? Relative?

Did she find her?

Was she still here?

Newton ran over the interview in his mind. His Jane Doe had handed Mrs. Todd a picture and letter dated a full year previous. It was definitely a high school picture—Mrs. Todd had seen more than enough of those pictures to be sure, but the picture had no date, no name, or writing on it at all. The envelope had no return address and, no, she didn't happen to notice who it was addressed to.

He would send a police artist over that afternoon to see if Mrs. Todd could come up with enough information to make up a sketch of the young lady. Then the search would start again. If they could find the girl in the picture, they would likely have someone who could identify their Jane Doe. It was their best shot at this point in the investigation.
His request made, Newton returned to the job at hand. He continued on with the local investigations of the buildings and their occupants. Sometimes he found someone at home, most times he did not. His notebook now contained entries about the areas he had canvassed and a look at his watch indicated it was time to meet Andy at a local restaurant.

Like most tourist destinations, there were a number of excellent eating establishments to cater to every taste. At this time of year especially, they were full of patrons and bustling with activity and noise. It was for those very reasons that Newton and Andy had chosen a small locally owned and operated place to have lunch. Coffee Mac's was a place that offered good service, a quiet place to talk—and Andy's favorite food—peanut butter and banana sandwiches. As it was open 24 hours a day, the beat man made it a regular stop during his shift. Newton found him at his regular table at the rear, with his back to the wall and his eyes on the door.

When Newton approached the table, Andy automatically slid over in the roomy booth and let the senior detective sit down. Like most police officers they both preferred to be in a position to observe folks as they entered.

"Any luck?" Andy asked.
"A little, I found a schoolteacher who can give us a lead on another girl who was looking for our Jane Doe recently."
"Really? Well that's a bit of luck; she didn't have a picture of her by any chance?"

"Nope, not that lucky—but we will have as soon as Robbie gets a sketch together. He will be heading over there this afternoon so it will be out by the time the evening shift starts."

"That will help—more possibilities, more leads."

"You get anything?"

"No idents, but I got some background stuff for you."

Unlike many of the newer detectives, Newton and Andy did not regard this part of the investigation as a dreary task. When there was no response to a knock on the door, he took the time to study the surroundings, what was it about this section of town that would interest a young girl?

"Not much on the west side to attract a girl of that age," Andy was saying. "There are no nightclubs, very few shops that catered to her age group, no hostels or points of interest that would attract out-of-towners. No cheap restaurants or fast food outlets."

"So the only thing that would bring his Jane Doe here had to be a personal connection." Newton added. "Maybe the new girl who was looking for her at the school teacher's house?"

"Could be," Andy replied. "If so, what had brought that girl here?"

"Well, that, my friend, could wind up being the 64 million dollar question."

"There is always one isn't there."

"Yes," said Newton. "There is always one—and it is always 'WHY.' You're off shift tonight, right?"

"Yeah, got a couple of days. Maybe I'll look around in the daylight for a change."

"I appreciate it, but the budget is limited with respect to overtime."

"No problem, Al, I'm not doing much else with my time, and it's a change from just keeping an eye on things. Besides, things are changing so fast around here it's good to get out during the day and see how the other half of the world lives."

"Working straight nights gives you a unique perspective, Andy."

"Not that unique anymore though, the city wakes up earlier now. Around 5:00 AM the first of the commercial vehicles, usually garbage pickup, start making their rounds, hoping to complete them before traffic made movement of the big trucks difficult. The cabbies start earlier too, hurrying to their first booked appointments. Even the early commuter rush gets here earlier now. Even with the growth in the city, the bedroom communities that surround us have kept pace."

"Don't I know it, when I come in I find the night crews heading home and the first city workers in their road and street vehicles are making their way to various sites to begin their day. Used to be they wouldn't hit the streets until 9:00 AM."

"Nothing stands still in this place at night anymore," Andy remarked. "But I guess that's the way of things everywhere."

The two men drank the last of the coffee and put away the notebooks. A quick check with the office from his cell phone brought no new information from the others on the case. Newton snapped the phone shut and slid it into his pocket.

"Remember the old radios we used to lug around?" Andy joked.

"Yes, I do, but when the batteries died, as they frequently did, you could always use it as a club if needed."

"Ever regret those cold wet days you spent pounding the pavement, Al?"

Newton smiled back, "Nope, not a minute of it."

Newton remembered the time when he was a young constable walking the beat. It was a time in his police career that he even now considered to be amongst the best he had for learning about life on the streets and in the city. Traveling the same paths day and day out at all hours gave him a full picture of what happens in a city as the day went on. Throughout the day the streets would be filled with all the myriad services that allowed a big city to function. Sidewalks would be clogged with workers, on their way to and from appointments, competing with shoppers and tourists for the ever decreasing amount of space on the concrete ribbons.

Later, around mid afternoon, the evening rush hour would begin with shift workers headed for home, or to school to pick up their kids. The regular workers joined an hour or so later and the rush would continue until the supper hour had passed. After a brief respite the streets would then fill with folks headed out to dinner, theatres or late night shopping. The sidewalks would be filled with the young folks looking for a night's adventure.

In earlier times, this would be the best part of the day for the young beat constable to learn his trade. Every spectrum of society was on display. The shopkeepers who catered to the evening and night crowd had their establishments to look after, and the patrons had the luxury of making their own schedules instead of responding to the demands of others.

Dinner at 7:00 PM, movie at 8:00, home by 11:00 PM.

They were relaxed and happy, talking with their friends and looking forward to the evening. Traffic was more relaxed. The streets were not as crushed as rush hour, and more people took cabs at this time than any other period of the day. This meant more cabbies worked this shift. Newton got to know all of them in his area over time, even the independents. As the night wore on, the beat changed subtly, the early show goers, the new parents, and the more elderly left the streets along with those young people who still had school to go to the next day. Those left were increasingly the hard core of the population who gravitated to the late nights and early mornings. Street people who couldn't find a place for the night steeled themselves to survive yet another night on the streets. Most had their favourite spots, under a bush in good weather, over a heating grate in bad. Some formed groups for mutual protection; some would sleep whilst others remained on watch. The drug dealers would begin their rounds, They had their favourite spots also. Instead of seeking out their clientele, they waited for the needy to come to them. This made it easy for the customers to find them and also easy for the police to spot them. A double edged sword, made duller by the increasingly lenient attitude of a court system swamped by a societal change in the way drug use was viewed, and increasingly addictive drugs like crystal meth.

Newton had seen the pattern change in his career; marijuana had given way to cocaine, cocaine to heroin, and heroin to crystal meth. His sympathies lay with the users, their world shrunk to a place where the time horizon was not days, weeks, or years, but the hours and minutes from one high to the next. Help was available to those precious few who had the strength to take it, but far too many did not. Their level of consciousness simply did not allow for the thought of getting clean. For them, the only hope would be some sort of compulsory treatment. A course of action that the courts had long ago decided violated their rights and in doing so, condemned them to a deadly downward spiral that led to an early grave from hepatitis, HIV, or an overdose.

The dealers were another case. Newton would quite happily exile them to a barren Arctic island and allow them to fend for themselves. The dealers had networks of runners, suppliers, and scouts like Rusty. Newton would see them start out on their rounds in the late evening, seeking the newly arrived street people, checking to see if someone had arrived alone, scared and hungry. Soon the word would get out "new targets in town."

After midnight, most of the restaurants had closed and the nightclubs were winding down. Those who had drunk too much and overstayed their welcomes were now appearing on the streets. The happy ones were destined for a cab ride home accompanied by friends; the angry ones were looking for a fight. At first the fights had been settled with fists, and a broken nose or black eye the result, but fists had given way to knives, and knives to guns. The angry patron whose alcohol consumption was greater than his self restraint had been replaced by the organized gangs of young folks carrying on a tradition born and practiced for centuries in another country. Too often the after midnight call was not for a paddy wagon to take someone to jail to cool off, but to the coroner to take them to the morgue.

As Newton got older, the streets got meaner, the population of the city grew, and with it the number of street folks. The number of predators grew also; gangs formed, flourished, and fell. Territories changed ownership and the pace of life quickened. Newton proceeded up the ranks to become a detective, beat constables left the streets to ride cruisers, losing touch with their communities and an invaluable learning tool was lost.

It was into this harsher environment that Newton's Jane Doe had stepped.

CHAPTER SEVEN

At the end of the day, Newton and not turned up any more information on the girl and he returned to the office to check with the artist. He was rewarded with an artist's sketch of the young lady Mrs. Todd stated was the one Jane Doe was inquiring about. The artist was impressed with Mrs. Todd's remarkable memory and attention to detail, a product of dealing with so many children over so many years. This gave Newton a greater degree of confidence that the picture was accurate.

Through long experience, the police artists had learned to place a degree of reliability on the final sketch. Some witnesses had difficulty in remembering small details like the shape of eyebrows or ears; others had trouble communicating what they remembered to the artist. Mrs. Todd had exhibited no hesitation at all, requiring little questioning about the small details that distinguish one face from a similar one. Like there being one eye higher than the other, or a small scar on the edge of a hairline. Very few people were blessed with perfectly symmetrical features, and Robbie knew how to get a witness to recall the things that made a face different from the main stream. Unlike many of compatriots, he used a custom set of templates that he had made himself, based upon his observations of the years. This had resulted in an amazing success rate for his sketches matching the suspect. With the possible relationship of her to his Jane Doe being his best lead, Newton would need that accuracy now more than ever.

Copies were made and distributed to his team and they would now begin their inquiries anew. While this may seem a setback to some, Newton knew it could have unforeseen benefits. People who had been interviewed already would have had some time to think and remember. The human memory process was a wonderful thing, most people never forgot anything, they just had trouble recalling it later. Many times the name of a movie actor would pop into someone's head hours after they visualized the role the actor had played. Often remembering a co-star would trigger the name. Now with a second person to think about, it was possible that the process would trigger someone's dormant memory and bring it into the forefront. For his part Newton knew who he would call on next.

He returned to the streets and began a search for Rusty.

The night was one of those summer evenings that brought people out of their homes in droves. The day had been warm and the night air was changing to a pleasant and cooling breeze. The sun had almost completed its journey to the West and painted the bottom of the clouds building on the western horizon a soft hade of cinnamon. Red at night, sailor's delight was the old refrain running through Newton's mind. A good omen perhaps, if one believed in such things. Newton put far more faith in hard work than a pretty sunset.

It took two hours for Rusty to turn up.

Rusty didn't keep regular hours.

Newton had instructed him to stroll through the park and sit on the same bench in case Newton had more questions for him. This time when Rusty sat on the bench the wildlife was not there to greet him. Newton sat beside him and passed him the new picture.

Rusty studied it for a few moments with an intent gaze. While he did that, Newton studied him with greater concentration. He saw Rusty's eyes focus on the picture clearly, and he also saw that the pupils were not dilated, as they would have been had he been on drugs. Alert for any involuntary flicker of recognition, Newton saw none.

"When was she here, man?"

"Probably two years or so ago, maybe longer, is our information."

"Yeah, well like I told you, I've only been here a year, maybe a year and a half, and I ain't seen her."
Rusty folded the picture and put it in his pocket.
"I'll show it around," he said. "Is there a reward or anything?"

"I'm sure we could arrange something." Newton responded. "Maybe some traveling money with that ticket out of town you want."

"OK, well, look, I'll show it around a little to some of them older guys like I said, but I gotta have something to offer them, you know?"

"All right, tell them $100 for a solid lead, $500 if they can produce an address or telephone number, and I'll give you the same."
"That's big money to some of those guys."
"And to you?"
"It's a new life, man, a new life."

Rusty nodded and left the park, Newton turned back to his office to check on the progress of the others on the team. He had his cell phone and could have used it to check in, but unlike the younger members, Newton found it to be intrusive to his thought process, and impersonal. Besides, he was forever leaving the silly thing in another pocket or desk drawer, unless like earlier today, he knew he would probably need it. Even then, he had carried it around turned off.

On his return he learned that Jack Strong and Willy Jackson were waiting for him. They had been canvassing the Inner Harbour region, including the hotels and various tourist traps. Willy, being the younger of the two, had a knack for connecting with the street kids and was dressed in his usual attire of ancient jeans, a good pair of leather boots, light shirt and his ever present Army jacket. Willy could be one of the Sally-Anne's best customers. Despite looking like a refugee from a '70s cop show, Willy got results. People were surprised to learn that he had spent a month of his vacation time living on the streets, getting to know the lives of the people and how they thought. During that time he had helped more than a few runaways avoid people like Rusty, and paid for more than one bus ride home. At the end of that month Willy knew more about the "night crowd" than most of the young constables trying for one of the few detective positions that came available each year as people rotated in and out.

Some of the upper management had learned about Willy's "holiday" after the fact and pressed him for arrests of the drug dealers that he came across. Newton had stepped in and convinced them that if that occurred, then they would no longer know who to watch and a lot of good intelligence would be lost. After a back and forth battle that was at times bordering on acrimonious, Newton prevailed.

On the street, news of Willy's true occupation was greeted with resignation by some that they would soon be in jail. There were some arrests of course, but these were the normal, if drug arrests could be characterized as that, day to day busts by uniformed and undercover police. Willy had been on the streets to learn the culture, gather intelligence, and develop a network of people that he could ask for information, and it was this network that provided the information he had learned today.

Willy had found two people who had seen Newton's Jane Doe.

Newton listened, sipping coffee, while Willy, notebook in hand, made his report. "This afternoon I went into the Empress to look for Pauley, my contact there. He is one of the doormen there. Has a position as one of the two relief workers who rotate in and out of the normal five-man cycle of doormen. Because he is a relief worker, he has a limited catalogue of 'regulars' and he works the position infrequently. Like the other relief guys his uniform is supplied by the hotel on an ad hoc basis, which means he doesn't have one tailored to him specifically, but depends upon whatever is available."

"Those are the guys with the top hats and tails?" Newton asked.

"Yep, they look like chimney sweeps to most folks, or an ad for peanuts, the tourists love it. In Paul's case he is someone who can look out of place at times. On most days, this is not a problem, he is of fairly standard build and matched at least two of the regular doormen in size and fit, except for his head."

"His head?"

"Paul is one of those guys whose head, for some reason known only to nature, was smaller than it should be. While he wore a size 6 7/8 hat, the nearest fit to that the hotel had in stock was 7 1/4. Now if he had been a regular employee, he would have been fitted with an authentic top hat."

"Who makes those things anyway," asked Jack, "some costume company?"

"Nope, they are the real McCoy, all the way from L.W. Wilson and sons, purveyors of fine hats and garments to the gentry since 1705. They are the hotel's regular suppliers of uniforms, and also supplied a large portion of the hotels in England. In the valet business, you were rated by what you wear."

"This story is getting a little long in the tooth," Newton chided. "Maybe we can cut to the chase here."

"Right, well to the point then," Willy said, holding his notebook up to his eyes and speaking as he would if he had been in court.

"On the day in question, the wind was unusually high, Paul Angelist stated he had just had a haircut, and thus spent most of the evening trying to keep the hat on his head with one hand, whilst opening the doors and unloading baggage with the other.

He found himself one hand short.

The top hat left his head and carried by the capricious breeze headed west across the broad lawns of the hotel towards the Inner Harbour. There it settled in one of the many flower arrangements that spelled out the name of the hotel in large letters visible for miles. The hat caught the attention of a girl walking on the broad sidewalk, and she retrieved the wayward headpiece and returned it to Mr. Angelist."

Willy paused for a breath, and then continued.

"Mr. Angelist recognized the young woman in the picture as the one who had retrieved the hat for him. On that day she had been dressed in jeans and a sweater. After speaking with him for a few minutes she had returned to the sidewalk, and the company of another girl. Paul had returned to his duties and not seen where they went from there, nor had he gotten a phone number or address."

"Too bad," Newton mused, "go on?"

"The second person who recognized the picture was the operator at the Undersea Gardens; this is a tourist establishment where folks can see various sea creatures swimming in glass tanks. The trade was steady but small in numbers and the operator took particular notice of two young women who spent longer than usual observing the various octopi and fish."

"Was this the same day as the hotel valet sighting?" Newton asked.

"No, it was eight days later. The operator had his attention diverted by various enquiries for scuba diving lessons and trips and so his recollection was spotty."

"So what is important here is that the two were amiable, not arguing in any way, and that this had taken place on a different day than the doorman at the Empress."

This led Newton to believe that perhaps his Jane Doe had successfully located the girl Mrs. Todd had described and that they had spent some time together.

"Entrance to the establishment had been paid for in cash, so there are no credit card receipts to trace."

Since there was an eight-day period from the time that they had been spotted at the Empress and the time they had been seen in the Undersea Gardens, there was a good chance they hung out on a frequent basis. That meant there was a good chance others had spotted them in the area as well.

"I went back and re-interviewed both witnesses once I got Robbie's sketches," Willy went on. "When shown the pictures of the second girl, the doorman did not recognize her. Not unexpected really since the second girl never approached him. The Undersea Gardens operator was not certain, but felt that she was familiar. She could easily have been the second girl of the two he had noticed."

"Good work, Willy," Newton said, "Now we have a definite area to search."

In light of this, the team felt they were finally making some progress.

CHAPTER EIGHT

"Settle down, folks." The sergeant bellowed to the assembled night shift. All over the squad room chairs were scraped across the floor and the general level of noise died away.

"Most of you already know what happened early this morning, and Detective Newton has asked to say a few words prior to your going on patrol this evening."

Newton took his place at the head of the room and quickly told them of the day's events, and the progress of the investigation up to the present time.

"What I'd like for you to do tonight is to check out the various night clubs and restaurants in the Inner Harbour area. Now most of the eateries are on the high end and it was unlikely the two would be patrons, so concentrate on the various fast food spots."

"Those places put a lot of people through in a short time." One of the younger constables remarked. "There is not much chance that they would be remembered unless they're regulars. Staff turnover was also high in such places and that would work against them too."

"Agreed," said Newton. "It's a long shot, but at present, it's the best we have. Pick up a copy of the sketch and the picture on your way out and keep your eyes open. Ask questions. And one other thing, don't forget the regular street people. There are indications that at least one of these girls was known to them, so the other may be also."

Newton stopped at his office and finished his paperwork for the day. Reports of what progress had been made on this and other cases, briefs for upcoming court appearances, personnel reports, daily car sheets and administrative tasks. All of them were essential to the running of the department and managed to eat up ever increasing amounts of his time. Such tasks as these made Newton's upcoming retirement seemingly more welcome. He would not miss the mindless day to day tasks, but he would indeed miss the daily challenge of trying to map out the events that led up to the crimes he had to solve.

Truth was, Newton had no idea what he would do in retirement. Whilst the financial end was taken care of, the personal part was not. Alone for many years, he had few hobbies, and most of his friendships had been made in the context of some branch of police work.

He reached out, switched off the desk lamp, and logged out of the computer system. He paused for a moment to look around his office.

Several diplomas and certificates hung in dusty frames on the walls, attesting to the various courses he had taken over his career. The filing cabinet was topped with a stained coffee mug and a couple of old shooting trophies from his younger days. His desk held the usual computer equipment, assortment of pens and pencils, another well used coffee cup, a pad of paper, some file folders and in a corner, a small plastic figurine of a police officer. It was painted blue and stood on a black plastic base with a small metal placard. "World's Greatest Policeman" was the inscription. This kind of knick-knack was available at any shopping mall for a few dollars. Of all the awards, commendations, and trophies that covered the walls and gathered dust in boxes at his small apartment, few would guess that this was the one thing that meant the most to Newton. He picked it up and his eyes lost focus, and his mind returned again to a happier time in his life. Replacing it on the desk, he switched off the lights and closed the door.

For Newton, life had pretty much two time periods: at work and not at work. He headed home and let his mind wander over the day's events. As investigations went, they had accomplished all the basic tasks. The wheels were set in motion to cover the needed procedures that were common to every inquiry. The external resources, such as fingerprint matching by the R.C.M.P., flyers and notices to adjoining departments, requests to the customs and immigration people for a record search of entries to the country—everything that needed to be done had been done. Leads developed by examination of the evidence, such as it was, would be followed, and now it was up to the two best tools of the investigator, determined police work, and pure blind luck. Often it was the latter over the former that provided the final keys to the puzzle.

Newton opened the door to his apartment and checked the two answering machines; one was for his work only number and the other for his listed home phone. Unlike most police officers Newton had not requested his home number be unlisted. This was for several reasons, the most important of them being personal. He no longer worked the beat, and so was not exposed to the public in the same manner as a traffic cop. Those who would call him now were likely to be in possession of some information that he wanted. To facilitate this information gathering he had his work number printed on his business cards, any messages on that line would be concerning some case he was working on. The messages on his regular line would likely be some sales pitch for carpet or furnace cleaning. Both machines message lights were blinking. Newton checked the personal line first.

There were two messages, one from his landlord advising him that his apartment would be painted at his convenience and to please let him know when that might be. The other was a hang up. Newton checked the other machine, there was one message and it was from Rusty.

"This is Rusty, are you there?" A long pause, Rusty was not the swiftest on the uptake.
"Well, I guess not. Hey, I got some more info for you on that other girl you were looking for. I'll be at the Tim Horton's on Robson and Main at about 10:00 tomorrow morning—meet me there."

Newton noted the time and place in his notebook and went to bed.

The next morning found Newton at his desk preparing papers for court. Every so often the paper trail police officers prepare gets changed in response to someone's latest and greatest idea of how to streamline the system. The current process required every investigation resulting in a court charge to be written up in a document called a court brief. This was to identify for Crown Counsel, the Canadian equivalent of the district attorney, the circumstances of the charge, who was involved, who was a witness, and what testimony each would provide. The idea was that Crown Counsel could read through the brief and derive everything needed to prosecute the case. It was the unanimous opinion of police officers that they were being called upon to do the attorney's job for them, and the briefs were typically submitted with comments of "See officer's report." This was because the department used a different format for its regular daily use, and preparation of the brief required duplication of the already written incident report. Like many such new ideas, Newton gave this one little chance of being in place after a year. Police officers disliked processes which kept them off the street doing "real police work" and usually found a way to sabotage those ones that were the most onerous.

One of the most recent of these in Newton's experience was the edict that incidents should be written up in as brief a manner as could be done to adequately describe the event. This occurred after Willy, in a brief moment of literary genius on a slow night, used seven pages of legal sized paper in single space typewritten prose to describe his response to an intruder call. The gripping narrative detailed Willy's investigative skills and attention to detail in pursuing the suspect for seven city blocks through black and rainy night to his ultimate apprehension of a 12 pound grey feline. In response to the new edict to keep the narrative as brief as possible, the next report Willy wrote simply had:

Complaint: Barking Dog
Action Taken: Bang

Both reports achieved legendary status and were circulated for months amongst the patrol sections of neighbouring police forces.

Newton finished with his "He said, They said, We say" narratives on a recent theft case and pushed the file folder back onto the pile on his desk. He stretched, looked at his watch, and rose to refill his coffee cup. As in all western police forces, Coffee was the blood that fueled the staff, and like most police officers, Newton drank too much of it. Lately some of the older generation had been switching over to various brands and flavours of tea. It was becoming the current fad, and although he was not a follower of fads, Newton had to admit that switching brews after noon had passed had allowed him a greater level of relaxation.

His paperwork completed, at least for the time being, Newton headed out of the office to his meeting with Rusty. True to his word, he carried with him a voucher for a bus ticket out of town. The destination was specifically Calgary, as Rusty had requested. The department had an arrangement with the bus company; the voucher would be honoured when Newton phoned them to give the OK. This procedure allowed him to demonstrate good faith, and keep his informants around for as long as needed. Actually, few ever took possession of the voucher, the better not to advertise their impending change of residence to their present bosses. Doing so resulted in their being ostracized at a minimum, and other more drastic things had been known to happen. They were on an island after all and some had been invited to make their departure from it doing the Australian crawl rather than taking the ferry.

To Newton's surprise, Rusty was there waiting for him, and his empty coffee cup suggested that he had been there for a while. This meant that either the information he had was hot, or more likely, Rusty was. The look in his eyes suggested the latter.

Newton ordered a coffee and sat down.

"What do you have for me, Rusty?"
"It's that new girl you're looking for—the one you showed the sketch of—I found her."

Newton's eyebrows rose slightly.

"All ready? That was quick, where is she?"

"Well, I didn't exactly find her, I found out where she works"
"And that would be?"

"The museum—she does those diorama things."

The museum was well known for its innovative ways of displaying artifacts in a scene depicting the era of their use. For example, they had a mining town, complete with tunnels, machinery, and local stores. The bakery even had the smell of fresh baked apple pies. Since the museum was also located close to the inner harbour, it was definitely in the right area.

"Go on," said Newton, taking out his notebook.

"She does the Indian village thing, you know, with the totem poles and the carvings and things like that."

"How do you know all this?"

"Well," said Rusty, with a conspiratorial look, "the boss has customers down there, you know? And one of them was a little slow in coming up with the payments, so he asked me to show this piece of stone, really nice piece you know, with carvings on it, to the boss for payment, said it was worth a lot of money."

Newton nodded, Argillite carvings were worth a great deal of money to the right person, if they were also carved by the right person.

Rusty went on,"But the boss, he's no art collector, besides after his recent, um, reversals and all, he needed the straight cash so's I told that he needed to pony up with the scratch. Two hundred or else the boss is gonna have to send Tony around to do the collecting, 'stead of me."

Newton nodded. Tony Ambrosio was the "muscle" for the group. Of course, as good as he thought he was against his usual clients, half scared out their wits and not in the prime of physical condition, Tony did rather poorly against the lads from Esquimalt. The Naval Commandos had little trouble with the overweight and overmatched thug. Seems the toughest part of Tony was his mouth, and that didn't survive the first solid punch.

"Isn't Tony still in the hospital?" Newton asked

Rusty brightened at the thought, "Yeah and he's gonna be there a while yet, they still ain't found all his teeth."

Tony, much to his misfortune, had swallowed a fair number of his suddenly extracted molars. Most had worked their way through his system, but various bits had hung up on his intestines during their journey. This extremely painful condition was being monitored daily, the docs having decided the risk of an operation too great as long as no blockage of the tract was present. Thus "Big Tony" was reduced to a liquid diet—and mouthing requests for morphine through his wired jaw. As with all bullies, Tony had from time to time practiced his skills of intimidation on other members of his crew, Rusty had not been exempted.

"So after the boss says no, I give the piece back to R.J., the guy at the museum, and we get to talking, he's all crying and scared that he's got no way to pay off the boss and now he thinks Tony is coming, 'cause he don't know about him being in the hospital and all, and he's asking how he can come up with dough. So I show's him the drawing and he gets all excited like. He says he seen that girl and how she's the one in charge of the display. So I tell him if that's the straight goods then he can use the reward money to pay the boss and everything is going to be cool."

"Is she there now?" Newton asked.

"Nah, she left for the North Islands about a week ago–some place called Sandspit."

Sandspit was the location of the commercial airport for the Queen Charlotte Islands, an often fog covered and stormy archipelago that lay just South of the Alaskan panhandle, west of Prince Rupert on the West Coast of British Columbia. Separated from the mainland by the treacherous waters of Hecate Strait, they were the ancestral home of the Haida, a gifted people whose wonderful stone carvings and totems were the current subject of the Provincial museum.

It all fit.

Newton reached in his pocket and produced the voucher for Rusty, who looked at it like it was an unexpected Christmas gift.

"Thanks," he said. "Does this mean I can go now? Things ain't too healthy around here for me."

"I'll make the call this morning if you like," Newton replied. "When you get to Calgary head for the Sally-Anne, they have a brand new building there and they'll help you get a start."

Newton reached in his wallet and took out $50 in small bills, "Here is some traveling money, the bus is reliable but you need to eat on the way."

"That ain't department money is it?" asked Rusty suspiciously. "Why you doing this?"

Newton leaned forward, "Call it a loan if you want, I've seen a lot of people on the streets in my time, some are too far gone, some are just starting to go, and some are coming back, you strike me as one who is coming back because you want to."

Newton got up and left the table, when he looked back at the table Rusty was carefully placing the bills in the same envelope that the voucher was in, he had a determined look on his face, and both were good signs.

Newton's bet on Rusty wasn't as far off the wall as it might seem to someone on the outside. Rusty had got away from the drugs his boss sold, and even stayed away from the alcohol problems of his clients. Rusty got his buzz from belonging. The gang was his family and the streets they worked, his home. It was the need to feel needed that turned Rusty's crank. If he made it to Calgary and if he made contact with the Sally-Anne, then he could stay live. Being alive meant at least he had a chance.

And what of his Jane Doe, did she have a chance?
Newton thought of the childhood she might have had. Would it have been the same as Rusty's?
Which "gang" did she join in school?

"Miss Jones, if you need me to stay and clean the brushes I can do that!"

The little girl in the odd clothes always sat in the front row. During recess she practiced her penmanship, making endless copies of the alphabet. Her hair was done in braids and her desk was always neat and tidy. Curiously she always tried to do her homework before leaving school, except for reading of course. She loved to read and probably had read more books from the school library than anyone else in the class, except for Alice Taylor, and Alice was a charmer wasn't she? Straight "A" student and never seemed to break a sweat. A natural leader you could call her. Alice sat on the other side of the classroom with most of the other girls.

"Honestly, June, did you ever see such an outfit in your life? What on earth could that girl be thinking?"

Patched jeans and sweaters made up her wardrobe. None ever seemed to be the right size.

"Well, girls of that age are still growing in spurts and all, hard to find a size that fits for more than a few weeks. Still, she could have a little more style sense, couldn't she?"
"Maybe she just doesn't care, bit of a loner too. A good student but spends too much time alone. It could be worse though, none of that weird hair and piercing some of the girls wear."
"Shall I pour you more tea, dear? At least we have lots of that here in the teacher's lounge." The teacher named June smiled and raised her cup.

"Nobody sits with me at lunch, Mom, nobody, I hate my clothes, I hate my life, I'll never be popular!"

The echoes, present in every case Newton had, brought to his mind the echoes of a life; sometimes it provided him an insight to what had happened. Sometimes it was just the hollow sound of what might have been. Sometimes it was a foggy veil that lifted every now and then to reveal where the voices originated. For this case the passage of time, as always, was the final arbitrator of which it would be. This also was Newton's law.

In those echoes scenes played out as an early cinema would, usually in a silent jerky motion. Black and white or in color—bright, fresh, and blood red, and always accompanied by disjointed voices.

Newton knew they were dreams. His mind told him that. But that fact did not make them any less real to his heart.

He remembered school, many schools, and many teachers. Of all the ones he had visited or studied in, one teacher stood out in front of so many. He was an older man, though most adults seemed old to him during his youth. Small of stature, he had been a teacher at a remote school, set in the middle of the Canadian prairie. English was his specialty, but life was what he taught.

One day they were in the lunch room, and Newton had sought him out to discuss an assignment, one which was not going particularly well. He had found Mr. Rumsford seated at the desk the teachers used to supervise the kids at lunch.
"Look around Mr. Newton—what do you see?"

Mr. Rumsford always addressed the senior high students in a formal manner, he believed it conveyed to them the sense that they were becoming adults, and should act that way. Newton found to his surprise that it worked.
"I see a bunch of kids eating sir," Newton replied, after gazing over the crowded room.
"You see too little, Mr. Newton, try to expand your vision beyond the obvious, it's what you see that others don't that marks your place in life."
Newton looked again, "I see groups, sir, groups of people eating and talking."
"Very good—for a start—and what does that tell you about the people who make up the groups that you see?"
"I suppose that they are kids with like interests, friends, and things like that."
Mr. Rumsford looked at Newton and shook his head. "Well, that's a start, but still too obvious."
"Lunch rooms are the court of public opinion in our schools, Mr. Newton. A week's observation will set the groups and cliques in your mind. Look over there where the sports teams gather in a herd. Notice how the footballers take over the tables in a loud raucous chorus, they are the biggest boys in the school. The cheerleaders and other general admirers are close by, a giggling flock of colors and perfume."
"What are they wearing Mr. Newton?"
Looking hard he saw some adorned with jackets much too large for them with the school name and tags spelling out their owner's positions.
"Tackle," "End," or "Linebacker."
Newton was about to answer when he stopped, turned slowly to Mr. Rumsford and said, "They are wearing their positions in school society."

Mr. Rumsford smiled, "Yes, Mr. Newton, yes, now what else do you see?"

It was as if a light had suddenly been turned on in his brain, and Newton gazed around the room with a different vision than just that of his eyes.

In the schools of today it had been the same, and Newton never forgot Mr. Rumsford and his words. When he was scheduled to give a talk to a school he made time to visit the lunch rooms. If he had been at the Jane Doe's school what would he have seen?

The baseball team is a lithe group that combines speed and power; they are close by as some boys play on both teams. They too have their cheerleaders.

The drama club is off in a corner, practicing lines from Shakespeare with a modern slang, much to the delight of an impromptu audience. Like peacocks they are preening their feathers and testing the reaction of others to their efforts.

Likewise, in a corner the chess club is meeting, a quiet group with punch clocks and chessmen. One of them is playing three others blindfolded, and the rest are taking notes and discussing the laws of probability. Their admirers are mostly the faculty, chess being an endeavour considered to be further up the evolutionary tree than mere sports.

The science club is voraciously running through the latest volumes of "Discovery" and "Scientific American," their table cluttered with homemade robots and computing equipment. They are oblivious to anyone who might be an admirer, including their girl and boyfriends. They are watched over by Mr. Portney, the physics teacher, who already realizes many of them have surpassed his knowledge in some areas and is undecided if this makes him proud—or just nervous.

The music club is deciding with their teacher what kind of a performance to put on at the end of the semester. The brass section is not as robust this year as last, but they have more violinists. One of the group is threatening to bring his bagpipes to "help" out the wind instruments. Most of them disagree, but their teacher is arguing in favour. "Amazing Grace" on the pipes cannot be beat and it would allow them to push the boundaries of the regular program.

In the middle of this are the majority of the students, gathered in groups large and small, chatting amongst themselves and changing places and tables. They are showing each other the latest in fashions, MP3 players, and gaming gear. Backpacks are a big item this year and everyone seems to have one.

 Well, not everyone. There are those who sit alone, or with just a friend or two, lost in their own world with a book, or just lost and unnoticed. A student or teacher will pass by and engage them in conversation for a moment and they brighten and respond or shy away, sometimes both. They are the uninvited to birthday parties and forgotten when Valentines are passed around unless there is a system to ensure everyone is on the list. But their scrapbooks hold every card received, every invitation that came in the mail, even if someone's mother insisted they be invited, every class picture is there, every poster and paper. These things are their proof that they matter.

 Which group would she be in, mused Newton? And which of the echoes reaching out to me, is hers?

 How much of a difference would it make to them if someone smiled, took an interest, got past the clothes and backpacks and surface clutter and gave them a chance? If sometimes a small rock can change the direction of an avalanche, what does it take to make a difference in a life? What would or did make a difference in hers?

 In nature, for each action there is an equal and opposite reaction, but with people the reaction is complimentary and compounded, good things usually resulted in better ones, and bad ones brought about worse.

This also, was Newton's Law.

CHAPTER NINE

The museum was a large airy building that gave off the feeling of a beehive in some ways. It was one of the first that made an effort to get things out from behind glass walls and roped off rooms and put them in a setting where they could be seen in context. Areas were remodeled to show how tools were used, life was lived, and why things were valued. Taking a step back in time allowed the visitor to appreciate the genius of a canning machine, or the hard work required to keep a team of horses shod, fed, and productive. The museum had discovered that actually watching a totem being carved with the use of traditional tools and decorated with colourings made from various natural materials enabled a closer connection between the public and the exhibit. This allowed them to appreciate more deeply the dedication and spiritual connection of the artists to their work.

One of the new exhibits was comprised of the artistry of the various aboriginal nations that inhabited the West Coast of Canada. Each had a place in the exhibit and one of the most visited was that of the Haida. Their Argillite carvings were intricate and beautiful. Like art everywhere, it said that a civilization had reached the point where the needs of its people had been met to such an extent that there was surplus time available for other things. It was this exhibit that was the responsibility of the girl in the sketch, and Newton made his way to the museum's offices to inquire about her.

Museums make an effort to exude a calm and studied atmosphere. The visitor is encouraged to study and learn by the unhurried pace of the exhibits. Behind the scenes things are much, much different. On the top floor, away from the crowds and carefully laid out posters, paintings, and exhibits there exists a world of carefully controlled chaos. No museum can store and display every artifact of interest to the public. The more successful a museum is at collecting, displaying, and educating, the more in demand its exhibits become. Collections that are in demand become part of a traveling display loaned from museum to museum in cities in many different countries. The responsibility for coordinating the preparation for receiving and exhibiting them and then sending them on to their next destination falls on the museum staff. This was in addition to their regular duties. Because no museum has enough room to show everything it collects, there is a constant cycle of exhibits being prepared for display, displayed for a period of time, then protected and stored away. Of course, collections are being added to every day.

This is what the girl in the sketch was doing right now, Newton learned.

Alicia Howell was her name, and she was 22 years old.

Newton was speaking to James R Worthington, a middle aged man who could be the poster boy for North American museums. He wore a turtleneck sweater, flannel slacks, loafers, and sported a beard and moustache. His accent and manner displayed his British ancestry. Sitting behind a desk cluttered with an eclectic display of bits and pieces he sipped tea from a translucent cup and saucer. Newton had the distinct impression that it was from a collection of fine china the museum owned.

"I would think it unusual to have someone so young with the responsibility of acquiring such valuable pieces," Newton was saying.

"Yes, quite, well it's a bit of an unusual circumstance you see," Worthington responded. "The artist is rather, well, set in his ways so to speak, and he will only release these carvings to her."
He went on, "You see, Elijah Longeyes is sort of the custodian for his people of these carvings and he is rather particular about who he trusts and so on. But as long as it is what he wishes, and it works, we can accommodate his conditions."

"When do you expect Ms. Howell to return?"

"Well, that's the thing, you see, there is no set time, she sort of goes up there from time to time and then returns with a new exhibit, or not, as Elijah sees fit."

"When did she leave?"

"Ah, that would be last Friday, and she should be back in a week or two if things hold as they have been."

"When you need to contact her, how do you arrange that?" Newton asked.

"Actually, we don't directly. We just leave a message at the hotel, and she calls us, when she's in town that is. You have to understand that most of her work up there takes her away from the phone and cell phones don't have the coverage to reach her."

"What exactly does she do in the field?" Newton looked from the notes he was jotting down in his notebook.

"Basically she collects new art on behalf of the museum. As I said, in this case she works with Elijah. He supplies us with the best carvings, but only a few at a time, and we have them for only a limited period."

"Does she take them back when you're done with them?"
"Um, yes and no, we send them FedEx to the hotel, and Elijah picks them up, although he has on occasion requested she bring a piece back personally."

"How do you notify him that they are on their way?"

"We don't."

"Excuse me?" Newton looked up from his notebook again with a quizzical expression.

"We don't let him know, we just send them FedEx and he is always there to receive them. Don't ask me how he knows, but he always does, I expect that FedEx calls ahead to make sure that someone will be there to sign for them. They are insured rather heavily."

"Insured for how much?"

"It runs a minimum of $50,000 U.S., sometimes up to $200,000 or more for some of the more select pieces."

"Really," Newton paused for a minute, leaning back in his seat, "and how often does this occur?"

"Actually, until Alicia came on board with us, we rarely had pieces of this quality. It's only been in the last two years that we have been getting these particular pieces, and that is why we decided to create the exhibit."

Newton left the museum armed with the latest itinerary for Alicia and headed back to the office. He would contact the local R.C.M.P. detachment in the Charlottes and see if they could arrange for an interview. With a little luck he might be able to learn the identity of his Jane Doe.

To his surprise, when he arrived he found a message already waiting for him on his desk. It was from the R.C.M.P. Cpl.in charge of the detachment in Queen Charlotte City.

TO: Detective Alfred Newton

FM: Cpl.Nels Taylor
    R.C.M.P. Detachment
    Q.C. City

        We have been contacted by a Mr. Elijah Longeyes who has requested that you make arrangements to travel here in the next two days. Mr. Longeyes does not have regular access to a phone and has made this request to me in person. I have known Elijah for two years and have found him to be helpful to the R.C.M.P. in the course of past inquiries. In anticipation of your acceptance we have made reservations for you at the hotel. Please respond directly to this office with any questions you may have.

Signed:
        Cpl.Taylor NCO I/C
        R.C.M.P. Q.C. City

"Well, well," thought Newton, "this is interesting." He picked up the phone and called the force's travel agent.

"Going traveling, boss?" asked Willy, looking up from the pile of paperwork scattered around his desk.

"Apparently," answered Newton, "and also apparently, I'm expected." He tossed the note over to Willy who read it through twice.

"Weird eh?"

"Interesting," Newton responded with a smile.

CHAPTER TEN

It wasn't that Newton didn't accept that some things in the world were unexplainable; in fact, he did. Often in his line of work, he had come across evidence at the scene which led to the conviction of the culprit. The presence of the evidence was sometimes as much a mystery as the original event. Sometimes solving that mystery would result in solving the main mystery. Why did that button have a particular and identifying pattern, how was it that a single hair could be lost, and more importantly found? Some would call it the Law of Averages. With so many hairs on a body, the chances of losing one or two were better than most people thought. Others would say Karma, it was meant to be this way. Still others chalked it up to good police work. There is always the presence of evidence; it just needs to be found. Newton had a different, more ethereal view that sprang from his belief that, just as there was abundant evil in the world, there was also good, and everyone chooses their side to be on.

So what of his Jane Doe, what side did she choose?

Was she a troublemaker in her youth? If so, there was little evidence of it. Her body bore none of the common indicators. No piercing, tattoos, evidence of unnatural hair colour, or permanent lip markings that the young of this generation used to signify their rebellion. Not that any of these in and by themselves meant the wearer had made any choice, other than to stand out from the crowd. There were also no needle tracks, no blood evidence of drug abuse, or anything else that indicated she was not just an ordinary girl in definitely unordinary circumstances.

What do ordinary girls, or boys for that matter, do?
They have families, siblings usually, and lead a life that would be marked at the top of a bell curve. Their school work would be returned with a "C" or "C+" grading in most areas, some things higher, some things lower. There would be certain activities that stood out, showing either a surplus, or a lack, of talent. Mostly they just plodded along from year to year, ending up in a regular job in a regular place doing regular things. Being found dead on a beach was not considered part of a regular life.

A return phone call from the travel agency confirmed his trip itinerary and departure time. The tickets would be sent over by courier.

"How long this time," Willy asked, "do you expect to be gone?"

"Couple of days at most I think. I'll just check out this lead and see what information Mr. Longeyes has for me that couldn't be given to the R.C.M.P. to forward on."

"Doesn't it seem a bit strange to you that he needs to talk to you in person, especially if you two haven't met before?"

"I suspect it's not just talk that is on his mind, there must be something up there he needs to show me—something that cannot be shipped or examined by the Mounties."

"Hmm," said Willy. "Well, as the rabbit once said to Alice—curiouser and curiouser. Anyway while you're off on your trip, I'll keep the investigation going at this end. We've been making progress at the marinas, and by that I mean in coverage, not results." Willy indicated the pile of reports on his desk from the night shift. "Not much new coming to light, but we have been able to eliminate all of the larger marinas and most of the small ones."

"Good, anything we can do to narrow the search is helpful."

His tickets were delivered by courier and the departure time left him but a couple of hours to throw together a suitcase and head for the airport. His journey would take him first to Vancouver, next to Prince Rupert on the West Coast, and then, if he was lucky and the weather was good he would land at Sandspit. From there he would rent a car and head north along the only highway to Queen Charlotte City. If he was not lucky he would have to wait for a cross strait flight in a charter aircraft. Of course, the R.C.M.P. could have one of their helicopters or fixed wing aircraft in the area and he might hitch a ride if it was available. Time would tell and the secret was to be prepared for whatever the circumstances dictated.

As he drove north towards the airport, Newton glanced at the countryside. The road which had been so deserted when he was driving it as a patrol officer in his youth, was now a highway lined with homes and shops for its entire length. It sometimes seemed as if the world had come to visit and then just stayed on. With it came all the problems of a crowded community. Land suitable for building was scarce, and so houses crowded in on one another, turning once pleasant communities into anthills. Where once you looked forward to meeting your neighbour and helping out, the trend was now to look upon him with suspicion and complain that his kids were too noisy or his car blocked yours.

If it was true that too much familiarity bred contempt, then what of too little contact with your neighbours—what was the end result of that? Newton knew the answer without having to think about it. The increasing volume of domestic disputes, neighbour problems, and general impoliteness was spelled out each day in the reports that crossed his desk. The job of the patrol officer had turned into that of mediator. From his perspective it had other consequences. There had been a time when he could get reliable information from anyone on a street about a strange car or person frequenting the neighbourhood. Now, it seemed, few knew their neighbour's name. Hopefully Mr. Longeyes would be more in tune with the happenings in his community than the locals folks here were. This would be one of the more unusual sources of information Newton had interviewed, but he had learned to keep an open mind. The truth could appear from any direction and any source.

This too was Newton's Law.

CHAPTER ELEVEN

Any trip to the Charlottes is an adventure in itself. Even if you live in the Vancouver area, the flight stood a better than even chance of landing in Prince Rupert rather than Sandspit. Anyone with experience in the aviation world would tell you the weather is enormously fickle in that area of the world. The water is a mix of the Japanese current sweeping eastward and the colder waters from the Bering Sea that flowed south along the coast of Alaska. They met, more or less, at the tip of the Queen Charlottes. This cauldron boiled down the Hecate straits, stirred by the winds which suddenly found themselves confined between the islands and Coast Range Mountains. The seabed itself was shallow and thus the wind could whip the water into mountainous waves in what seemed like minutes.

It was between these waves that Newton now found himself. He was strapped into the right hand seat of a Yellow Grumman Goose. The twin engine plane was a charter from the island that happened to be in Prince Rupert when the Air Canada flight had diverted there, being unable to land, yet again, at the fog shrouded Sandspit airport. George Thompson, the pilot of the Grumman was happily humming to himself as he expertly piloted the amphibian just under the clouds and rain and just above the waves. It was as if he had done it dozens of times before, and of course, he had.

Most passengers would be in a state of panic, gazing upwards at the tops of the waves whilst flying at an indicated airspeed of 120 knots t. It would be terrifying to most. Newton however, was enjoying every minute. In his teens, he had learned to fly in Vernon B.C., the airport there was guarded on the East by power lines and trees, to the West by a trailer park and Okanogan Lake. Landing was usually from the east, requiring an approach over the City followed by a side slip on to the airport runway. The rivers of air that swirled around the strip were influenced by the moisture and moderating body of the lake, and the rock canyons of the surrounding mountains. If you learned to fly there, you could pretty much fly anywhere.

George, a long time resident of the Charlottes, was enjoying the flight. For once his passengers were neither sick, scared out of their wits, or frantically looking around for a place to hide. He had noticed that Newton took the time to conduct an instrument sweep every few minutes, with his glances resting on the outside air temperature and engine RPM gauges. He was alert for changes in the sound of the engines that might indicate the presence of carb ice forming. When the air is sucked into the carburetors, it speeds up and loses some of its heat. Any moisture in the air would tend to form ice if the amount of heat loss took it below freezing—such as on a day like this with fog, cloud, and rain. The ice could block off the carb, the engine would lose power and the plane would suddenly become a boat. To prevent this, the pilot would apply carb heat, diverting some of the heated air generated by the engine to the carb to keep the air temperature above freezing. The problem with that was the heated air was then less dense, and the engine developed less power. So it was a balancing act, but today with the aircraft lightly loaded, the loss in power was not so critical and George kept the carb heat open a little more than necessary. Conscious that the altitude they were flying at, mere feet above the water, allowed him no room for error.

When the cloud level lifted, he eased the aircraft higher, maintaining visual contact with the sea. If necessary, he could have climbed into the clouds and navigated by instruments as he had done many times before. The Charlottes were home to an air force navigation station. A giant ring of antennas laid out in a circle, known as a VOR. Through the magic of radio signals it broadcast a signal that aircraft instruments could interpret as an electronic compass. It would display the heading to the antenna, and the distance the aircraft was from it. George knew exactly what bearing to take to the VOR and when on that bearing, what distance reading would place him in the harbour.

But like most pilots, he enjoyed the feeling of speed that only came when you were flying close to the surface. If the day was clear and he was alone, he would be flying like this, with the side window open, listening to the roar of the engines and the rush of the air. As the aircraft climbed higher, Newton began to pay more attention to the outside of the plane. The storm-tossed waves below him were growing in height as they neared the center of the strait. The wind almost always blew from the north here, and these waters had claimed many a fishing boat, especially when the herring run was on. Canadian fisheries regulations limited the time available to catch the little silvery fish to mere hours. That meant that the captains had often only a single chance to fill their holds. A full catch would pay for the season while anything less would usually mean another talk with the bank. So they filled their holds to the brim when they could; risking a heavy sea could cause the boat to roll past the point of stability, and the weight of the catch would doom the boat to capsizing. A man could last but minutes in the cold Alaskan current, if they made it out of the wreck at all, and not many did.

There were no boats to be seen today, however, since the run was not on and the local salmon were not plentiful enough to risk fishing in this weather. To the north was the Alaskan panhandle, an archipelago of islands that hosted some of the last stands of virgin timber on the coast. Islands to the north and east were the home range of the Komodo bears, a strain of white furred black bears believed sacred to the Haida and other native groups. Further north, the cities of Skagway and Anchorage prospered with oil revenues and the crab fisheries of the Bering Sea.

This was truly the edge of one of the last frontiers on the North American continent. Like all frontiers it attracted both those searching for adventure, and those fleeing from it. Some came to make a life and some to start a life anew. People here placed more value in action than history.

Newton wondered how he would be received here, as an outsider. Around for a short time, applying rules from a community many sought to escape from and many more didn't care to know. It takes time to be accepted and for people to open up, especially on a frontier. That is not to say folks wouldn't be hospitable; the hospitality of the North is legendary, people gave freely, like your life depended on it, in the realization that at any given time circumstances could reverse the roles and it may be their own life at risk. There are no fire stations in the bush and relief agencies are few and far between. When you lose everything up here, it usually means just that, everything. The detachment of the Royal Canadian Mounted Police would provide a base position to work from and Newton would be depending upon the legend of the Mounties to some extent to open doors that otherwise might be closed against him. Cpl.Taylor promised to be a good resource, and also there was the mysterious Elijah Longeyes, whose role in this case was yet to be determined.

The clouds lifted rapidly now, and as they neared shore, the waters calmed below them as George brought the Goose in for a landing. Soon the familiar bump of the flaps and the changed attitude of the aircraft signaled the start of the let down. Newton watched as George's practiced hands went from lever to lever, checking the gear was up for a water landing, adjusting the prop speed and engine power, nudging the trim wheels and easing the flaps into full landing configuration. That done, George searched for, and found the landmarks on the shore he was looking for, called his intentions over the Unicom, and settled the twin on its final approach.

Water is surprisingly hard when struck at speed, and a hard landing is a hard landing whether on land or water. Seaplanes require extra reinforcement to take the repeated pounding, and the surface of the water can be hard to judge. Many a pilot has landed above, and below it, causing a bounce on a good day, and a swim on a bad one. On this day George landed the craft like it was made of paper. A small bump indicated contact with the surface of the sea and the roar of the engines was supplemented with the swish of the water and the increasing drag on the hull as the twin settled like a welcome lover.

The Grumman taxied across the water towards the dock. Equipped with a water rudder, the aircraft steered like a boat, and applying power to one engine or the other assisted in the maneuvering. When he was about 25 feet from the shore, George lowered the wheels from their positions on each side of hull, and headed for a concrete ramp that was more commonly used to launch a fishing boat off a trailer. The aircraft, with its wheels down and locked, traveled up the ramp and parked over to one side.

George shut down the engines and looked over to Newton who was unbuckling his seat belt.

"How many hours?"
Newton smiled, "Just over 100, 20 or so in twins."
"Thought so," said George. "If you go back over with me, I'll let you take her for a while."
"Thanks, but only if the weather allows a little more altitude, I'm usually expecting to troll for salmon when I can see the top of the waves above me!"
George smiled back, and nodded to a tall man standing at the edge of the ramp, "I think Elijah wants to talk with you, he sent me over to Rupert to pick you up. I'll get your luggage unloaded."

The Grumman had a rear door for the luggage hold and George fished out Newton's single bag and brought it to him.

With that, George motioned to two young kids, "ramp rats." Fascinated by aircraft, they hung around the tie down for the plane doing odd jobs in hope of getting a ride from time to time. Wherever they were in the town, the sound of an aircraft approaching brought them lemming-like to the dock. Eagerly they broke out a couple of hoses and proceeded to wash the salt water off the twin. George supervised, making sure they played the water into every nook and cranny to chase out the salt. Just as water is a universal solvent, salt water is a universal corrosive, even to aluminum.

CHAPTER TWELVE

Newton sized up the man awaiting him. Elijah Longeyes was a tall, well muscled individual standing just over six feet tall. His hair was black, well kept, and covered with a felt bush hat. He stood with a self assured ease resting on one leg. His arms were crossed in front of a simple jacket, dark blue in color, and he wore a pair of jeans freshly washed and well worn. His boots were the typical work boot marketed by any number of stores, leather with steel toes. The left boot was more scuffed than the right, so he was probably right handed.

That was confirmed when they got closer and Elijah stuck out his right hand.

"You must be Detective Newton."
"And you must be Elijah Longeyes."

The two men shook hands as an R.C.M.P. cruiser pulled up beside them.
Cpl.Nels Taylor exited the car and came around to them.

"I see you two have met."
"Just arrived." Newton said turning to Elijah. "Nice of you to meet me."
"Well, you know how it is," Elijah said with a chuckle. "You white men always need a guide, even in a small town like this."
Taylor smiled, "Elijah would be the best guide in these parts, he always seems to know what is happening, and to whom."
"Speaking of that," Newton responded, "what can you tell me about this girl?" fishing in his pocket for the sketch he brought.

"Ah, yes, you want to know about Alicia," Elijah said immediately without waiting for Newton to produce the sketch. "She is out in the field, looking for the golden spruce."
"Golden spruce?"
"It's a local legend." Taylor said as he motioned them to take a seat in the cruiser. "There is a single golden spruce tree in a stand of regular green pine trees, that the locals say was touched by the great spirit which caused its needles to turn to gold."
"Actually, that's the tourist version." Elijah said with a wink. "We locals have a different explanation." The men chuckled and the cruiser soon pulled up in front of the detachment building. Along the way the weather had cycled from sun to rain and to snow, which was typical for

the Charlottes at this time of year.

The detachment building was a typical rural R.C.M.P. setup, a small office, a couple of meeting rooms and a cell off to one side. Living quarters were attached to one side for the NCO in charge and separated by a pair of stout doors. The ever present coffee maker in one corner of the office gave off the welcome smell of a fresh pot brewing. The shelves were packed with versions of the Canadian Criminal Code going back ten years or so, also customs and fishing regulations. While the myriad of other enforcement responsibilities set out in statute that the R.C.M.P. are required to attend to took up the rest of the available space.

Sitting in the Cpl's office with the customary cup of coffee, Elijah turned to Newton.

"You will want to talk to Alicia about the dead girl I expect."
"How did you know that?" Newton looked up sharply.
"My fault," Cpl.Taylor chimed in. "I showed the picture of your Jane Doe and the sketch of Alicia to Elijah."
"And do you think she has any information, did she ever mention a girlfriend to you?" Newton asked Elijah.

"Not by name certainly, and that is what you are seeking I'm sure, but she did mention that there was a friend of hers back in Victoria that was interested in acquiring a carving. It was someone who had also asked if there were some other pieces from a particular artist that could be purchased."

"And are there any?"
"For sale? No. And in this case it would not be necessary." Elijah replied.
"Not necessary? Why would that be." Newton asked
"Because," Elijah said leaning back in his chair. "Alicia is already the owner."

At this point, seeing the expression on Newton's face, Cpl.Taylor jumped in.

"Elijah is one of the Haida elders, a respected shaman and leader. One of their core beliefs is that an object has a spirit. The spirit of the original artist is embodied in his creations, and that spirit may select another person as a sort of caretaker after the original artist passes on."

Newton turned to Elijah, "And you believe the carvings have selected Alicia as their caretaker?"

"It is so." Elijah said. "The carvings are old, very old, hundreds of years in some cases. They were lost to us until Alicia arrived two summers ago. She found them in a cave on the west side of the Island, since then she has taken a few to the museum for viewing."

"Do you know how she came to find the cave?"
"Sure," replied Elijah, "The carvings showed her the way."
"There is a map?"
"Of sorts," replied Elijah with a grin. "You are one of the few to see it that way. One of the carvings given to the museum had a scene on it that she recognized."
"Ah, from a dream or vision?" Newton asked with a smile.
"It was a National Geographic article on these islands four years ago. Alicia recognized the scene from a photograph and found it. A rock fall had in the meantime revealed the old cave entrance, and the rest, as they say, is history."

"The museum tells me that you only allow a few pieces out at a time, and that the previously viewed ones must be returned before new ones can be put on display."
"Actually, that was Alicia's plan; she knew that too many on display at one time would saturate the public's desire to see them, better that they should be parceled out in small lots and keep an air of mystery around them."

"Really?" Newton responded. "I would not have expected that of one so young."
"Ah, yes," Elijah winked, "She is young, but the spirits of the carvings are much older."
"So she could take as many of the carvings as she wanted, and do with them as she wished?" Newton asked.
"Of course, and she knew that. She intended on giving one to her friend, but something happened at the museum, a piece went missing and she didn't want to risk taking another one down there. The carving was recovered later and I believe she was going to select another one on this trip, but, well, now I suppose that won't be happening."

"Does Alicia know her friend is dead?" Asked Newton
"No, at least not from me she doesn't. As I said, she has been out doing fieldwork."

The ringing of the phone interrupted the conversation and Cpl.Taylor picked it up.

"Right," he said after listening for a few seconds, "Which beach is this?" "OK then, I'll head out there. Tell Tony to get the wrecker out there as soon as possible, and, Sheila, better let the doctor know."

The last sentence got the attention of Newton and Elijah, and they looked expectantly as Cpl. Taylor put the phone down. Taylor looked over at Newton. "You better come with me, in fact both of you, we just got a report of another 4x4 turning up on the beach, out on the flats."

As they headed to the cruiser, Newton asked "What are the flats?"
"The flats are a tidal sandbank where folks gather clams at low tide." Elijah replied as they climbed in.
Taylor added, "That wouldn't be bad if that's all they did, but some of the younger ones use the flats as a race track in their 4x4 trucks, and even that wouldn't be so bad." He continued switching on the overhead lights and headed out to the west of town towards the military communications post. "But when the tide comes in the flats turn into quicksand, and more than a few have got stuck there. Sometimes Tony gets there quick enough with his tow truck to get them out, or someone else runs a winch line and hauls them back to solid ground. Every now and then they don't make it and have to wait until the next low tide to recover the vehicle. Not much usable at that point after soaking in the salt chuck for 12 hours."

"And this time?" Posed Newton.
"This time it's not just a truck they found when the tide went out, they also found a body—and they think it could be Alicia."

CHAPTER THIRTEEN

The road to the beach was a short drive and the traffic was typically light. When they got there a few minutes later, there was already a crowd. The usual group of kids with their Toyotas and Jeeps, and some of the town elders had arrived. Somehow word had reached folks who didn't have a phone. The red and blue flashing lights of the cruiser were joined by Tony's amber tow truck light as he pulled into the parking lot. Out on the flats, still covered with water, the top of a 4x4 Jeep Renegade could be seen, around it two canoes and an aluminum boat circled. The boat had two young men in it, each canoe had one of the elders. On the beach was a Toyota with its winch cable trailing from the front mount out to the water line. It was owned by one of the kids from the military camp, he was sitting on the hood, with his arms wrapped around a shaken young girl.

Taylor switched off the cruiser's lights and all three headed down to the young man's jeep where a crowd was slowly gathering.

"Hello, Peter." Taylor said walking up to the young man. "What's going on here?"
The young man nodded towards the beach.
"We were driving down the beach road towards camp, when Nancy saw the top of the truck in the water. So I figured one of the guys got stuck last night and I rolled out the winch to help," he said indicating the played out cable. "A couple of the guys showed up in that boat," and pointed at the aluminum boat circling the truck. "Then when they went to see if they could attach the cable, they came speeding back saying there was a body in the truck, a girl, and I called it in to you." His companion nodded in agreement, saying nothing out loud, the scared look on her pale face was the same as both officers had seen many times before. It was the first time she had been this close to a fatality.

The occupants of the boat had by now noticed the cruiser's arrival and headed their craft into shore. Taylor walked down to the beach and waited there for them to arrive. He knew them both; they were from town, a couple of native kids who spent most of their time on the fishing boats. Both of them good kids and apart from the usual hijinks kids pull off, neither had been in trouble. Even though both were of legal drinking age, he couldn't recall that he had ever seen either of them in the one and only hotel bar.

The boat's motor sputtered to a stop and the crunch of gravel

announced its grounding. Taylor and Newton grabbed hold of the front
and pulled it further on shore. The two kids, Johnny Wilson and Eric
Littleknife, scrambled out of the boat and stood in front of Taylor, both
started talking at once, their voices tumbling on one another like the
incoming tide.
"There's a girl in there!"
"Yeah and she's dead!"
"We tried to get her out, but her seat belt is stuck."
"I think that truck is Mel's."
"Yeah it's his truck alright, got both tail lights missing and there's the
dent from where he hit the rocks last winter."

"OK, OK slow down, one at a time, Johnny, you go with this fellow
here," he said, indicating Newton, "and tell him what you saw and did.
Eric you come with Elijah and me."

Newton reached out and shook Johnny's hand, "Hello there, young
man, I'm Detective Newton, why don't we step over here and you can
tell me what happened."

Newton could see the excitement and fear on the young man's face.
Most people never see a dead body up close in their lifetime, except in
the movies, a TV screen, or at a relative's funeral. It took some time
for the shock to wear off. After you see enough of them, it took some
time for the shock to begin. Newton could still remember every one
that he had been required to attend to. From the natural passing of
the elderly, to the victims of traffic accidents or the evil man does to
man. Some had the look of peacefulness about them, as if their
passing was a relief from the turmoil of their lives. For others, the
shock that they were dying was still etched on their faces, and in the
very young, for whom there was no understanding of death, there was
a sense of wonder, as if a new door had been opened for them. No
regrets at leaving a life barely begun, of expectations not realized.

His Jane Doe on the beach had displayed a resigned look, an
acceptance of what had to be. "Maybe I'll do better next time?"

The young man was talking excitedly.

"Eric and me, we were heading out to check the crab traps and we
saw someone on the beach waving us over, so we get there and says
there's a truck or something and wants us to run a cable to it. So we
head out there to it and Eric starts to climb out to the roof so he can
get down and hook the cable to the bumper and then he screams at

me that there's a dead girl in the truck."

"OK, slow down a bit, take a deep breath and relax for a minute." Newton said. "Now then, which way were you coming from?"
"We headed here from the marina," Johnny said, pointing towards town. "We have some crab traps set just outside the low tide mark."
"And what time was this?"
"Oh man, about an hour ago."

"You say you saw these folks on the beach?" Newton said, indicating Peter and Nancy, "Did you see anyone else?"
"Nope they were the only ones."
"OK, so you saw them on the beach and they called you over, is that right?"
"Yep. Soon as we passed that point over there. They were waving their arms and calling us."
"What were they doing exactly?" Newton asked
"Well, the guy was pulling out the cable from the winch, and the girl was waving her arms."
"OK, then what?"

"We come into shore and they point at this thing in the water. You couldn't see it much from the water, but you could just see the waves breaking over it from the shore up where they were parked. When we got up to the end of the cable, Eric grabs it and we hook it up to the end of the boat, I held it away from the motor 'til we got close to the truck and then Eric tries to get onto the roof."

"How much was out of the water at that point?"
"Not much, just the top of the roof, maybe a couple of inches."
"OK, what then?"
"Well, Eric grabs hold of the roof and then he looks down and then he yells that there's someone in the truck and drops the cable, and then we head back into shore."

"When did you see the folks in the Canoes arrive?"
"Well, the guy in the truck on shore, he uses his cell phone and calls you guys, then the girl, she phones her folks, then before you know it all kinds of people show up. The elders came in their canoes just before you arrived."

"And you know the owner or the truck in the water?" Newton asked.

"Yep, it's Mel's truck, Mel Lonepine, he lives in the East Village, works

on the fish boats with us from time to time."
"Do you know him well?"
"Off and on, we don't hang out together or anything, just see him around."
"Did you recognize the girl in the truck?"
"No, I've never seen her before."
"OK, thanks, we will need a complete statement from you, please wait right here."

Newton headed over to Taylor, who was also finishing up talking to Eric. The Cpl.arranged for both boys to be transported separately back to the detachment office where they would give formal statements and answer any other questions that may come up.

The tide was ebbing faster now and the water was half way down the windows of the truck. Taylor grabbed a camera and a yellow plastic blanket from the cruiser and made a call requesting the detachment summons an ident team from Prince Rupert. So far it simply looked like an accidental drowning, but you could never be sure. That done, they headed out in the boat to the scene.

Peter had by now reeled in the cable the boys had earlier taken out to the truck, and a screech from the winch announced Tony was preparing to run out the cable from the wrecker. By now a couple of the other constables had arrived and were taking control of the gathering crowd. Like crowds anywhere, they were drawn to the unusual. Newton noticed that several of the elders had gathered together and had begun a quiet chanting. Prayers for the dead?

Newton estimated the distance to the truck from shore to be about 150 feet. The bottom seemed to be mostly sand and mud.
"Not much on the bottom for a tire to grip." He said to the Corporal.
"Not around here, no rocks of any substance, that's why the kids wait for low tide when the sand is packed."
The boat made the journey in a few minutes and when they reached the truck, Newton observed both windows were down. As the young men had reported the lifeless body of a woman was still sitting on the passenger side. He confirmed the shoulder harness from the seat belt was still in place. Face hidden by the water, her long hair floated on the water, moving in time with the current as it ran through the open windows with her.

Using the bowline from the boat, they secured their craft to the door handle on the passenger side and tied off both the bow and stern to give them as solid a platform as possible. The click of a camera and the swish of the waves was the only sound for a few moments.

"Ready?" Nels asked, as he passed the camera over.
He peered through the viewfinder and focused the lens on the back of her head, then nodded.
Taylor reached through the passenger window and turned the face of Alicia Howell towards Newton.

The camera clicked again and the motor drive advanced the film to the next frame.

CHAPTER FOURTEEN

That evening Newton was once again sitting in Cpl. Taylor's office. The Jeep had been recovered from the flats when the tide had receded and towed to the locked compound at the rear of the detachment. The trip took only a few minutes and was accompanied by an R.C.M.P. cruiser. The body of Alicia was left inside, wrapped in the yellow blanket that most police forces carried for such purposes. Once there, the ident team from "K" Division was waiting, having flown up from Vancouver on an R.C.M.P. Beaver aircraft. They went about their work in the quiet deliberate way they always did. Carefully taking pictures and material samples from the Renegade, placing anything that might be of some evidentiary value into plastic bags and sealing them. The vehicle had not been in the water long enough to get coated in anything other than a light film of sand, allowing the team to examine the vehicle thoroughly. Alicia's body had been taken to the local hospital for examination, and both Taylor and Newton were awaiting those results. When the vehicle was winched to shore, they had both made some observations about the body. No obvious signs of trauma were seen, no bruises, cuts, or other outward signs of force. One of the ident team members along with one constable had been detailed to attend the examination. As in the case of Newton's Jane Doe, a camera would record the results on film, and a pen on the paper in the police officer's notebook. This would be backed up by the audio recorder in the mortuary—a final official acknowledgement of her life.

Newton had grown accustomed to such waits in his career, such as he could. He always found his mind focused during this period on the life of the victim, like he did with the young girl, whose death started this case in motion. There was another young girl on his mind, the one Rusty had identified as being in Bellingham. Like a ghost, thoughts of her swirled on the periphery of his mind. Where was she now, what was she doing, was she well, unhurt, and happy?
Was she even alive?
Newton was fairly confident on the last point, he would have heard if it was not the case, because after all, he was her father

And he would always wait for her.

They were also waiting for word on the whereabouts of Mel LonePine. They had gone to his home of course, but there was no sign of him there. He lived alone, in a trailer parked on the edge of the reserve. His father had died long ago and his mother was an invalid living with her relatives who could care for her. Mel received a government cheque each month as part of his band's treaty settlement, and he supplemented his income by working on the docks or shipping out on a fish boat whenever one was in need of crew. An aspiring carver, his trailer housed pieces of his work dating back several years. Each one traced the evolution of his talent in stone, from the earliest attempts to the last piece he worked on. Occasionally he put a piece up for sale in one of the tourist spots. Some sold, most didn't.

Cpl.Taylor and Newton learned that Mel was considered in the community to be a shy and quiet kind of guy. He didn't spend his nights in the bar nor had he any history of violence with the detachment. Elijah knew him best as a loner, whose ambition was to improve his skills as a carver. His weekends were likely to be spent looking for Argillite to carve.

Elijah joined them as the ident crews were wrapping up their day's work.
"Mel is not in the village, and he has not been seen since yesterday," he reported. "The elders will call when he returns."
"Any idea of where he would go?" Taylor asked.
"You mean "go" as in run away?" Elijah asked. "If so, nowhere. He's not the running kind, never has been, as long as I've known him."
"Well, there are only two ways off this island, and he was not seen at the airport in Sandspit, and the Grumman is still tied up, so that leaves a boat of some sort." Newton added.

"The fishing fleet is more or less tied up, no season at this time of year, though there may be the odd crab fisherman checking traps. Not much of a commercial crab fishery around here, I have one of the guys checking the docks now, so we will know soon. That leaves a small boat and perhaps a camp or cabin on the coast somewhere," Taylor said.
"Possible, though not likely," Elijah responded. "Not in his spirit."
"Folks do things out of character sometimes when they get in over their head." Taylor noted.

A knock at the door interrupted the men.

"We're done for tonight Cpl." It was Sgt. Johansen of the ident team. "Preliminary findings are here," and he passed over an envelope. "We'll take another look tomorrow with fresh eyes to see if we've missed anything."

Elijah left with Newton and headed for the hotel. Cpl.Taylor did not show him the contents of the envelope. He would look at it overnight and discuss the results with Newton in the morning if there was something he needed to know. Officially, this was an R.C.M.P. investigation and he was the lead. Newton's connection and interest in the case was obvious and there was no doubt in Taylor's mind that his request to keep the city detective fully informed would be approved. R.C.M.P. detachments were always undermanned and depended heavily on the cooperation of those municipalities and cities whose borders they shared. In return, they made the resources of their force of 14 thousand plus members and the experts in their labs available when needed. Still, protocol needed to be followed and thus he had made the formal request through "channels" as required.

Once at the hotel, Elijah said good night and headed home, Newton headed to the desk to check for any messages. Not that he was expecting any, but it was his habit to do so whenever he was out of town. Anything to do with any cases he was working on would likely come through the R.C.M.P. Canadian Police Information Centre terminal at the detachment office unless there was something personal or private. He was a little surprised then when the clerk handed over an envelope with a fax message in it. Tucking it under his arm, he headed up to his room.

The room was typical for a hotel, a small bathroom just off the main door, and a double bed. A small desk and two chairs completed the furnishings. The window, framed in heavy curtains, looked out on the ocean. On a clear day it was said you could see Alaska from it. This was not one of those days. At night all you could see was the lights of the town, and off to the west, a smaller glow from the military camp. An air conditioner took up the lower corner of the window. Newton could not imagine it ever being used.

It had been a long day, and after a quick shower, he phoned down to order something to eat. He was not surprised to learn that room service had ceased for the day. Most small towns did not have the business flow to warrant keeping the kitchen open past the regular dinner hour. Changing into a comfortable set of jeans and a shirt, Newton headed down to the restaurant.

Typical of smaller hotels, the restaurant occupied part of the lower floor, with a doorway off the main reception area. There was no door to the outside street save the mandatory fire ext. This forced any street traffic to walk pass the front counter, and all the advertising the hotel had on exhibit in the foyer. Still, for a small hotel, it had a good feeling about it. The tables and chairs were set in neat rows; the carpet was fresh, clean, and without the wear patches that he found in so many places. The lighting was good, and the walls devoid of any grease, smoke, or other signs of neglect. For all its commercial fittings, it still managed to have a welcoming ambience. The lone waitress was sitting at the counter looking at her watch when he walked in. Newton glanced at the sign on the open door and saw that the restaurant was due to close in 15 minutes. He took a seat in a booth as she came over.

"We'll be closing soon," she said, "but the coffee is fresh, can't say the same for the daily specials though."
Newton chuckled, "Same thing in my house, how about one of those sandwiches over there," indicating a deli case with wrapped sandwiches, pie and muffins.
"You got it," she said. "Just as long as your choice is either roast beef or egg salad."
"One of each will do, and bring a piece of that pie with it"

As she went to get the food, Newton tore open the envelope. A two sheet fax with a cover sheet fell out. It was from Willy.

Hi, Boss, hope you're having fun up there in the sunny Charlottes, Just a note to let you know we have recovered a Haida carving in a drug raid in Esquimalt. Museum says it is NOT one of their pieces though, but since you're up there I thought I'd send you a picture to show around, can't be that many carvers. Maybe you can find out some more info. Enjoy your stay!

- Willy

The other sheet was a scanned print of a canoe with paddling figures, set against a beach with tall cedars. Newton judged it to be not in the same league as the museum pieces he had seen, but it was still good, better than most of the tourist pieces he had noticed in the hotel lobby. He was still studying it when the waitress came up to serve him. He put it down face up on the table.

As she placed the sandwiches in front of him, she glanced at the picture.

"Hey," she said, "I know that piece"

Newton looked up at her, "Really, who is the artist?"

"That would be Mel," she said. "He was peddling that piece about four months ago, I thought it was pretty good, but he wanted more than the hotel was willing to pay."

"Does the hotel usually pay for them up front?" Newton responded, motioning her to sit down across from him.

"No, that was the strange thing about it, usually they just take a commission but for this piece Mel said he already had an offer, and he wanted the money up front."

"When was the last time you saw Mel?" asked Newton.

"Ah," she said. "I should have guessed, you're the cop from Vancouver Island aren't you?"

"Yes, you're right, guilty as charged. My name is Alfred Newton, and I'm from Victoria." Newton extended his hand across the table. "But folks call me Isaac for some reason."

"I'm Frances Miller," she replied. "Folks just call me Fran, and I haven't seen Mel for a week or so. I heard about them finding his Jeep in the salt chuck today, and that there was a body in it, it's so sad."

"Did you ever meet someone called Alicia?" Newton continued.

"Oh yes, she stayed at the hotel when she was here, well not that much really, she was usually in the field."

"Did she know Mel?"

"Sure, he was a carver looking to sell his stuff, and she was from the museum. If he could have got a piece on display down there he would have it made. But his stuff wasn't as good as what they already had, though I always thought it was pretty decent. Mel did mention that Alicia was going to see if one of the galleries down there would display his work and that of other "up and coming'"artists, but the museum was only interested in the best works they could get."

The cook came out from the kitchen, "Hey Fran, I'm going to take off now, lock up will you?"

"Sure Henry, Have a good night."

"So what brings you up here to the Charlottes?" asked Fran, taking a seat across the booth from Newton, "It can't be what happened today because you were on your way already."

"I came up here to look for Alicia, to ask her about another girl she was seen with. I have a picture up in my room."

"And what was your interest in that girl?"

"She was found dead on a local beach, and we can't yet identify her."

"That's terrible; somewhere her parents are going through hell!"

"Did you ever see Alicia up here with another girl?"
"No, she always came alone, stayed alone, and left alone, In fact the only one I've ever really seen her with for any length of time is Elijah." Newton took a bite of his sandwich and leaned back. "What can you tell me about Elijah?"

"Aren't you the one with all the questions!" Fran laughed. As she did she threw back her dark hair and her brown eyes twinkled. "Well, I should expect that I guess, given your line of work. Elijah is sort of everyone's grandfather, even though he's not a lot older than you. Even the tribal elders seek his advice on things. He's sort of the spiritual flying doctor in these parts. When someone has a question or problem they can't work out, he sort of appears on the scene without being asked and tries to set things straight. It can be weird at times."

"And Alicia spent most of her time with him?"
"Actually, no, whenever I saw her with someone it was with Elijah, but she spent most of her time alone."
"Do you know what she did exactly, "in the field?" I thought she just transported carvings for the museum."
"It's kind of complicated, but she did that in part. She would bring pieces back from the museum and hand them over to Elijah, then she would go out for a couple of days or so and come back with a new piece or two. Elijah would meet her here and they would talk and sometimes argue a bit, and she would either leave with one of those pieces or go out again and come back with something different."

"Did you ever see the pieces?"
"All the time, she would show them around the hotel asking people how they liked them."
"Like she was the artist?"
"Exactly, and according to Elijah, she was."
"I'm not sure I understand that part" Newton said.
"You have to understand the people to understand that!" Fran laughed.
"And you understand them?"

"Heaven's no! At least not entirely. You have to spend much more than the five years I've been here to do that, if it can ever be done without actually living your entire life here. But I've picked up a few things, an open mind does wonders to open the soul, as my mother used to say."

"You've spent five years here?" Asked Newton, "What made you

decide to come here anyway?"
Fran laughed back, "Curious are you? Well, truth is I'm a West Coast girl myself. Grew up on Vancouver Island just outside of Victoria, familiar stomping ground I'm sure for you. I went to Ottawa, came out here for a vacation, and never felt the need to get back onto the plane."
"Really? Didn't your family object?"

"My my, Mr. Detective, you have so many questions! Oops, look at the time, I'm afraid we'll have to continue this at a later date, it's well past closing and I have to get my beauty sleep."
"Not much of that needed from where I sit," in a response that surprised them both.
"Are all you southern boys such charmers?" Fran responded in a southern drawl. "Y'all are just too much for this gal."
"I'm sorry," said Newton, "I didn't mean to embarrass you."
"Looks to me like you're the one who's embarrassed!" Fran laughed, clearing the dishes from the table.

Newton got up from the table and paid his bill, "Thank you for all the information," he said, assuming his detective persona.
"Well, if you have any more, I'm off tomorrow," and she wrote a phone number on the back of the receipt, "You can reach me at this number."

Newton pocketed the receipt and left the restaurant. For the first time in a long time, as he headed to his room and prepared for bed, his mind was not on a case.

CHAPTER FIFTEEN

The morning dawned bright and clear as Newton placed a couple of calls from the phone in his room. It was only 6:00 AM, his usual time for getting the day started. The first call was to his office, where he left a message for Willy, acknowledging the fax, and confirming the piece of art was from the Charlottes. He asked Willy to check with the museum and see if they had ever heard of Mel LonePine, and if they had considered exhibiting his works. Next he phoned the detachment office.

"R.C.M.P. detachment office," Cpl. Taylor's voice responded.
"You're up early."
"Hey, I live here remember."
"Yeah, I sometimes get that feeling at my office too, but unlike you my living quarters aren't attached to the cell block. I hope I didn't wake you, I was just going to leave a message about my itinerary for today."
"Actually, I'm glad you called, I wanted to set up a meeting for later this morning, say around 10:00 AM to go over everything and see where we are with things. Will that fit in with your schedule?"
"No problem—your office?"
"May as well, the coffee is free."
"I'll be there at 10:00 then."

Experience told Newton that the ident team had probably turned up something that might be of interest and even have a bearing on Newton's case. That meant he now had four hours until the meeting. Heading down to the restaurant he found himself the first customer of the day. Henry the cook was still banging around in the kitchen, setting out plates, pots, portions of food, and punctuating the process with a humming tune best described as "self taught." A pair of waitresses were on duty, one fixing her hair by the cash register, and the other bringing the coffee makers on line. Outside the weather was just switching from a squall of snow, to rain and wind with bright sunshine and a rainbow etching its colours onto the windows—another day in the Charlottes was beginning.

He took a seat in a booth and examined the menu, all the regular breakfast choices were present, and he elected to have just toast and coffee. The waitress brought him his order and put a carafe of coffee on his table so he could refill his cup at his leisure. The window allowed him the opportunity to watch the town wake up. The first thing he noticed was that the vehicle traffic was greater than he expected. It was certainly not the overwhelming amount of any big city, but still, a steady stream, with a good mix of new and old vehicles. The only concession to the remoteness of the location was that they were chiefly four-wheel-drive models. All heavy goods to the islands came by barge. Every summer RivTow Straits, a barge and tug company, shepherded a string of barges from its home port of Vancouver and Prince Rupert to the island. Tons of goods, building materials, household appliances, and vehicles made the journey. Folks leaving the islands would likely sell what they had rather than pay the shipping costs to have to it hauled to the main land, and there was always a demand for used goods.

Newton wondered how many hands a vehicle would go through in a community like this. Was Mel the original owner of the Renegade, or were there previous owners? Owners who might have made enemies? But on the other hand, this was a small community. Who would not know in short order when a vehicle changed hands? News of such things was announced, not found out, especially amongst the younger crowd where the type of vehicle you owned was a badge of sorts.

That would be chiefly among the guys of course, with a few women in the group. Newton understood the thinking for guys, what was it for women? What would it have been for his Jane Doe? What were the markers of status in her circle?

Generally, women regarded clothing as the currency of choice in main stream society. It mattered less what you did than how you looked doing it. Boyfriends were another sign of status. Dating the hottest guys was as important to your social status as the daily outfit you wore. Even if you didn't really date them they did have to show an interest in dating you.

His Jane Doe didn't have a car as far as Newton knew, at least none had shown up so far. Her clothing was just run of the mill K-mart and Wal-Mart stuff, not brand new but nothing too worn either. What did that mean? Was she unable to get better or just uninterested? As for boyfriends, that too was a blank and the only other person that Newton knew she had been seen with on a regular basis was now dead.

Two dead girls in the same week, both found in or near water, both apparently by drowning, there must be a common thread here, there always was, and it was up to Newton find it.

Breakfast done and with still a couple of hours to go, Newton headed out towards the dock. George was there tending to the Grumman and the two "ramp rats" were getting a lesson in how to pre-flight a twin. The engine nacelles were open and George was pointing out the various fittings that needed to be inspected at regular intervals.

The Grumman was a commercially operated aircraft and as such the Department of Transport laid out strict rules regarding frequency of inspections and each item that needed looking at. George was also a rated airframe and power plant mechanic. Thus he was entitled to make the inspections himself. This was one of reasons he could afford to operate the Grumman, it was not an inexpensive aircraft, being close to 50 years old. The engines were still in service in many different types of aircraft the world over, so parts were available. The aircraft itself was another story. Spare parts were nonexistent, usable parts could be had, and almost every part could be handmade if needed. If not on site, then at a reasonably equipped overhaul facility. The labour costs involved made that a very expensive proposition, and George was an adherent to the mechanic's code that stated "the easiest part to fix is the one that never gets damaged." This was one of the points he hammered home to his helpers every day.

On this day, the aircraft and engines were going through their 100 hour inspection. Various access hatches had been removed to expose cables and fittings on the airframe, and George had both kids' undivided attention as he explained how to check a magneto for cracks and wear.

"What does this part do?"
Both kids replied together, "It provides the spark to fire the cylinder plugs!"
"Right!" George said with a smile, "how?"
"A coil and a magnet!"
"Right again, and what are we checking for?"
"Cracks in the case and wires."
"How many do we have?"
"Two for each engine."
"Why?"
"More Power!"
"Reliability!"

And so it went with George carrying on a running lecture.
In an automobile you normally had one spark plug per cylinder, but better combustion was achieved using two. In addition that produced

more power, and power was the first part of the Holy Grail of any pilot. More power meant you could take off in less space, carry a larger load, climb out of danger quicker, and reach your destination in less time—all attributes a pilot looked for. The other advantage of a magneto was that it did not require a battery to function. It generated its own spark. This meant a battery failure would not affect the engine's power output as it would on an automobile. The constant change in altitude and temperature that an aircraft battery suffered through meant they had less reliability than their ground-bound cousins. Reliability of aircraft systems was the second part of a pilot's Holy Grail.

The usual method to check a magneto's performance was to run up the engine and switch from one magneto to another, the normal drop in engine speed would be less than 200 RPM. Any reading greater than that indicated a problem in the ignition circuit of that magneto. It could be the magneto, the lead to the spark plug, or the plug itself; thus the need to visually inspect the components.

The magnetos were mounted on the body of the engine itself, the internal components were mechanically rotated by the engine crankshaft. They were held to the engine block by two bolts through the plastic body of the magneto. Over time the plastic body would succumb to the engine vibration, temperature stresses and the torque placed on it, developing small cracks. George was pointing out one of these hairline cracks to his two students, oil had seeped into the crack and allowed it to standout against the brown plastic of the case.

Holding the magneto in his hand he was explaining how the rotation of the internal flywheel inside generated an electrical current that fired the sparkplug. He paused when he noticed Newton come up to the side of the aircraft.

"Are You up for another flight today?" he asked

"You bet," Newton replied. "I have a meeting in a couple of hours, but it should be over by noon."
"Perfect," George replied. "I have to flight test the new magneto I'm putting in, and these two are itching for a ride."

Newton looked at the expectant faces of the two kids and smiled, remembering his days hanging around airports. He had also been a "ramp rat."
"When are you going up?"
"I figure about noon, the inspection part is done and I just have to

make sure neither one of these two left bubble gum inside the engine or some such thing." George replied, nodding towards the grinning kids.
"Great," said Newton. "I'll see you then," and turned to head towards the detachment.

He took a couple of steps, turned around and said to George, "Would it be OK if I brought a friend?"
"No problem," George replied, "lots of room."

The Grumman had seats for eight people.

"See you around noon then."

Newton found a pay phone, and reached in his pocket for the slip of paper he got from Fran the night before. The phone rang three times before an answering machine picked up.

"You have reached 555-1212, please leave a message."

"Hello, this is Alfred Newton calling, I was wondering if you would care to go for a flight this afternoon? If you have the time, meet me at the seaplane dock at noon, I'll be down at the R.C.M.P. detachment 'til then. Thanks"

Newton hung up and continued to the detachment where the smell of coffee greeted him as he entered.

"Have a seat," Cpl. Taylor said, sitting behind his desk. "You're early; the ident gang will be here shortly."

The two passed the time waiting by going over what they had so far. Alicia's body had been recovered from the Jeep, and taken to the military hospital. A preliminary examination revealed some bruising around her wrists and shoulders. Also she had a few minor cuts on her legs. Death had been caused by drowning. There were no signs of major trauma, and still no signs of Mel LonePine. The Jeep had been stuck up to the axles, but that could have been from the action of the tide as it came in or went out. Her room at the hotel had been searched and nothing found other than personal effects. No letters notes or messages.

No luggage or overnight bag was found in the Jeep, although anything of that nature could have floated away. Her room held one suitcase and one carryon bag containing makeup and daily needs. No carvings were found either. She had been in the Charlottes for over two days, and had not yet picked up anything for the museum. Her return air ticket noted a flight back to Victoria booked for two days from now.

The museum had been contacted of course, and they were faxing next of kin information. Her parents apparently lived in Vancouver.

The detachment constables had been out to the village during the night, attempting to locate anyone who might have seen the two, or have any information about where they were going and what for.

The ident crew arrived, and tossed a sheaf of papers onto Taylor's desk. Taylor looked up at them. "And when I get through all that, what will I know that's different from what I know now?"

"Probably not much, it's still not complete though, "K" division has some work to do yet, they should be finished in a day or two. We have pretty much finished here, better keep the Jeep in impound for a while though, you never know what might turn up." For the next hour the team went through the details of the report with both Taylor and Newton posing questions as various points were covered. It was evident that the team had done a thorough job and covered all the bases. In the end, their original comment had been accurate. There were no big surprises, both Taylor and Newton were left with the same impressions that they formed at the scene. The facts were the Jeep was found on the beach, it was apparently stuck which was not an unusual occurrence, and Alicia had been found still in her seat, dead, and the cause of that death was drowning. The questions were much larger in scope.

Why was she in Mel's Jeep?
Why was Mel not there?
Why had he gone and where?
Why didn't she get out?

The forensic team said its goodbyes, packed up their equipment and left, heading douth to Sandspit to catch the flight to Vancouver.

Their report had provided a framework of facts that Taylor and Newton could flesh out by making inquiries in the community. The most significant information would come from Mel, either in person, or depending on the circumstances, by the discovery of his body. This was an R.C.M.P. matter, and Taylor's case to proceed with. Newton was both relieved and bothered not to be the lead detective. Instead of starting out on his usual path of investigation, he would have to take his lead from the corporal. He could only participate to the extent the R.C.M.P. member allowed. Newton did not sense this would be a problem. If Taylor was a territorial sort, he would likely not have allowed Newton to attend the briefing. As if reading his mind, Taylor looked across at Newton, and paused for a minute.

"I don't suppose I could get you to stay on a bit and help me out with this?" he said with a grin.
"Always glad to lend a hand, and I always welcome an opportunity to learn something."
"Welcome aboard then."

Newton wasn't joking about the learning part; every investigator has his own style. Just like any other occupation, different things come easier to different people. The scope of an investigation, any investigation, involves many different aspects of forensic science. It is, for this reason, the larger departments have experts in several disciplines, be it fingerprints, pathology, chemical analysis, or even entomology. Manpower constraints meant the smaller departments have to rely on their investigators being sharp in more of those fields than just one or two. Both Taylor and Newton would have the opportunity to learn the techniques of the other, and so increase their knowledge overall.

They went over the report again together. There was not much new in it, the Jeep had been found, not surprisingly, full of sand. Fingerprints had been taken and were now being looked at by the lab. Alicia's body had been fingerprinted and the cards faxed to the lab to match with those from the Jeep. No weapons had been found in the Jeep, no blood of any kind, no new damage.

The preliminary report from the base hospital was added to the ident file and along with the investigators notes, went into an even bigger file folder. There were the usual pictures of the scene, the Jeep, and the body. So far it was officially a suspicious death—one that may turn into a homicide.

There was also the usual discussion about circumstances, motive, and cause. Mel was the chief suspect or rather, person of interest, for two reasons. He was the last one known to be with the victim, and he was not at the scene. The fact that he was nowhere to be found was another mystery, as if Newton was not involved in enough of them already.

Taylor directed his team to renew their investigations in the village, and then check the businesses in town. Everyone would know what happened by now anyway, but just to be sure no one was missed. It was a small place, and nothing remained a secret for long. Eventually, Taylor would learn everything anyone knew. It was only a matter of time.

Newton sent a fax to his office, requesting that he be kept informed on any further developments down there. He had planned return to Victoria today, the official R.C.M.P. request for his assistance had changed that, and the trail had led here and he had a hunch that here is where he would find his next lead. He had requested that his Jane Doe's picture be shown to Alicia's parents on the off chance that they knew of their daughter's association with her and could provide some help. It would also afford them something else to focus on than their own painful loss. At the least he might get an up-to-date list of Alicia's friends, and that might in turn lead to something.

He wondered what the parents of the young girl might be thinking, and where they might be. They didn't know yet that their daughter was dead, and thus they still had hope. How cruel that solving the mystery of her identity would lead to extinguishing of that last glimmer. Some said closure was better, Newton wasn't so sure.

Leaving the detachment he headed back down to the seaplane dock. George should be about ready to test out the new part, and flight always gave Newton a new perspective on his earth-bound problems. Even if his namesake had discovered the laws of gravity, it was nice to escape them every now and then.

CHAPTER SIXTEEN

As Newton suspected, George had the Grumman buttoned up and ready to go. The two boys were already aboard, sitting in the cockpit and fingering the levers and gazing at the instruments. They called out to each other the name and purpose of them. No doubt imagining the day when they too could "slip the surly bonds of Earth" with an aircraft under their control.

Chatting with George was Fran, dressed in Jeans and a Mackinaw shirt. Newton thought he had never seen simple clothes looking so good.

"Hello," he said, "I see you got my message, I hope I didn't wake you."
"Not a chance," she smiled back, "I'm an early riser."
"Do you like flying? I never thought to ask."
"Absolutely! George here says you're an intrepid birdman also, are you going to be the pilot?"

"Ah, no, I'll leave that in George's capable hands and that of his crew." Newton said indicating the two boys. "If it's OK with George, we'll sit in back, I think the young fellows here would prefer the right hand seat this trip."
"OK by me, I think they will enjoy that." The two boys were small enough to both sit in the co-pilot's seat, and big enough to argue about whom was going to get the window seat. A flip of a coin settled who got that for the first half of the trip, with the "loser" given the job of helping with the engine controls and scanning the instruments. Suddenly, not having the window didn't seem so bad.

The two lads nodded their agreement, the look on their faces showing relief at not being confined in the rear where all they could do was sight see. They would get a chance to see the aircraft perform from the front office. If they were very lucky, they might even get a chance to actually put their hands on the flight controls!

After climbing aboard, Newton and Fran took a seat just to the rear of the big wings. The windows afforded a fine view, and although noisy, it was close to the centre of gravity of the aircraft and that would lessen any feelings of turbulence. One of the boys slid into the co-pilots seat by the window, the other took a seat directly beside him where he could observe the instrument panel. They had done this before, and during the flight they would change places so that one got to be the co-pilot for takeoff, and the other for landing.

George handed the lad the takeoff check list, and had him read out the steps. He pointed to each lever and instrument as it was called and gave them a reason why it had to be where it was supposed to be.

"Flaps 15."
"Allows more lift from the wings so we can pull loose from the water's suction."

"Check magnetos."
"Makes sure we have full power from the engines."

"Mixture full rich."
"Cools the engine and prevents them going lean."

"Carb heat on."
"Prevents the engine from dying from picking up carb ice when taking off ."

"Props at fine pitch."
"Lets the engine develop maximum RPM and horsepower."

So it went, with George continuing his commentary as the twin taxied down the ramp into the water.
"Now what do we check here?" He asked.
"Gear up!" The response came in unison.
"And why is that?"
"Because you can't take off or land in the water with the wheels down more than once in your life!"
"You're learning." George said.

With that he advanced the throttles to full power and the Grumman accelerated across the water. It soon reached a point where it broke free from the water's suction and got "on the step." That meant only the keel of the hull was in the water and the acceleration increased quickly. With a bump, the noise of the water rushing past the aluminum hull ceased and the aircraft was flying.

Newton never failed to get a rush when he felt the weight of the aircraft was fully transferred to the wings, his senses came alive and even though he was not flying the airplane, he was at once in tune with every motion and vibration.

Fran looked at the light in his eyes, "You really get a kick out this, don't you?"

"Always did, it's the greatest feeling of freedom in the world, nothing else like it, and you?"

She smile back, "I've had my wings for 10 years now, learned on gliders, then got my fixed wing ticket."

"I should have guessed! You're way too relaxed for being just a passenger."

The Grumman banked south, heading over the east coast of the Island. To their left Hecate Strait was unusually calm. The odd fishing boat making its way from one spot to another trailed their wakes in the waves. To the right the coast road wound down the shoreline. They passed over an old ranch, said to have once belonged to Bing Crosby. The docks reputed to have provided berthing space to the Duke's "Wild Goose," a converted minesweeper John Wayne owned. Over the years the islands had provided a place of rest and spiritual renewal for many of its visitors. Further down the island narrowed and the hills disappeared, leaving a large sand bar. This was Sandspit, the only place a modern passenger plane could set up to approach an airport of sufficient length to take them. It was also prone to lengthy and cloaking fog.

The island protected its privacy well.

Newton and Fran spent the time viewing the Islands from the air, even long-time residents rarely had the opportunity to see the whole place from the air without clouds and rain blocking some portion of the view. Although the plane afforded the passengers windows on both sides, they seemed to find sharing one to be just right.

The Queen Charlottes were an archipelago made up of several small Islets and larger islands. There was some argument in the scientific community whether or not they belonged to the Pacific plate moving in towards the main land, or the continental shelve of North America. The standard answer was that only a really big earthquake would decide the issue once and for all. In any case, they were home to several micro climates. Areas where the weather could and did change at a moment's notice, and in so doing was separate from the weather experienced just a few kilometers away. The varying climates supported many different species of animals all living under a varied canopy of trees that were now under the passing shadow of the Grumman's wings.

Newton always found the sights, sounds, and smells of an aircraft to be intoxicating, but on this occasion he was hardly aware of them. The scent of Fran's perfume filled his senses, and her sitting so close with his arms around her shoulders brought back feeling he had believed to be so long gone as to be irretrievable. When she slipped her hand in his he thought his heartbeat would drown out the engines.

Christ, he thought, it's like I'm a schoolboy on his first date. I'm too old for this stuff.

Completing the trip down the east coast, George turned the plane in a sweeping 180 degree turn to head north back up the Pacific side of the islands. The twin swung out over the west side of the island, while below them the forest below changed from a mix of soft and hardwoods into stand of fir and spruce. In the sea of green below, a golden tree stood out from the rest.

Fran place her lips close to his ear.
"Did you ever hear the story of the 'Golden Spruce'?
She turned her ear to him, and he bent closer till his lips touched her cheek. "Yes, Elijah told me."
As she turned back, her lips briefly touched his.
Newton froze for a moment, did she just kiss me? Damn, what the hell do I do now?
Fran smiled as she noted the look on his face and squeezed his hand slightly, turning back to the window as if nothing happened, but with a little smile on her face.

Newton, of course, was completely lost.

Moving further to the west, George brought the twin out over the coast and then headed north back towards the town site. He was checking his charts; the military had a "no-fly" area over part of the base. Everyone knew the base was more than just a navigational facility. The forest of communications antennas lent itself to the view that it was one of NATO's western radio hubs. Accordingly, the swing out to the west was necessary to skirt the restricted zone, and then allow them to come into the town from the northwest. A small archipelago of islets that were home to seals and birds lay in their path. It used to be a favourite site for Russian seal hunters in the last century, but had long ago had become a protected area.

George brought the plane down in a curving descent to line up with the westernmost island. At a height of about a thousand feet, they were safe from collision with the birds, and still had a view which encompassed the entire islet. Clouds of seabirds, disturbed by the approaching craft, rose and fell in multicoloured waves over the rocks. There, families of seals could be seen basking in the sun before returning to the sea to feed.

"Oh look!" Fran cried out, "whales!"
George had seen them too, and set the Grumman into a descending circle above the sea going mammals. Spouts of water rose as the animals surfaced to breath at regular intervals.
"Orcas, a pod of seven I think," Newton remarked.
"Yes," Fran added, "two calves among them."
The Killer Whales swam north at a steady pace, and George kept the plane centered above them in a constant left hand circle. The two boys in the front had a restricted view from their side of the plane, and George switched rotation to give them a better view. After circling for ten minutes or so, he brought the aircraft back on course and they continued their trip.

"Do they frequent these waters?" Asked Newton.
"Every now and then the fishing crews will report seeing them when they come into the hotel. Some of the boats are even offering sightseeing tours for the visitors. Makes up for the diminishing fisheries."

The whales had led them away from the shoreline, and George had altered course to bring them back towards the coast. Stretches of cliffs and offshore rocks marked the western coast of the island.

Each of the little outcroppings of rocks seemed to hold their own contingent of birds and seals. Like black sentinels rising from the sea they guarded the entrance to the only sandy beach on the largest islet. The beach was cluttered with the flotsam and jetsam of the North Pacific. Logs from long broken booms, or trees from some distant place, that had been ripped from their shores in a past storm. An ever increasing amount of plastic bottles and bags, and occasionally a much prized glass float from a Japanese fishing net dotted the sand. It was this last item that enticed folks to make the trip from the main island to comb the beach. Thusly, the sight on an aluminum boat on the sand was not an unexpected occurrence.

The body beside it was.

CHAPTER SEVENTEEN

George called to Newton to come forward to the cockpit. Thinking it to just be some point of interest, he was reluctant to let Fran's hand go and make his way up there, and that surprised him almost as much as the urgency in George's second call to him.

The boys had also spotted the body and on George's command moved back into the passenger compartment to let Newton take the right seat. As the plane banked over the beach, George pointed the body out to Newton, whose next thought was, oh no, not again.

"I'm going to come in low over the bay," George said. "Take a look for rocks and logs. I've never landed here before."

Newton nodded his understanding, striking a submerged object on landing was a constant worry for an amphibious aircraft pilot. Luckily the water was still calm, and as they made their sweep, he saw no dark shapes that signified something dangerous to the aircraft or its occupants. However, the opening to the bay was narrow and the wind was coming from the side of the aircraft. George pulled out his sea charts from the leather bag that stored all his flight gear to check the tide tables. Landing on the sea, or a river, was different from a lake. You not only had to allow for the wind, but also for the current of the water. Satisfied, George set the plane up for landing and brought the plane in over the mouth of the bay and touched down gently in the swells.

With the engines at idle he taxied up to the beach, keeping the wheels locked up, cutting the engines off when they were about twenty feet from shore. Quickly he opened the hatch above his head and grabbing the paddle mounted on the bulkhead beside him, prepared to get out onto the nose of the plane. Once there he un-stowed an anchor and rope and let it over the side. The hatch also held a small life raft, and a pull on the cord inflated it. George took the end of a rope attached to the bow of the raft and tied it off on the ring located on the nose of the aircraft. By this time Newton had also grabbed a paddle and followed him into the bobbling rubber boat. A few strokes had them onto the beach, where they pulled the raft up on to the sand.

The aluminum boat was grounded on the sand with the outboard tilted up out of the water. The body of a young man lay in a fetal position, curled against it. Newton checked him for a pulse while George pulled the rubber raft higher onto the beach.

"I have a pulse!"

The young man was alive, but barely, a feeble pulse beat at his throat and his breathing was shallow and quick. Newton tried shouting and shaking him gently, but he could not rouse him. The young man's clothes were soaked and his lips had a bluish tint. Placing his hand under the young man's armpit, Newton felt for some indication of his body temperature. Even in the cold wind, the boy felt colder and appeared to be in the late stages of hypothermia.

"He's freezing!" Newton said to George, and the pilot quickly grabbed a blanket from the plane's life raft. They wrapped him up as best they could in the silvery "space blanket." It was designed to keep a person's body heat from escaping and Newton prayed it would live up to the manufacture's claim. George started to rub the boy's arms and legs attempting to increase the circulation. To his surprise, his hands and fingers began to feel sticky.

That was when he noticed the blood.

A small but apparently deep wound was evident on the man's abdomen, a clot had formed with the fabric of his shirt caught in the edges. This had evidently staunched the blood flow, but swelling around the area indicated possible bleeding internally.

"Damn, look at this." George called to Newton who was setting about to build a fire. In response he dropped the bundle of wood he had collected and came over. A quick look was all he needed; Newton had seen his share of knife wounds.

"We need to get him back to town," he said to George

"And quick!"

"Use the raft," George said. "This boat is too high on the beach."

"That means we'll have to move him more—and that bleeding could start again."

"A chance he will have to take," George said, "it will be quicker that way."

The raft was re-floated and together they placed the unconscious boy on the floor of it. It was necessary to keep his movements minimized as much as possible to prevent the wound from reopening. George crawled in with him, and placing his knees on each side stabilized the bobbing craft.

"Careful now, push off gently, I'll keep him stabilized as much as possible."

While this was going on, Fran and the two boys were standing in the

cockpit, staring out of the hatch at the activities on the beach. As soon as George and Newton began to load the boy aboard the raft, Fran made her way out to the nose of the plane and grabbed the end of the rope. When George had boarded the raft and pushed it off into deeper water, she began to haul steadily on the rope. In a few minutes the raft had reached the side of the plane. George scrambled aboard the aircraft and kneeling on the flat area just ahead of the cockpit windows, managed to get his hand beneath the boy's arms, and thus lift him into the aircraft and laid him on the floor in the fuselage.
A few minutes later he returned to the beach for Newton and they both clambered into the plane. Sinking into the pilot's seat, George's hands flew about the cockpit, going through the pre takeoff list by memory, and even with the urgency of the situation he was deliberate and methodical. A missed step here would not do anyone any good.

 In the back, Fran and the two boys piled blankets and coats on top of the unconscious young man, and Newton felt gently around the knife wound, checking for any sign of renewed bleeding. Satisfied the wound had not re-opened, he left him in Fran's care and rejoined George in the cockpit.

 "Follow through with me." George told him and Newton nodded, buckling up the seat belt and testing the rudder pedals with his feet. Putting his hands gently on the yoke, he nodded to George, "Ready here."

 The Grumman taxied out of the bay and turned into the wind. As soon as it was lined up George pushed the throttles fully forward and soon the noise of the water on the hull died away and they were airborne.

 Once they had gained enough altitude, George switched the radio to the international distress band.

"Pan Pan Pan," he spoke into the mike, "Grumman Charlie Tango Romeo Yankee."
"Aircraft calling an emergency, this is Charlotte Base go ahead," responded the controller at the military base immediately.

"Charlotte base, this is Romeo Yankee, 10 K north of you, inbound with a severely injured man, and I require clearance to land at your dock and an ambulance."

"Roger Romeo Yankee, winds west at 14K altimeter 019, and we will roll the ambulance."

The roar of the engines did not diminish as they would normally have done, because George kept the throttles pinned to the top of their quadrant. He adjusted the pitch of the props for best speed and with an eye on the engine temperature readings headed for the base at an altitude of 100 feet. Newton glanced back at Fran and saw her bending over the boy's face, a mirror in her hand, searching for a sign that he was still alive. Seeing a slight coating of mist on the glass face, she turned towards the cockpit and mouthed the word "hurry." Outside the beat of the engines drummed against the sea.

Normally entrance to a military base would require all sorts of bureaucratic hoops to jump through, especially one with sensitive equipment, but the people of remote regions had long ago established their own way of doing things. George was well known to the military folks, he had more than once provided transportation for someone based there whose child needed a quick trip to the mainland, and had brought injured fishermen from some desolate spot in for emergency treatment at the better equipped base hospital. He had been granted a de facto permit from the base commander to land there when circumstances required it. The military had left it up to his judgment to decide which cases needed the skills available at the military base, and which could take the slightly longer trip to the town hospital. The paperwork could be sorted out later.

Within minutes the seaplane was making its approach to the base dock. An ambulance was already standing by along with a military police jeep, their red lights beating a pattern against the surrounding buildings. Newton had left the cockpit, and he and Fran were attending to the injured man, keeping pressure on his wound less it start to bleed again, prepared to begin CPR if he should stop breathing. They had not spoken but a few words, each aware of the thin thread that the young man's life was suspended on.

A bump and change in engine noise told them George had touched down, almost as quickly as it died away, the engines started up again, he was keeping the twin up on its step, like a racing boat, as it approached the dock. This would save them some time, but it was a dangerous maneuver as the water rudders were largely ineffective and steering the aircraft required an expert hand on the throttles. With a final roar, the engines were cut off, and a solid thump announced the arrival of the Grumman at the dock side.

Within moments of the engines being shut down, the unconscious man had been transferred to the ambulance and was on his way to the hospital. The attending medics were already on the radio relaying his vitals to the physicians awaiting his arrival. His core temperature was dangerously low, and he had lost a lot of blood. Already in deep shock, the only thing he had on his side was the resiliency of youth.

CHAPTER EIGHTEEN

After seeing the young man off in the care of the medics, Newton and George boarded the twin for the short flight back to town. There was not much time for conversation, George was busy with flying the plane, and Newton was organizing yet another investigation in his mind. George did have time to tell Newton the identity of the young man. It was Mel LonePine.

Cpl. Taylor met them when they taxied up the concrete ramp to the parking area.
"I got some of the details from the tower operator at the base," he began, "and the doctor will phone when he has the time. For now, I'd like Fran and the boys to give a statement to Eddie here."
He indicated a constable who had accompanied him to take statements from the two boys and Fran. Taylor started removing an ident kit from the trunk of the cruiser and checking its contents. Fran had not said much during the short hop from the base, and came up to Newton as they were waiting for George to refuel the Grumman and ready the craft for a flight back to the island. There was still blood on her hands from Mel's wound and she had tried to wash off as much as she could in the cold ocean water.

"So is this what life is like for you?" She asked Newton.

"Rarely," he said, turning his face to hers. "Mostly it's just slogging through the evidence and trying to figure out what everything means. The usual 99% routine and 1% excitement that makes up police work."

"Well, if you get done by this afternoon, I usually have dinner at five, give me a call. I'm sure the young man will pull through, the doctors at the base are very good and he was lucky enough for us to find him." She looked up into his eyes, "I enjoyed the plane ride." With that she turned and shepherded the boys into the second cruiser for the trip to the detachment office.

Newton and Taylor joined George in the Grumman for the return trip to the island, The weather was now turning gusty and the plane rocked from side to side as it maneuvered down the ramp. Taking the right hand seat, Newton slipped on the headset and automatically began reading out the pre-flight checklist. He had gone into "detective" mode again, all business. He glanced back at Taylor to see that he was strapped into one of the passenger seats and holding tightly onto his ident bag. The look on his face revealed that the corporal was not likely to be a frequent flier. Of course that could just be small planes; many folks did just fine in a commercial airliner. George keyed the intercom, "How's our passenger doing?"

"Looks like he would rather take the boat."

"At least he's not barfing like he did when he first got here," George laughed. "But just in case, behind your seat you will find a sic-sack, grab it and toss it to him."

Newton swiveled around and found the white plastic lined paper sack. Universally known as a "barf bag," it was one of aviations greater, if less heralded inventions. Taylor, whose complexion had turned slightly green, nodded with thanks when it landed on his lap.

The roar of the engines announced their takeoff and soon they were back in the familiar airspace to the north of the city. The flight to the Island was just a few minutes long and they quickly let down into the bay. As before, they anchored the plane off the shoreline and used the still inflated raft to get to the beach. The aluminum boat marked the spot where they found Mel. And Cpl.Taylor, the colour returning to his face, broke out his camera and other equipment. George and Newton stood back and let him do his work. The only sense of urgency now was the ever changing weather. Bands of clouds were gathering to the northwest and the wind was rising. The air temperature had dropped a few degrees leaving Newton wishing he had a warmer coat. He had been feeling warmer earlier in the day, much warmer.

The R.C.M.P. training academy, located in Regina Saskatchewan, was arguably the best in the world at what it did. What it did of course, was train men and women to a high level of competency in many skills. Skills they would need in the small detachments scattered across the length and breadth of Canada. Whilst the Quantico training establishment for the F.B.I. turned out great people also, it tended to slot people into specialist roles. Out of necessity, R.C.M.P. members were required to be skilled at a greater number of tasks. Unlike their southern cousins, their powers, and thus their responsibilities, were greater, because they were often the only law enforcement official for hundreds of miles. One of the skills taught was how to take pictures at a crime scene. To the untrained eye, it often appeared to be nothing more than a random series of shots, with a few graphic pictures for effect. Nothing could be further than the truth. Every crime scene has a story to tell, and the photographer must not only know how to read that story, but also how to record it on film. This included how to use the available light to highlight the tread pattern of a tire, or footwear. Fingerprints are fragile and require that the photograph display each ridge in order to make a match later in the lab. Blood spatters tell the story of who moved where and how things occurred and even the order that they did so. Most important of all was that once the scene was disturbed it was gone forever, and the only record a follow up investigation could rely on was the one being etched on celluloid.

Newton waited patiently on the beach until Taylor had finished his first set if pictures and was reloading the film cartridge. Both investigators worked in silence, concentrating on their tasks. Needless conversation distracted the mind and they would speak to each other only when required. There was seemingly not much to take pictures of, the footprints and the beach. The interior of the boat had blood in it indicating that the boy was bleeding before he got to the island. There were no paddles nor oars, and the gas tank for the engine was empty. No life jackets or any other clothing was present. Satisfied he had recorded everything that he saw, Taylor invited Newton over to take a look. Everyone sees things differently because of their past experiences and training, and an extra pair of eyes was always a benefit.

Newton started his scan of the scene, with the near ground first. What did he see that stood out? There was the boat of course, and the blood. It had dried now, but there were differences in colour, indicating he had bled for quite some time. The blood was centered in one spot, so he likely was not involved in a struggle with someone. Newton imagined the young man in the boat, sitting just above the pooled blood. The wound was to his abdomen, so he likely would be doubled over, clutching the wound with his hand, head down. The amount and position of the blood indicated he had not tried to run the engine after being injured. The gas tank was empty though, indicating the engine must have been running and in the water. The engine was now out of the water, held clear by the mechanism common to all outboard motors that allowed the prop to be raised from the water for storage and trailering. Could someone with such a wound have managed to lift the engine without causing his wound to open up and bleed? Newton suspected the nature of the wound would cause him to go into shock and lose consciousness in a short time. Mel had not been dressed warmly, only a shirt and jeans, no jacket; the water was always cold and the air above it the same. Likely that worked in his favour, causing the blood to congeal quickly, probably saved his life.

So it was possible, but not likely.

Another explanation could be that the leg of the outboard had struck some object. If it had done so hard enough, that could cause the engine to pivot upwards, far enough to engage the catch. Taking the camera, Newton focused on the front of the leg, and found scratches indicating the prop shield had indeed stuck something hard, like a rock. He pressed down on the shutter release.

Newton walked around the boat and changed his perspective. The wound appeared to him to have been caused by a knife. If he was in the boat when he was stabbed, then where would the knife be? If he had been stabbed by someone else then it would probably be with them, if not, it could have dropped and lodged under the floor boards. Newton bent down and carefully examined the bottom of the boat. He straightened up and motioned Taylor over. There, under a loose piece of wood, lay a pocket knife.

Taylor focused the camera and took another series of pictures, then reached in and recovered a folding pocket knife with a two inch blade. It was covered in blood and he put it into a plastic bag and marked it with his initials, the date and time. The rising wind now carried spits of rain with it, making it difficult to do any further detailed forensic examination of the craft.

Newton switched his focus to the middle ground, taking a picture in his mind and going over each feature. Checking the position of each object against his memory of what a hundred other beach scenes looked like. What was here that shouldn't be, and what was missing that should be here. There was the boat of course, and the footprints from their earlier arrival, but other than that it looked like a calendar picture of a thousand other beaches. The tide line just below the halfway mark of the boat, and the craft would likely be reclaimed at the next high tide and floated away. That told Newton that the boat was likely at the same spot it had been when it grounded on the beach. Mel had been found beside it, so he must have got out sometime after the grounding and when the plane landed. The tide tables for the region would tell him to within a few minutes when the boat arrived. From that they would have a time span back to the low tide period when the Jeep got stuck. That would be the amount of time the boat had to get from there to here, a distance of what? Ten, twelve kilometers, how fast did the current run in these parts? How much gas had been in the tank?

After completing his middle ground scan, Newton switched to the far ground. The definition of far ground was dependent upon the topography. If urban it could mean the surrounding houses, lane ways, garbage containers, etc. It would mean the far walls or adjoining rooms of a large building if the scene was indoors. Here it meant the ground spreading out from the scene for 100 feet or so, Newton judged it unlikely that there had been anyone else on the little islet, nothing had been seen from the air to indicate it, and of course no parking lot and roads as there would have been down south on the mainland or the bigger islands.

That's when he saw the stick.

He stopped and pointed to it, Taylor came up to his side and sited along Newton's outstretched arm.
"See it?" He asked
"Not seen yet." Taylor replied, then "Yes, I think so, to the right of that whitish rock by about a foot."
"Yes, that's it."

Taylor took out his camera again and fiddled with the lens and focus. In the viewfinder the top and bottom semicircles slid into alignment and the stick suddenly grew in size. "Well, it's definitely not a natural feature, that's for sure. I can clearly see saw marks."

Taylor snapped a few frames and the two men walked up to the position. Newton noted no footprints in the sand and dirt, and if there was a path it was little used and not apparent. Taylor knelt down beside it and took a few more frames. It was a definite marker of some sort, only a few inches above the ground, and neither man knew its meaning. Taking this new position as a starting point, Newton began his scan anew. Near ground and middle ground revealed nothing to him but two dead gulls, scrub vegetation and a plastic bag blown in on the wind and caught in the branches of some shrubbery. Taylor followed with his own examination and this time it was he who first noticed the next marker.

About 100 feet from them sat a stone, upon another stone. It was only noticeable because the strengthening wind caused it to move slightly about its balance point. This meant it was placed there recently because the winds in this area would soon move it to a position where it would no longer rock to and fro, and it also meant that it had to have been placed there by someone. There being no larger or higher rock formation from which it could have fallen nearby.

Cpl.Taylor continued taking pictures as they walked up to it and Newton scanned the ground continuously for signs of passage from whoever had placed it there. But the wind packed ground had turned hard and rocky and revealed nothing to them. Standing on the spot, both men began searching the area for another marker, or other sign of something out of place. This time it was Newton who spotted it.

The ground near the exposed roots of a bush was darker in colour than its surrounding soil. Darker ground usually meant digging had taken place and there were no animals here that were of the burrowing variety. As they carefully made their way there, Newton felt that familiar feeling of being on a chase. The quarry being ultimately the motives of a person's actions but the recovered treasure was the artifacts of those actions. For every action, he thought to himself, there is a clue.

Newton's laws of evidence.

Once again Cpl. Taylor changed film cartridges and once again he began the painstaking procedure of documenting in film what their eyes saw. Only after the pictures were taken did they bend down to examine the site. Time was usually on the side of the investigator. A small piece of cloth, oiled cloth by the looks of it, and very old, had been exposed by the wind. Carefully, like an archaeologist at a dig site, which when you thought about it, was exactly what they were, he removed the loose dirt. Loose dirt meant recent digging, or in this case recent burial. The action of the rain and snow had not compacted the ground. Soon they had unearthed a cloth-covered bundle, heavy and wrapped in the oil cloth. More pictures and Newton carefully undid the bindings of the ends, and the contents were revealed.

Eleven carvings lay before them.

As Taylor examined them, he murmured "These are exquisite, I've never seen better."

"And you likely never will" a voice rang out from behind them.

CHAPTER NINETEEN

Both men turned to see Elijah Longeyes standing behind them.
"How the hell did you get here?" Taylor asked.
"Your office requested someone come and tow that aluminum boat back, so here I am, and no I have not wandered about your crime scene leaving a confusing trail of footprints."
"Well I'm glad you're here, what can you tell me about these" said Taylor indicating the carvings.
"Those are Alicia's," Elijah responded.
"And she buried them here?"
"No, I did."

Taylor and Newton looked at each other and turned to Elijah for an explanation.

"Later my friends," Elijah went on. "The weather is turning quickly and we should get that boat back to town while we can, or George will have to find room for it in his plane."
With that he turned and headed back to the beach, followed by Newton and Taylor, carrying the wrapped carvings with them.

Off the beach was a fishing boat from the village and it had already attached a line to the towing ring of the aluminum boat located in the prow. As soon as the little boat was pushed back into the water, the journey to town could begin. Taylor and Newton slid it into the water and Elijah waved to the fishing crew to take up the slack. Taylor would ride with them back to town to provide for continuity of evidence, Elijah and Newton would return with George and the carvings. The weather gave the whole process an air or urgency.

George stowed the raft in the fuselage again, he would let the air out and replace the Co2 cartridges when they got back to town. The paddles were secured in their holders in the cockpit, Elijah took a seat in the rear and strapped in. Newton had placed the carvings back in their oil cloth wrappings and strapped them down in the cargo hold. He took the right hand seat and dug out the pre-flight check list. George retrieved and stowed the anchor, with the engines running he turned the aircraft around and taxied out into the middle of the bay. The wind had now shifted and was coming directly off the bay entrance.

The waves were choppy, bad for a boat ride but good for seaplane operations as they helped to break the suction of the water on the hull. George paused for a moment and reached over and took the check list from Newton.

"I'm tired," he said. "You take us home."

Newton looked at him and replied, "I'm a little out of practice and I don't think my medical is exactly up to date."

"You look OK to me, but if you decide to keel over and die, I'll land the beast," George said. "So quit yakking and start flying, I'm hungry and I do believe you have a dinner date, and there is still work to do."

Newton nodded his head and took a breath, "All right then, it's your plane, and your hide."

"My hide too," came a voice from the back. "But if George says you're good to go white eyes, it's OK with me—and thanks for asking!"

Newton chuckled and George began to read from the checklist, pointing out each setting and instrument in the same manner as he had done for his ramp rats. Newton was much more relaxed than he thought he would be. It's like riding a bike he thought, you never forget, and your senses adapt quickly to the particular plane you're flying. Flaps cranked to takeoff position, Newton checked the gear setting one more time, set the carb heat, selected fine pitch on the props, and advanced the power levers to their maximum. The roar of the twin engines filled the cockpit and the plane began to pick up speed as the hull carved its way through the water. As the speed increased, the wings began to take more of the weight of the plane and the craft rose higher in the water. Soon it was on the step and the water rudder lost its effectiveness and Newton was able to control the yaw with the air rudder. The noise of the engines seemed to abate a little as the speed increased and the sound pressure waves struck further back on the fuselage. Holding the twin steady into the wind, Newton felt the water release its hold and the Grumman was airborne. Newton kept the plane in climb configuration until it had gained 1,000 feet of altitude and then cranked the flaps full up. Next he selected cruise pitch on the props and brought the throttle levers back to cruise RPM. That done, he banked gently to the right to head to town.

"Nicely done," George said. "I think we still have all the original parts we came with."

"Bonus," Newton replied.

"Can I open my eyes now?" Elijah chimed in.

"Hell, no," said Newton. "We still have to land."

"Oh, yeah," Elijah responded. "I guess we do."

"Takeoffs are optional, landings are mandatory." George added.

"What goes up, comes down," Newton laughed.

"Clever," Elijah said. "That must be one of 'Newton's Laws—no?"

"Right now, it's one of my laws," George announced. "Make your approach a sweeping turn to line up the dock on the left side of the aircraft, and set your approach speed to 95 knots, reduce that to 90 on final."

Newton began the checklist for landing, essentially the same as takeoff with a reduction in power. He cranked in the flaps for landing, ensured the gear was up, and set the power and prop levers. On landing, he would be prepared to advance the power, then the props to full takeoff power if debris in the water required that they abort and go around for another try. No logs, boats, or other obstructions were present and Newton brought the twin in over the water, allowing the speed to bleed off until a thump announced the hull had made contact with the water. He kept power on until the hull had settled solidly, then reduced it and allowed the water drag to slow the plane down.

"Nice job," said George. "I never even felt the bounces."
"That's because there weren't any," smiled Newton. "If you don't count the wave tops."
"Never do," said George.
"I did," said Elijah. "There were five of them, the first one was the biggest, I want a refund, and there was no meal on this trip."

The three continued their lighthearted banter with George taking over the controls to guide the plane up the ramp to its parking area. When the engines were shut down they exited and the moment was gone, time to continue with their work, two young girls were dead and a young man lay in critical condition in hospital.

CHAPTER TWENTY

It was not often that Newton let this side of himself be seen amongst civilians. Police officers understand the necessity of seizing whatever relief afforded itself to keep the insanity at bay. Pilots understood that too, seemingly relaxed on the outside, their minds were always occupied with the constant checking and rechecking of myriads of details that could cascade into a deadly situation if not attended to. Attention to detail was an absolute requirement in both jobs. Elijah was another factor altogether. He had the ability to fit in no matter what the situation and he always seemed to know what was happening, and also what was likely to happen, no matter whose world he happened to be in at the time.

Elijah, though Newton, would make a good cop. Right now though, there were other things to attend to.

"George, you will have to go down to the detachment and give a written statement, Taylor will need that to finish his report."
"No problem, I'll do that as soon as I get the plane squared away, why don't you head over there in an hour, they should be by with the boat then."
"That will be fine, until then, Elijah, let me buy you a coffee and you can tell me all about these carvings." Newton said holding up the bundle he had retrieved from the plane.

"As long as you include pie," Elijah said with a smile.

They made their way to the hotel restaurant, the wind picking up as they went. Even though the trip was short, only a few blocks, they experienced a snow squall and a light rain on the way, topped off with a rainbow and the re-appearance of the sun. Elijah seemed not to notice. Newton just enjoyed the changes and marveled again that only in the Charlottes did you get every season's weather in five minutes. Then he wondered to himself what effect that would have on any evidence that remained on the boat. As he slipped back into his police persona, he went over the past day's events. It all seemed to swirl around the package he carried under his arm.

They entered the restaurant and took a booth by the window. Newton ordered coffee and pie for himself and Elijah, surprised at how hungry he was. He reminded himself to phone Fran and confirm dinner plans. Is this going to be an actual date? He thought momentarily to himself, I haven't been on one for years. Just what are the dating rituals for folks of my age anyway? The world has gone around the sun many times since last I did this sort of thing. I suppose I'll find out in the time honoured way. With that thought he pushed it to the back of his mind into one of the many compartments that seemed to reside there, and cycled the day's events back into focus.

The two men ate without much conversation; one of the effects of stress is the body reacting to fuel itself in order to handle the added workload. The large sections of pie disappeared in a remarkably short span of time. With the pie out of the way, Newton spread the carvings out on the table.

"So what can you tell me about these?"
"Every carving tells a story, records a piece of history, or marks an event. At least, that's what they did in historical times. Now they are made by the young as just art to sell to the tourists, and in doing that, they have lost a piece of their history, and clouded over some of the old legends. Luckily, these are, as you would say, 'from the old school'."

Elijah looked them over, "Well now," he said, pointing to one, "this one is about 250 years old, carved originally by a craftsman named 'Shqua' as a gift to the spirit of the bear. He was on a fishing trip with his son and they were netting salmon. The winter had been a hard one with much snow and very cold, and both the people and the animals were starving. They were lucky enough to net two salmon, the only ones of the day. And as they were returning to the village they came upon an injured bear and her two cubs. The bear could not travel to the stream for salmon and her cubs were dying. Shqua's son took one of the salmon and offered it to the bear for her and her cubs to eat. The bear took the offering and let them pass on the trail. The next day they returned to the stream and netted more salmon. Again on the trip home they came across the bear and again his son shared their catch. This continued for two weeks, and gradually the bear healed and her cubs became stronger. One day they were at the stream and the bear, now recovered, was teaching her cubs to fish. The spring runoff had begun in earnest and the water was flowing fast and strong. This was not a problem for the bear and her cubs as they were now strong and healthy. Shqua's son fell into the water and was swept downstream faster than Shqua could follow. The mother bear dove into the water and grabbed the boy and brought him to shore, leaving him unharmed at Shqua's feet. This was in return for his saving her young when they were starving. Ever since that day the people and the bears have been able to fish in peace at the same stream when the salmon run. To celebrate this Shqua made this carving to be placed in the longhouse of the elders so that all could know that the spirit of the bear was the token of Shqua's clan, and to do harm to the bear would do harm to the clan."

"So it is with all of these, they tell a history of the carvers and their clans. This one is from a female carver, QuonTa, who tells of the birth of her son who became a great whaler." Elijah pointed to another carving. "This one is newer, only 100 years old or so, it tells of a great meeting between the people of the North and South Islands."

"You said they were Alicia's?"

"Yes, the people believe the spirit of the carver lives in the carving, and the spirit selects someone to reveal itself to after the carver passes on."

"How is this done?"

"These are kept within the clan, by the elders, when they find someone worthy the carvings will speak to them, and they are passed on."

"And they feel that Alicia was the one who they pass them onto?"

"No mystery in that, the people needed someone to speak for them to the greater world, what better place than a museum where thousands visit, to tell their story?"

"Can't argue there." Newton continued. "You said she only brought one or two pieces back when she returned to the museum, but there are more than that here, and why on earth did you bury them?"

"These are the ones that she had not yet seen, the elders don't want to flood the museum and saturate the market so to speak, so they gave them to me to pass on to her. I buried them because it is a little known spot that is safe. She knew about it of course, and may have been planning to retrieve them. Sad to say, there are those among our people who would trade away their heritage for a few dollars."

"So you put them there for safe keeping then."

"We all return some time or another to the great mother earth for safe keeping, do we not? What better place to keep them than a protected island that no one visits?"

"Makes sense, but don't the elders want them to display at their ceremonies?"

"As a people we have been here a long time; there are carvings enough for the ceremonies. They are kept in a similar fashion, brought out from time to time when needed. There is a ceremony tomorrow at sunrise to pray for Mel's recovery, why don't you and Fran attend? I'll pick you up at 8:30 AM. That's in the early morning in case you needed to know."

"Thanks a bunch, I'd like to go for sure but I will have to ask the lady."

"She'll go, white eyes, trust me," Elijah winked, "and speaking of going, I must drop in and see how the young man is doing, and I'll give the Queen's Cowboys a call later and see if they need me."

Elijah rose from the table and Newton motioned to the carvings, "I'll need to take these down to the detachment so they can take pictures."

"No problem," Elijah said, "I know where you work," and with that he left.

Newton gathered up the carvings, wrapping them carefully, paid the bill, and headed off to the R.C.M.P. office. When he arrived the boat had still not arrived, so he waited while the constable on duty there took pictures of each carving. Since he didn't have a convenient piece of ground to bury them in for safe keeping, he had them placed in the evidence locker until Elijah could retrieve them That done, he used the phone to call Fran and confirm his arrival time for dinner.

Next he headed back to his room to clean up and get ready. At the desk there was another message from Willy, simply stating that the investigation was continuing and nothing of note had been uncovered. There was also a reminder of a court case that he had to attend on the coming Tuesday. Hate to cut short your "vacation," boss, but the Crown wants a meeting on this on Monday, Willy had added. Newton used the room phone to call the airline for a flight out on the coming Sunday, just two days from now. He would also let George know, in case the weather prevented the commercial flight from operating. The Crown took a very dim view of police officers missing a court date, whilst the system seemed to grant defence counsel adjournments on demand. It was a crazy system, and as Sir Winston Churchill had often remarked about democracy, the problem really was no one had come up with a better one. It was a simple case really, and Newton wasn't convinced he should even have been called. The officers at the scene had better evidence than he to give.

It started as a stakeout of sorts in an area where car prowling was rampant. For two weeks residents had reported vehicle break-ins and theft of gas. Although the value taken in any single incident was low, the accumulated amount was significant, and the real volume was the number of complaint calls to the city councilors. Accordingly, a number of extra officers had been marshaled in plain clothes and their own cars, and told to patrol surreptitiously in the area. On the second night, complete with the requisite rain and gloom, one of residents had called in a car prowling complaint. Now the chief problem in these cases was to gather enough evidence to tie the suspect to the scene. Which meant you pretty much had to catch them the act, or with identifiable property from the vehicle. Simply finding him with a half filled gas can was not enough. "Of course it's my gas, I ran out and now I'm going to get my car going." Invariably the suspect's car was a wreck where the gauge didn't work and his story had just enough plausible elements to avoid prosecution. The homeowners realized this was the case and urged a speedy response with whatever command of language they could muster. All which fell upon the ears of the police dispatcher, and little of it fit to be broadcast on the radio.

On this night a marked patrol car responded and met a very calm and jovial homeowner at his door. A truck was parked in the driveway, a red gas can and tank cap was on the ground and there was a black hose protruding from the gas filler neck of the truck's tank.

"So, what's the problem then?"
"Well, officer, I was watching TV when Rascal here," said the homeowner indicating his Jack Russell terrier, "began to kick up a fuss, so I peeked through the curtains and sure enough there was a kid with a gas can and hose taking the cap off the side tank of my truck."

"Can you describe him?"

"Sure, about 18 years old, red and black checked jacket, L.A. Kings cap on backwards, carrying a red gas can with a black hose, but he should be easy to find."

"Why is that? There are a lot of kids wearing those clothes around here."

"Well, the thing is that this truck has two gas tanks, and a while ago I put a camper on and changed one of them into a holding tank for the toilet. Guess which tank he tried to suck gas out of?"

The suspect was found, still retching, in a ditch just down the road. It was easy to trace the trail of vomit back to the truck.

Case closed.

Jesus, Newton thought to himself, a first year law student could win this one, what the hell do they need me for? As the senior investigator at the time he was limited to moving the paperwork through the required channels and his name appeared as the approving officer. Sometimes he wondered if the Crown attorneys ever took the time to properly read things through. Probably not, he mused, because they rarely had the time to do so, and come to think of it, he never saw them leave work early.

A quick shower later, he was dressed and ready to go. He hadn't packed any good clothes for this trip, just his usual working outfit of slacks and shirts. He had used the coveralls supplied by the detachment for his investigative chores, and other than a pair of jeans and a warm pull over, his wardrobe was pretty limited, nothing really suitable for a date. A date was nowhere in his thoughts when he took the flight up, as it had not been anywhere in his mind for years. After his divorce, he had immersed himself into his work and there just never seemed to be the time or opportunity or even the desire to get involved with anyone. Newton found himself taking a look in a full length mirror. The paunch he had developed over the years had almost completed receded now. Two years ago he had made the decision to change his eating habits. This was after he had purchased new slacks and found he had gone up yet another size. Either the cutting houses were cheating on the fabric, or he was gaining too much weight, and he doubted it was the former. So he had made a few simple changes, lunches were now salads spiced with tuna or salmon, a handful of raisins or grapes, and a light dressing. Snacks were now apples, bananas, or some other fruit. Gone were the pizzas, burgers, and fries of previous years and even donuts, the staple of the police officer's diet, were relegated to a rare treat. Slowly the change worked, and the weight had come off. Fact is, he thought, he didn't look half bad for a guy of his age. The fact also was, he hadn't much cared, at least up 'til now.

He had Fran's address, but no idea of where it was and so he picked up the phone to call for a cab. For what time though? He didn't want to arrive too early, or too late, but he had no idea of how long the ride would be. At home he would probably allow half an hour or so, but here five minutes took you out of town. Maybe he should just get some directions and walk, but who to ask? If he asked the staff at the hotel they would know where he was going, and he was not sure if that information was for public consumption at this point. Damn, how could one woman complicate his life so?

In the end he decided he would phone Taylor and get directions, surely he would know where any place in town would be. He dialed the detachment and found that Taylor was still at the dock. Nothing for it now but to go and ask for a town map, maybe he could find out from there. He slipped on his jacket and closed the room door behind him, went down the stairs and headed for the desk. The girl on duty told him that they normally had maps, but they were out at the moment. However the gas station across the street usually had them. He started to head for the door when she stopped him and handed over a slip of paper.

It was written in what could only be described as feminine handwriting.
Alfred, it occurred to me that you don't know where I live, so here is a map - Fran.

A hand drawn map followed. Newton read it and put it in his pocket, when he looked up, the girl behind the desk gave him a knowing smile. So much for being discreet he thought.

A few minutes of walking brought him to Fran's door. It was a nice little house, about 40 years old by the look of it, in very nice shape with a white fence and a gated walk that led from the street. The driveway on the side did not appear to have seen a vehicle in months, no tire tracks or oil puddles. The house was sided with horizontal cedar boards, the bottoms of which had a decorative edging that had been all the rage years ago. They were painted a grey colour and the trim for the windows and door was in teal green. The front door itself was what appeared to be a solid piece of cedar, cut from a single tree. The darker colours at the edges gave way to the lighter coloured heart wood in the centre. An iron door handle and hinges complemented the setting. The entire doorway was set into an alcove that sheltered it from the almost constant wind and frequent rain. The whole feeling was that of a country cottage. In the main window, curtains were drawn back to the edges, a table sat in the centre with a very large cat cleaning itself sitting on top. The aroma of wood smoke permeated the air, and Newton couldn't shake the feeling he was Hansel knocking at the door of the gingerbread house.

A rap at the door brought the sound of footsteps coming closer, the door opened and Fran greeted him wearing a pair of jeans, and flannel shirt and an apron that she was drying her hands on.

"Come in Alfred, you're a little early—or I'm a little behind, I'm still cooking."

"I'm early I think," said Newton, and thinking, my God she looks lovely.

"Well, have a seat in the living room if you like, don't mind Horatio, he's always looking for a lap to curl up on. I hope you're not allergic to cats, I didn't think to ask you beforehand."

"No problem," Newton responded. "I like cats, but haven't had the time to look after one."

"You can follow me into the kitchen if you prefer, I'm still puttering a bit."

Newton followed her. Even though he didn't mind cats, he much preferred her company.

Fran poured him a glass of wine from an open bottle set on the counter. The kitchen was a cook's dream. A pair of wall ovens, an island mounted cook top and wide open counters. An expanse of cupboards and a large stainless steel sink complemented the look. An assortment of copper bottomed pots and pans hung suspended in a rack above the island. One of the ovens was on and delightful odours emanated from it. A pair of pots simmered on the cook top, and a pile of freshly washed greens lay on a cutting board by the sink.

"Cooking must be a hobby of yours" he said gesturing at the kitchen's professional appointments.

Fran laughed, and her eyes lit up with a sparkle, Newton felt his own spirits lifted by just listening to her. "Oh my no, I didn't do all this, I bought it from one of the cooks at the hotel when he moved back to the mainland, I really don't do it justice at all."

"Well, on that I must disagree, I think you would do justice to any endeavour you choose" Newton replied.

"Aren't you the gentleman!" She said, squeezing his hand. "Why don't you grab a knife and slice up some tomatoes for the salad?"

Newton made his way to the sink, carefully put down his wine and struggled to get his heart back to something approaching a normal rhythm. Taking a deep breath he willed his knees to hold him up and tried to slice the tomatoes without cutting off a finger, accidentally committing Hari Kari, or otherwise embarrassing himself. They chatted back and forth, with Newton trying to sound relaxed and normal, when in truth he was nowhere near it.

Fran set the table, "I hope you don't mind eating here in the kitchen, the house was never built with a dining room," she said refilling his wine glass and handing it back to him.
"Not at all, it's the company that counts, not the setting."
"Why than you, Sir Galahad," she replied giving him a peck on the cheek. "Or should I call you Sir Isaac, I suppose you get that a lot."
Newton made some sort of stammering thank you reply whilst trying to control, his legs, his heart, and his breathing all at the same time. "Umm, yes sometimes, but I don't mind, I guess it's a compliment to be thought of like that."
"Have you ever traced your family history? Do you know if you are a descendent of Isaac Newton?"

Newton took the suggestion to have a seat in relief, "I tried once, but the records are somewhat obscured. I believe we may have shared a common branch of the tree, but some of my ancestors seemed to have chosen a life of purloining horses and such."
"Don't they say it takes someone who thinks like a thief to catch a thief?"
"Only the really good ones, most thieves are too lazy to think far enough ahead to plan adequately. A really good thief thinks of everything as a game, him against the authorities, and they all have an inherent belief that they are smarter than everyone else. A good police officer on the other hand, knows he is not the smartest detective on the planet and works hard at not missing anything that may help him solve a case. Given enough time, the detective will always win out, it's only when the amount of work overwhelms the resources available that things slip between the cracks and a case is not solved."

Newton was feeling more relaxed now. Back in his own world he was sure of himself and in control of his emotions. As long as he didn't gaze too long into her eyes, or see her smile, or hear her voice, or smell her perfume. When that happened, well he drifted off a bit; his voice lost tenor, words escaped half formed and stumbling from his mouth. His palms would sweat, his heart performed Beethoven's fifth, and there was this strange roaring sound somewhere in the back of his head. At the same time he felt comfortable in her presence, and that he should be standing beside her, holding her and if he could do that then, well, things would be as they should.

But here he was on the other side of the table, babbling like some academy instructor, and trying to sound like he had some clue about what he was talking about. Well, he did know what he was talking about, it was his profession, and had been for years, but he didn't know a damn thing about how he felt, except it was good, and confusing, and natural, and unnerving, and a thousand other things all swirling about at the same time. Given all the times he had faced the wrong end of a gun or knife, or pulled a lifeless child from a car wreck, or listened to some bent and twisted mind describe the things he did to a child, you would think, he would think, that he could handle this, but he couldn't, not well, not really.

A point brought home by the amused look on her face that told him he was sitting there like a fool having completely lost his train of thought. He realized that he had stopped talking, and had no idea when, or what he had said last.

"I'm sorry, I must appear to you to be, well a little foolish, I apologize, but I must admit I haven't felt this way in a very long time."
"And how would that be?"
"Like a teenager on his first big date, I suppose. That's the only way I can describe it."
"Well, thank God for that" Fran replied with a smile, "I thought I was the only one. Shall we eat?"

Newton smiled back, and visibly relaxed, he decided that he would let things develop as they would. Dinner went off without a hitch, the conversation was light and flowing, and the topics centered on things they had in common, flying, walking, and an interest in the craftsmanship and art of the Haida. After dinner they did the dishes together, and it seemed that there was more than one occasion that they took the opportunity to touch hands. As she took the last dried dish from his hands, Fran slipped her arm around Newton's waist, without another thought he wrapped her in his arms and they kissed for a time that was both too short and too long. She laid her head against his chest and murmured "For a detective Alfred, you can pretty dense at times."
"Practice" he replied, "practice, practice, practice, besides, I have no idea of the pace of these things anymore. It has been years and years

and years since I felt anything like this," holding her closer and gently stroking her hair.

"Me too Alfred, me too, but face it, we aren't getting any younger."
"I have to get back to Victoria day after tomorrow," Newton said.
"Well then, let's make the best use of the time we have 'til then."

And they did.

CHAPTER TWENTY ONE

The ringing of the phone woke Newton from the first deep sleep that he could remember having in months. He rolled over in bed and fumbled for the receiver.

"Good morning, Newton, hope I didn't wake you," Elijah's voice boomed over the lines.
"Actually you did," Newton replied. "What's up?"
"The meeting at the village this morning, all the elders will be meeting after the general prayer ceremonies. I thought you might wish to have a word with them about the carvings. Don't tell me you forgot already. What happened to that steel trap of a mind you police folk have?"
"Rusted shut I expect. Damn, what time is it?"
"Seven-thirty."
"I'll be ready in half an hour, but aren't these meetings restricted to tribal members though?"
"Usually, but we can make exceptions from time to time if we think it's warranted, and since you have a direct interest in Mel's recovery, we would like you to come. You will get an opportunity to do some background on Mel, and we feel that will help."

"I have to be there before the chiefs arrive so I've arranged for you to ride over with Taylor and Fran. They will pick you up in an hour, so get ready." With that Elijah hung up leaving Newton once again with more questions than answers.

A quick shower later and Newton was down in the restaurant finishing his toast and coffee and watching the window. He had hoped to check with Taylor on whether or not the aluminum boat had yielded anything more of an evidentiary nature, but that would have to wait. After the ceremony was over hey would meet back at the detachment office to go over both what had transpired since his arrival. It had been a very busy few days, and with his flight tomorrow back to Victoria, he was little closer to discovering the identity of his Jane Doe. In addition he had been involved in the discovery and investigation of another girl's body, a suspect who was clinging to life in the hospital, and the recovery of some very valuable carvings. What more could happen? Well, he thought, perhaps the most improbable thing of all.

He could fall in love again.

Newton was by nature a cautious man, this was due to more than his training, it was the way he lived his life. He could point to several times where not rushing to conclusions had led to an initial feeling about something, or someone, being proven wrong. His astrological sign was that of the balance scales, a Libra who carefully weighed all available information before deciding which way the scales swung. The few times in his life he had disregarded this natural inclination had not proved to be to his benefit. So when it came to affairs of the heart, he had been found to be somewhat reserved in the past. As he grew older, this had been interpreted by others as being cold and distant, lacking passion and purpose in his personal relationships. He thought of last night and smiled—whatever would they say now?

At that moment the object of his thoughts was walking through the door of the restaurant accompanied by Cpl.Taylor. She was dressed in a skirt and matching blouse, with a scarf and jacket. Taylor was wearing the dress serge of the R.C.M.P. He looked every inch like Nelson Eddy and Newton half expected him to break out in a song and dance routine. For himself, Newton wore slacks and a shirt with a tie he had picked up from the hotel desk. He should by rights be dressed in the light blue dress uniform of his home department, but he had not brought it with him. He got up from the table and joined them at the door. Without any apparent thought, Fran took his hand and gave him a quick kiss on the cheek. With a great deal of thought, Newton slipped his arm around her waist and pulled her close. Taylor studiously pretended not to notice. Outside they climbed into a freshly washed and waxed cruiser, driven by one of the detachment constables, who was also dressed in the scarlet tunic, riding boots, and "Smokey the Bear" hat of the force. Taylor got in the front passenger seat and Fran and Newton got in the back. The cruiser was not equipped with rear door handles, so it meant their doors would have to be opened from the outside. Newton grinned inwardly; it would be the first time in his life that a uniformed member of the Queen's Cowboys had opened the door for him like he was royalty.

"Elijah will meet us at the ceremony," Taylor said. "Have you ever been to one of these things?"
"No, can't say that I have."

"The first part is all scripted according to the traditions of the people, there will be a gift exchange of tobacco and such, that will be my role, and then the elders will pray according to their customs. And at the end of it, you will be introduced to them. After the lunch you will have an opportunity to ask questions which they may or may not answer. You can consider any answers you get as gospel, for them to do anything other than that at such a ceremony would bring dishonour on their clan and people."

With that, they pulled into the village centre and parked on the grass field surrounding the largest building. This was the meeting house. Constructed of modern materials but finished in traditional cedar board siding and set into the earth. Around the long house were large totems marking each clan and its position within the societal order of the people. The smell of wood smoke permeated the air, and everywhere the people were dressed in the finery of their respective clans. Large masks of cedar and walrus tusk adorned with feathers and passed down from generation to generation were in evidence. Some carried carvings in both cedar and Argillite. The children were similarly dressed, their costumes the result of long hours of work.

Taylor led Newton and Fran to a waiting area beside the main doors. Newton noticed the number of young people that came up and chatted with the Mountie, it was obvious that he was a respected member of both communities. For his part, Taylor joked and laughed with the kids, and seemed to know not only their names, but also the names of their family members, never failing to ask how this elder or that was feeling.

This continued until the time for the ceremony to begin.
From inside the lodge came the muted sound of the drums, summoning the people to attend. Taylor took his place in line in behind the elders. Along with the other constable, he carried a small leather pouch of tobacco, and a scroll wrapped in red ribbon.

The drums lasted about five minutes by Newton's watch, and then went silent. All those who wished to attend had by now taken their seats and waited silently for the procession to begin. It was led by the elders, oldest to youngest, followed by the two R.C.M.P. officers. They walked between the rows of benches to the far end of the building, where a low platform served as a stage of sorts. Once there, the elders took their respective positions, turned and faced their people. Cpl.Taylor and his party waited until they were ready and at a nod from the elders, stepped forward and offered their pouches of tobacco. They were accepted and in return a carving of cedar given to the Mounties. Newton and Fran had been shown to a seat in the front row along one of the sides. Around them were families of the Bear clan, their totem marking their assigned spot, as did the totems of the other clans, including the Eagle, the Salmon, the Raven, and other venerated spirits. Each represented some special strength or food source essential to the survival of the people and their pledge to live in mutual respect and harmony with each other. Elders carried carvings of wood or stone, as did many of the people in the seats. The drums began again and the elders circled a large pit where a fire of cedar and pine crackled. A section of the roof had been withdrawn and served as an escape for the smoke. With chants and drums the elders called upon the spirits of their ancestors and the guardians of their clans to watch over and heal the young man who lay injured in the hospital. They also called upon the Great Spirit to provide guidance for the people so that they could continue to live in peace with those around them.

Each senior member of the clans called out in turn a ritual greeting to the spirits and pledged continued support for the peace and harmony of the tribe as a whole. A gift was offered, and prayers made. As the ceremony continued, young men dressed in costumes and wearing masks representing the clan spirits danced within the sacred circle. Newton scanned the assembly for Elijah, but could not see him anywhere. The chanting and drums died away. This signaled the end of the formal ceremony and the elders and R.C.M.P. left the floor through the same door they had entered. The floor was now open to the children, and they seized the opportunity with the enthusiasm of kids everywhere. Some lined up to try the drums under the supervision of older kids, some danced, showing off their handmade finery. Some just gathered around the fire pit to enjoy the magic of the flames. Parents took the opportunity to show their kids the totems of the different clans, explaining the legends and meaning behind each. The formality of the ceremony had given way to a social atmosphere you could find in any religious gathering anywhere in the world.

Newton and Fran stood off to one side, waiting for either Taylor to come back or Elijah to show up. Taylor was at this moment in conversation with some of the elders. They were explaining the details of the carving they had given him, and the story behind it.

"Well, what did you think?" Came a muted voice from behind.
Newton and Fran turned to address a large figure clad in a bear skin; the head was carved from cedar, with large eyes and real bear teeth.

"Very impressive, Elijah, I didn't notice you dancing out there though."
"For good reason, this rig weighs a ton, it's hot inside and I'm not the young man I once was."
Fran laughed "I'll bet you did a wonderful job when you did dance in

it."

"That was a long time ago, I'm afraid, now I just wear it to impress the tourists and scare small children." Elijah replied with a chuckle as he removed the carved head from his shoulders and placed it on a nearby seat. "Give me a hand will you? This thing takes a crew to get in and out of."

Both Newton and Fran helped him out of the costume and Elijah breathed a sigh of relief as he folded the heavy skin and put it beside the head. "Let me introduce you to Mel's relatives," he said indicating a group of people gathered expectantly at one end of the hall. "They are anxious to talk with you."

As Elijah led them towards the group, Newton cocked his head towards the costume and asked "Are you just going to leave that there?"
"Why not? It's community property, there is only one like it, it's too heavy to run away with, and everyone and his dog will recognize it."
"Does this mean you are of the Bear clan then?" Asked Newton.

"No, I don't have a specific clan, I sort of belong to the people as a whole, even though my ancestors were from the bear and eagle clans, I'm not aligned with anyone in particular." Elijah steered the couple to Mel's relatives. Fran took his hand and slipped a small pouch into it, it was pouch of tobacco, the traditional gift of greeting, and he had forgotten all about getting one. He turned and whispered a thank you to her and she smiled back.

The first thing Newton noticed was the respect that they had for Elijah. He was treated as both an elder and a Shaman. The next thing he noticed was the eagerness they had to talk to him. Even so, it began with the eldest of the group, the rest holding back until their turn to speak. He offered the pouch to the eldest member and the group nodded their appreciation of their customs and the talking began.

"I am Mel's uncle, Eddie Little Bear, Elijah has said you are one of the people who found Mel and brought him to the hospital, for that we thank you."
"No thanks necessary, I hope he will make a full recovery."
"The doctor's say he is doing well, for the moment. I understand you wish to learn what kind of a person Mel is, so I have asked his relatives here to speak for him."

Newton acknowledged each family member as they were introduced, aunts, uncles, and cousins—the entire living family tree. In his world Newton usually would have to track each family member down over a period of days or weeks to get an interview with them. Here they all turn up as a group, eager to help.

The message was the same from all, Mel was a good boy. He had worked hard to look after his relatives after the deaths of his parents. His life had not been tainted with excess drinking, though he, like teenagers everywhere, had tried both alcohol and tobacco, but found no attraction in either. Instead his passion was carving, and he was becoming good at it. His early work had not been so, and he rarely showed those pieces to anyone, but he kept them just the same. In the last two years he had improved greatly, as if the spirit of a carver long dead had found a home in his hands. If anything, Mel was too trusting. They had noticed in the last year or so that he had become friends with someone whom he thought could help him sell his carvings. The change of focus from artistry to tell a story, to art for sale had begun to trouble them. Mel never mentioned the newfound friend by name, and never brought him into the village. This also troubled the elders of the family. But it was normal for the young people of any culture to try to go their own way. In that journey, we all stumble around a bit before finding our true paths.

Newton asked if they knew anything about Alicia and yes they knew that he had been seeing the lady from the museum and asked her to take one of his newest carvings there, but beyond that there was nothing between them. Alicia was older than Mel, and though that did not have any significance age wise, the difference in worldly knowledge was vast and would not have allowed for a romantic relationship to develop. They had told all this to Cpl.Taylor, and were pleased to repeat it now. Mel was one of their clan and anything they could do to help, they would gladly do. One of them showed Newton a carving, it was one of Mel's latest and Newton thought it to be of very good quality. He could not judge if it was sufficient for museum exposure, but it would surely bring a good price in any of the tourist stores.

Throughout the conversation, Elijah kept to the background, chatting with the elders and making faces at the children, who laughed and squealed with delight when he did so.

After the relatives had had their say, Newton and Fran left them and

Elijah to enjoy the rest of the day and went to find Cpl.Taylor. They found him waiting by the cruiser and headed back into town. Once again they were treated to the feeling of being royalty as Taylor opened the door for them at the hotel. Newton resisted the temptation to put a dollar bill in his hand, and promised instead to go down to the detachment office later that day to review everything that had happened and the evidence collected. He and Fran went into the restaurant and ordered lunch. This time they sat side by side instead of across from each other, and despite the best efforts of the cook, ate very little. Instead they talked about the ceremony and each other, leaving the restaurant to take a walk on the beach. Hand in hand they strolled away from town towards the flats where the tide was still going out. Some of the young folks had their trucks on the flats, and were busy harvesting clams for the village feast to be held later that afternoon. As they passed one of the trucks, Newton stopped abruptly, turned around, and approached the passenger's seat. The seatbelt had been removed by cutting the strap. The owner was in the process of hoisting a bucket of clams into the back of the truck and came up alongside them. After introducing himself, Newton asked about the seat belt.

"Why do you cut them?" He asked.
"It's the salt; it gets in the lock mechanism and rusts it so bad it can't be opened even if you can get it to close in the first place." Newton nodded his understanding and thanked the young man for his help. Fran studied his face, "I haven't known you that long Alfred, but I can tell when you are thinking deeply about something." Newton blinked and replied "Sorry, just had an idea flash into my head; it happens occasionally despite my best efforts!" They laughed and continued their walk, "So what were we talking about?"
"We were talking about your having to leave tomorrow, that's what we were talking about," Fran said wistfully, "and I don't really want you to go, but I know you have to."

"Can't be helped, I can't stay here any longer, I have work to do back home."
"I know," she said, holding him tighter, "I just wish it wasn't so soon and so far away."

"Nothing is that far away anymore, they have airplanes now."
"I know that silly boy, it just seems so far."
"Not really, a few hours and poof you're there, you should try it sometime."
"Oh my, Mr. Newton, is that an invitation?"

"Yes." Newton replied, his mouth suddenly dry. "Yes, it most certainly is."
Fran gripped his hand tighter and smiled up to him, "And me with nothing to wear in the big city."
"Ah," Newton said "I can help there, I've heard they have stores now, marvelous things they are, and lots of them, in something called a "mall", and I have a map."

They continued their walk for an hour chatting about everything and nothing, then turned around and headed back to town.

CHAPTER TWENTY TWO

Cpl. Taylor, now dressed in his regular service uniform, was waiting for Newton at the detachment. There were two files on his desk, one for Alicia and one for Mel. Between them was the forensic report from "K" Division, it was open and Taylor was making notes on a legal pad.

"Come in, sit down - coffee?"

"Thanks—no, those drums left me wide awake. Something primordial in the beat of a drum."

"Sure is. That's why every culture features a drum beat in one ritual or another. Anthropologists relate it to the beat of our mother's hearts from our time in the womb, it's the first sound we hear in our lives. I always wanted one when I was a boy, but my parents wisely said no. Did you get any further information from the elders?"

"Some, mostly it was 'he was a good boy, works hard if not steady, and wants to be a carver,' certainly nothing that leads me to believe he was capable of cold blooded murder. Especially Alicia, she was the ticket for his flight to stardom, without her help getting his work on display—well, he had very little chance of ever selling much on his own."

As Newton sat down, the two began to review the information that had surfaced thus far.

The examination of the boat revealed several sets of prints on the aluminum surface. They had eliminated Newton, George, Fran, and Elijah's prints along with one of the crew members of the boat that towed it in. One set remained besides Mel's to be identified, and as yet there was no match. Fingerprints by themselves of course could only say that someone had been at a scene, not when. It took something else to set the timeline, something that could only be present during a certain period. Newton had been able to set the timeline by identifying incidental materials in the fingerprint impression, dirt from a garden, paint from a wall, even cleaning solutions could provide an acceptable method of establishing a window of time. If he was lucky he would find such a fingerprint, even better was a fingerprint outlined in blood, and the best of them all was a fingerprint containing the blood of the victim. The photographs before Newton clearly showed such a print, and the forensic report matched the DNA in the blood to that of Mel.

The print was found on the bottom of a seat, and the picture had been taken using a mirror. It needed to be reversed and run through the NCIS computer system for a match. It was as yet a match that had not been achieved.

"Any ideas on who this could be?" Newton asked Taylor.
"Not at this point, but what we do know is that whomever it is, they are likely still here, there hasn't been a commercial flight out for two days now, and the fishing fleet is still in port."
"Who owns the boat?"
"Ownership is something that is not that well defined when it comes to the people of this island, things like small boats are regarded as communal property and used by all. This boat was last seen prior to our finding it, at the common dock area. It would be used, along with half a dozen or so like it, by anyone who needed it at any time. The registration numbers are simply recorded to the tribe as a whole rather than a particular person."
"So do you feel we are looking for one of the people or someone else at this point?"
"Could be either; fingerprints have no racial characteristics."

"So let's go over what probably happened," Newton continued. "As I read it, Alicia and Mel were out on the flats for some reason not yet known, the Jeep gets stuck and Mel gets out and Alicia doesn't, first question is what were they doing out there in the first place?"

Taylor produced a series of photos, "Take a look at this."
"What am I seeing here?"
Taylor spread them out on his desk.
"What we have here are a series of four pictures of the same area of the left front fender of Mel's jeep. They are one of full colour, and one each of each colour channel, red, blue, and green. First look at the full colour one. Notice anything?"
"This is one of those new whizzy things that the ident folks have come with isn't it?" Newton muttered as he examined the photo with a practiced eye. "I see a number of dents on the fender and....one that looks like it could be fresh. See there, the metal is brighter on that spot—not completely rusted yet."
"Good eye detective. Many would have missed that, especially since we recovered it from the salt chuck where the rate of rusting is accelerated."
"Hmm, the rust that is there tends to blend in with the paint scheme though. Hard to tell from the distance the picture was taken if there is anything else of interest."
"This may help with that, forensic found traces of fresh paint scraping on the fender of the Jeep. The condition of the vehicle made that hard to find, we don't have a body shop here and any vehicle that gets a

dent or suchlike tends to remain in that condition. The paint is consistent with an early model Ford Bronco, a vehicle that I can't recall seeing here."

"OK, but I can't really see it well."

"Look at the next series of photos, where the colours have been separated into the primaries."

Newton examined the three pictures closely, "Aha! I believe that's how my ancestors said it, or maybe it was egad! Either way I see the red channel photo shows a different shade right over the dent."

"It is even more evident on the computer over here," Taylor said motioning Newton to the side desk. On the screen was the same series of photographs, along with a program that allowed the user to control the hue and saturation of each separate color.

Taylor used the mouse to move a slider bar and the area of the dent took on a different hue than the rest of the fender.

"Now we can expand on this area and bring out the damaged area even more."

In a few moments the area of the dent filled the screen and two scratches were readily apparent, and the paint residue plainly visible. A few clicks of the mouse isolated the revealed colour.

"Was this from those fancy new digital cameras the ident crew brought with them?" he asked.

"Actually, yes, but any good 35 mm camera picture would do the same, The magic is in the software, not the picture. As long as you can scan the photos into the computer you can use this program to do a detailed examination."

"We gotta get one of those then," Newton pronounced.

"You're on the list already. 'K' division will be sending every force in the province a copy so we are all on the same page as far as court presentations go."

"Will it identify the paint also?"

"Nope, you still need to do a chemical analysis on the samples, just as before, but you can narrow down the search area quickly with it. We still have to find the suspect vehicle the old fashioned way."

"Maybe we need to just look for the paint, not the vehicle, if there isn't a body shop, chances are that owners do their own body work, and for that they would get pre-packaged paint cans from some big box store on the mainland."

"Good point, I'll ask the boys to keep their eyes out, but that colour of white is probably close to any number of makes."

"So it would be a white 4x4 with fresh paint, or fresh scrapes on the side, like a fender, given the location of the marks, that should narrow it down a little."

"OK, so they are out on the flats, and there are fresh scrapes on the vehicle, nothing to indicate when it occurred though could be something as simple as a scrape in a parking lot."

"I've seen your parking lots, they just aren't that busy, and the rate of oxidation on the fender means the scrape must have been made fairly close to the time the jeep went into the water."

"Right, so most likely it occurred at the same time, let's go with that then, what happens next—they get stuck."

"Now you told me that these kids know each of the flats pretty well, and they would know where the areas to avoid were, correct? So why did they end up there?"

"I think we will have our answer to that when we trace that paint," Taylor said.

"So then, we have them stuck, that would occur when the tide has turned and is coming in, correct?"

"Right, as the tide floods, the pressure of the water loosens the sand and turns it into a quicksand-like material, and anything sitting on it sinks. Mel would know that and probably told Alicia to sit tight while he went for a boat."

"How far would they be from the communal dock, I mean, could Mel make it there and back in time?"

"It's about 1.5 kilometers, so, yeah, probably, so he leaves Alicia in the Jeep and returns in, say, about an hour. At this time of the year that means the tide would flood in enough to cover the floorboards of the Jeep, so there would be plenty of time to get her out."

"Unless he was delayed, don't forget the unidentified fingerprint, which indicates that there could have been someone else in the boat at some time."

"Hmmm, let's say he was delayed, but how and for how long, and why didn't Alicia just go with him at the start, or just climb onto the hood of the Jeep?"

"I may have the answer to that," Newton replied. "I noticed a lot of the kids have cut off the seat belts on their cars because the buckles get rusted out and won't release, so if that's the case maybe Alicia could not get the belt undone, did they examine the belt yet?"

Taylor ran through the reports in front of him, "No, nothing here."

"Get them to do that then, I'll bet they find the buckle won't release, and have them check for cuts on the belt."

"What's your thinking there?"

"Well look at it this way, Mel is in the boat, at the side of the Jeep,

and he and Alicia realize that the buckle won't work, so he takes out his knife and tries to cut the belt, but the knife slips."
"OK, that works, the angle of the cut to his upper abdomen could have come if he was bent over the boat rail, that would mean though he got there a lot later than we think."
"And that would mean Alicia would be very panicky, and there should be tell-tale enzymes in her blood to confirm that."

"Right. Then Mel gets back late, the Jeep has sunk to the frame due to the sand shifting underneath it, that would affect the time line also, Alicia had tried to get out of the belt, but it won't budge, the water is rising and she is in full panic. Mel is leaning over the boat, she is grabbing for him and he misses the belt and stabs himself. Then he falls to the bottom of the boat and it drifts to the island."
"Not quite," said Newton. "There is that other fingerprint, it has Mel's blood and must have come after he got stabbed so maybe there is someone else in the boat, or they come by just afterwards. Also, there's the gas tank, it was empty and the motor was up. Two choices there as I see it, first the tank was empty at the start and Mel can't get it running and he lifts it up so he can paddle the boat. That would explain the timeline. It would take much longer for him to get back if he had to paddle it all the way. And he would be tired too."
"And the second point?"
"Someone set him adrift with the engine running and pointed the boat out to sea, hoping it would sink and Mel would just disappear."

Newton and Taylor moved to the big whiteboard in the office, and quickly drew a time line.
"Now, we know when the tide turned, and when the Jeep was first spotted by the kids from the base. We know how far it was to the boat dock, so we have this period here." Taylor said pointing to a space on the board, "When Mel could have arrived back at the Jeep."
"We can narrow that down from the charts perhaps, when would he have to be there for the current to carry him to the island where he was found?"
"Right, because if he could not have got there on the current alone, then the engine on the boat must have been running."
"I'll track that down today," Taylor said.

"Any word on Mel's condition? He could clear up a lot of the 'ifs' and 'buts'."
"No change yet, but the doctors say his condition is improving and he should make a full recovery."
"Well, let's hope it's sooner rather than later."

With things progressing about as far as they could for the moment, Newton and Taylor called it a day. The Mountie would contact "K" division and ask for their help in answering those points still outstanding. What they had now was a plausible theory, backed by certain pieces of evidence, and so far not contradicted by anything they had uncovered. Like all good detectives, they would not lock themselves into any particular avenue, but allow the evidence to act as a guide, defining the limits and directions of their travel. Always keeping an open mind to other theories that could fit.

It was now the evening of the last day that Newton could spend in the Charlottes and if he followed his normal patterns, he should be spending the time in his room going over everything that happened since his arrival, and what he had found that could aid in the primary cause of identifying his Jane Doe. So far it didn't look as if he had come up with anything except more questions. Starting with the discovery of Alicia's body, then coming upon Mel on the island, add in the carvings, and what did one come up with?

A coincidental series of events?

Or interconnected happenings that followed a natural course from one to the other? And then there was Elijah, just a spectator? Or was his involvement somehow deeper, it did seem odd that every time that he turned around, Elijah was on or near the scene. Last but not least, there was Fran. Why here, why now, and why her? After all these years of being on his own, was it time for him to love again? To live again? To feel that wonderful sense of completeness that only comes when you share your life with someone? The Charlottes were always regarded as islands of mystery by those who visited them. The changes in the weather, the relaxed pace of life, the isolation and natural beauty of the place changed all who touched her shores.

Why me? Newton thought.

He reached for the phone.

CHAPTER TWENTY THREE

The next morning found him waiting with Fran at the seaplane dock. Sandspit was once again fogged in and the Grumman offered him the only method of air travel to the mainland. George and his ramp rats had the twin prepared and ready for takeoff.

"Got room for one more?" Newton asked George, nodding towards Fran.
"You bet, always enjoy company on the way back, maybe we will see some whales."

Newton passed up the chance at flying the right hand seat and instead he and Fran buckled in seats in the passenger compartment. George taxied the plane out onto the water and soon they were on their way.

To Newton, the trip to the mainland was much quicker than the original trip to the island a few days before. He hardly noticed the waters below the craft; instead, he and Fran spent the time holding on to one another. Before the Grumman landed at Prince Rupert, she had promised to visit him within the month, and the tone of their conversation signaled that she was not planning to return afterwards. There were a myriad of details that both needed to attend to. She had a house to sell, he had to look for a bigger apartment, and although the time apart would be short in time to their minds, it was endless to their hearts.

George busied himself on landing, delaying the takeoff until Newton had boarded the Air Canada flight to Vancouver, giving the couple all the time there was available. When at last they took off to return to the Charlottes, Fran was, for the first time, not interested in taking the controls of the plane, or racing the waves in a fast low level flight. George left her with her thoughts and tended to the routine of guiding the craft to a safe landing.

CHAPTER TWENTY FOUR

The stack of messages awaiting Newton at his office made him wish he had gone straight home instead of stopping to "check on things.:" He spent the next hour sorting out the trivial from the important. There were no messages from Willy, and that in itself was odd. He rose from his desk and headed for the coffee pot to refill his cup when his partner came in and sat down opposite Newton's desk.

"So did you enjoy your vacation in our misty and mysterious Northern Islands?" Willy asked.

"Somewhat, got more questions than answers though, how did you do with the museum inquiries?"

"Got some questions there too" said Willy. "Someone named Elijah sent me this."

Willy tossed a message onto the desk top.

Alfred is busy with things up here, but he has mentioned that you are looking after things while he is gone. I thought that you might want to look up this chap, his Name is Reginald Johnson, and works at the museum. Mr. Johnson sent a note to Alicia Howell from the museum. Alicia was out in the field at the time and the staff at the hotel re-addressed the message to me, knowing that I would likely run into her sooner than she would return to the hotel. Unfortunately, as Alfred has surely informed you, Alicia is now deceased. The message simply requests Ms. Howell contact Mr. Johnson at her earliest opportunity and lists a telephone number at the museum. I will forward it to the R.C.M.P. detachment here. Please convey my regards to Mr. Newton and let him know how much we all enjoyed his company even though the circumstances were less than auspicious.

"So who is this Elijah guy anyway, some sort of English professor who washed up on the shores of the distant colony to study the natives?"

"Actually, Elijah Longeyes is a Haida elder, and a medicine man to boot, you would like him, he thinks like we do."

"He's a cop?"

"The Haida have no police force per se, never needed one, and hope to God never will, but if they did, he would certainly be one of the ones they would pick. I found him a good logical thinker with his feet on the ground and good instincts."

"And I can see he has the ability to influence young impressionable minds of people like yourself," joked Willy. "Anyway, both you and he would no doubt be interested to know that the recovered piece of

Haida art came from the premises of none other than one Reginald Johnson, museum guard. What were the odds, eh?"

"Well, well, isn't that interesting, Rusty mentioned a museum guard with the initials R.J., so where might I find Mr. Johnson at this moment, in jail perhaps?"
"Alas, no, Mr. Johnson was not in residence when the drug boys came a-calling, bad manners. What?" Willy replied in his best Sherlock Holmes impression. "The riff- raff on the streets, having been interviewed at the yard, let it be known that Mr. Johnson has fled to the northern reaches of our fair province. As he happened to be returning from a local buy and unfortunately spotted the coppers making inquiries as to his whereabouts. In fact you may have run into him, his destination of choice was the same charmed island upon which you have spent the last few days chasing crime and or evil, and chatting up the local women folk."

Newton was genuinely surprised at the last comment, and to his chagrin, it immediately showed on his face.

Willy grinned "No mystery there boss," seeing the look in Newton's eyes. "That wasn't the only message we got." With that he tossed a second envelope to Newton. "Apparently the NCO I/C of the Charlottes detachment, Cpl.Taylor, felt this was of some importance and added it to some official dispatches from the frontier to the local lads, who obligingly dropped it off scant hours ago. We couldn't help but notice the salutation on the envelope."

Newton picked it up and saw it was addressed to "Sir Isaac Newton," and the return address read "Frances Miller." Very few people ever called Alfred by his nickname, and Willy had never known a woman to do it. When he saw the envelope he immediately suspected a more than casual relationship, and happened to let that be known to Cpl.Taylor when he phoned the Cpl. to let him know the envelope had been received. That was a totally unnecessary action on his part, but his curiosity has been piqued and Willy had learned that following hunches was an integral part of good police work, and Willy had been trained by one of the best. Besides, a chance to get something to tease the boss with was much more than opportunity knocking. It was a clarion call bellowing for a response. Cpl.Taylor had filled him in with the events that occurred during Newton's visit, and also added his assessment of Alfred's blossoming relationship with Frances. Willy could not have been more pleased, he genuinely liked Alfred, as did those detectives and uniformed personnel of the force who were not adverse to hard work and constructive criticism. Since his divorce years ago and disappearance of his daughter, Newton had been too alone for far too long, even for such a lonely profession as this.

Willy's grin said all that needed to be said and Newton accepted the unspoken congratulations. He was not used to feeling this way, a little embarrassed and little apprehensive, and for one of the few times in his life, he was short of words.

"So what do we know about Mr. Johnson?" Newton said, changing the subject.
"He has been working at the museum for close to five years." Willy said, flipping a picture of a man in his twenties, wearing a guard's uniform and cap, staring at the camera in the requisite identification pose. "No problems with him until about two years ago. He started showing up late for work, and taking sick days off. That was the same time the museum started the Haida exhibit, things started to go missing from the museum, they always do in an enterprise of that size. Some would show up later, having been simply misplaced by some worker or another, or taken by a curator for examination and the paperwork not filled out properly."

Newton nodded. Every organization had those who did not recognize the need for creating a paper trail to track valuable objects, whether it was pieces of evidence as in his department, or artifacts in the care of the museum. This situation was routinely exacerbated it seemed, by those senior persons who tried to micromanage everything and created paperwork that was not necessary.

"By the time they figured out what was really missing and was just misplaced, there were rumours of Haida carvings suddenly showing up in the hands of private collectors, carvings that never went through an agent or auction house. Not all were from the museum though, and that muddied the waters. Part of Alicia's task was to find out if some of the Haida were selling their carvings directly, and if so who to."

"So Mr. Johnson was buying from them and selling to the collectors," Newton said. "Nothing illegal in that."
"True," mused Willy. "But some of the pieces coming out of the Charlottes were not the prime pieces promised. Reginald was doing the bait and switch game, showing the buyers pieces from the museum, and then switching for pieces of poorer quality. If the buyers squawked then he would steal the museum piece for the buyer and leave the copy at the museum."

"Eventually, the museum would discover the switch, especially when the pieces were returned, and then it would, as they say, hit the fan."

"Ah, but the museum didn't want a public investigation, ruins their reputation, and we were never informed this was going on," Willy added. "So that allowed Mr. Johnson more time to carry out his plans. Eventually he got involved in drugs, and then he started using the pieces to pay off his drug debts."

"Do you have anything to indicate that he was connected to Alicia?"

"No, nothing other than they worked at the museum, and it was the same pieces of art. She must have twigged to the scheme at some point. He would have to convince her as well as the museum that the pieces they were returning were the real McCoy."

"Which means she was either a partner, or in the way. Add drugs to the mix and you have more than enough motive to engineer Alicia's demise."

"Oh?" said Willy, looking up in surprise, "I thought that was an accident with the tide coming in and a car getting stuck, wasn't it?"

"Could be," said Newton, "But things are beginning to take a different turn, and this new info about Mr. Johnson puts things in a much different light. Make sure you send a copy of your report up to the detachment in the Charlottes, I think Cpl. Taylor would like to see it." Newton got up from his desk, stretched and announced he was heading home. He stopped at the door and turned around to face Willy, "By the way, did you get any fingerprints?"

"Dozens. And the museum supplied the set they have on file for Reggie so we can match them to the ones in the house and on the carving."

"Good, send a copy to Taylor also, I have a hunch we may have a line on Mr. Johnson's travels." With that Newton headed home, the note from Fran in his pocket, close to his heart.

CHAPTER TWENTY FIVE

The next day was bright and clear, and Newton was at the office early to prepare for his court appearance. The case file had been reviewed a dozen times and the arresting officers were present and sitting in the coffee room. The "holding tank" bandit had become a bit of a celebrity amongst the departments in the Greater Victoria region. There was no lack of criminals who would score at the lower end of the bell curve in intelligence, and it took something leaning towards the spectacular to gain this unwelcome notoriety.

"Hello Andy," Newton said taking a seat in the squad room. "What do you have on this morning?"
"Night prowler at the parliament buildings, wanted to leave a political message for the government."
"Really, he couldn't just mail a letter like ordinary folks?"
"Nope—had to use a paint spray can."
"How did that work out?"
"Not so good, seems like he forgot which side of the nozzle the paint came out of and wound up with a snoot full of fluorescent green."
"Man, they seem to be getting dumber lately don't they?"
"Yeah, that stuff he used was industrial strength—almost killed him, coated his lungs real bad and doctors weren't sure he was going to make it for a while."
"Almost one for the list I think."

The discussion had turned, as it usually did, to other candidates for stupid stunt of the day. The list even had a semi-official status. It was called the "Darwin" list, and those on it gained entrance by succeeding at an act of incredibly shortsighted thinking that turned out to be fatal or near fatal. Thus removing themselves from the human gene pool and advancing the species along the Darwinian path of evolution. The candidates of the moment were down to three for the "best of the year" award.

"Well, it was definitely not the brightest thing to do. And depending upon the rest of the crowd, he might make it to number one for this year. But the guy with the J.A.T.O. rocket still had my vote for best of the decade."

"Which one was he again?" Newton asked. "There have been so many."
"He was the guy from Bremerton," Andy began. "An employee of the naval air station who had a need for speed, and light fingers to boot.

The availability of a number of rockets normally used to assist aircraft in short takeoff roles proved to be too much of a temptation for him. The genius calculated that the rocket's 15 seconds of extra thrust would propel his 1965 Chevy to a new speed record for his group of buddies and give him the ultimate bragging rights. So the thief mounted his stolen prize in the trunk and choosing a long straight piece of road he announced to his equally bright circle of friends his intentions to secure those bragging rights for acceleration on the coming Sunday. A late night party Saturday led to a small delay in the commencement of the run until 8:00 AM on the appointed day. To the cheers of his peers the Chevy accelerated under its own power to the marked spot where the crowd had gathered and then the rocket fired."

As near as the authorities could figure out, the less than bright thief had purloined a rocket with a burn time of 60 seconds, not 15 as he thought. The still accelerating Chevy had probably achieved the desired speed long before the rocket burned out, unfortunately the road ran out before the rocket engine propellant, and when it took a sweeping left turn on the edge of a cliff, the Chevy, having long since lost full contact with the road surface, continued across the canyon to embed itself in the opposite face. There, having arrived with a solid rock wall impeding any further process, the rocket propellant promptly incinerated the car and its occupant.

"Hard to beat a performance like that," Newton mused. "Did he not read the label on the damn thing?"

"Probably, but the military likes to obfuscate things with their own cryptic way of writing things. So it likely said something like "J.A.T.O. – Rckt – 60" instead of "J.A.T.O. – Rckt – 15" and he didn't catch the difference."

"Well, he has my vote then," said Newton.

"Not so fast Alfred, give the others a chance."

"There's more like him?"

"Yep. Let me present to you candidate number two, a young man who had been partying with his friends at the end of a country road. An argument ensued, where upon he had felt the need to take a case of beer and climb to the top of the nearby power line tower to sulk. The trip up was apparently tiring, and once the beer had done its work, a trip down to relieve the pressure in his bladder seemed to be a waste of energy. He therefore decided to see if he could direct said bladder contents upon the heads of those partying below. The wires were charged with 140,000 volts of electricity, and the bright flash lit up the countryside for hundreds of feet all around. The accompanying swan dive was well off the mark, resulting in a low score from the chap from Snohomish County, but then he was always difficult to please."

"Just where do get these stories Andy?"

"Off the internet Alfred, there's a ton of them, like this next guy for instance. Our candidate number three was a resident of California, so some adjustments in the entry standards were required. In any case, he decided that he would like to watch a local baseball game floating above the crowd from the comfort of his lawn chair, with a couple of beers in hand in case the day was warm. A trip to a local surplus yard yielded four weather balloons of the required size, and several cylinders of helium supplied the lifting portion of the formula. After the game, to return to ground level, he planned to fire a couple of rounds from his handgun into the balloons and the helium would be, he calculated, slowly released and since he was tethered to the ground he would sooner or later gently be embraced in the loving arms of mother earth."

"Well, I can see a few holes in that plan already," Newton shook his head. "Where do these folks come from?"

"Oh, it gets better." Andy grinned.

"His plan got off to good start, with the lawn chair rising the required 100 feet or so and view of the game was impressive. Our candidate congratulated himself on his brilliance and used his cell phone to call his friends and boast of his accomplishments. Alas, in doing so he lost his pistol overboard and now had no means of releasing the helium from the balloons. Undaunted, he attempted to haul himself down by pulling on the rope that tethered him. It seems his knot tying skills were just not up to snuff, and all he did was succeed in pulling the rope loose from its anchor. The balloons exerted their upward force, and in accordance with Newton's law, the whole contraption began to rise. As it did, two things began to happen, the sun warmed the helium further expanding it, and the outside air pressure began to drop. The result of which was an ever accelerating rate of ascent into the very busy approach path of L.A. International airport."

"You were right Andy, this is getting better."

"It is a known fact that LAX has a first rate radar installation, and it didn't take long for the whole mess to light up the screens over at air traffic control. This was followed by several pilots reporting the sight of our less than intrepid birdman headed out to sea in the offshore winds. A hurried discussion with the Coast Guard resulted in a visual confirmation by a USCG helicopter. The lawn chair was now rising past 20 thousand feet. This altitude featured two facts of physics detrimental to the survival of candidate number three. First and most important, the amount of oxygen in the air is less than that required by humans to sustain life, and unconsciousness soon resulted. This then meant our balloonist never fully felt the effects of fact number two; the air temperature is well below freezing. An F16 finally succeeded in puncturing two of the balloons and the increasing descent of the lawn chair began. A subsequent search recovered the remains of one of the balloons."

When court began, the consensus was that candidate number three was the winner, in that he had to screw up more things than either of the other two.

Court was scheduled to start at 9:30 in the morning. The names of people and their cases were posted outside each court room on what all called the "lists." Willy found Newton searching through the court lists pinned to a corkboard. Each listed charge, accused, accuser, and their respective counsels each morning and again in the afternoon. Those who had their cases put off to another date, cancelled, or otherwise removed had lines drawn through their names.

"Morning, Alfred, looks like an easy one for you."
"You can never tell Willy, I've been surprised before."
"Yeah, I remember last year when that set of twins threw everyone off."
"What do you have today?"
"Actually, nothing, I'm just checking the lists to see if any of my "clients" are here. Sometimes they show up for a different case, sometimes they don't."
"Are you after any in particular?"
"No, just thought I'd make some inquiries about our Jane Doe."

The court building was an ideal place to question a reluctant informant, he had to be there, and anyone watching would be expecting him to have contact with the police.

"Say, isn't this the guy you were looking for up in the Charlottes?" Willy said pointing to a name on the traffic court lists.

The list read "Reginald Johnson sect 113.c HTA Speeding in a playground zone."
"Yes, that's the same name all right; I'll check with the Crown, you wait by the door here."

As was usual in the lower courts, Crown counsel held a roll call prior to the proceedings to give each accused the opportunity to give their side of the case informally, check on witnesses, and play "let's make a deal." Newton hoped that all the accused had checked in with them already.

The Crown was busy with a line of people standing and waiting to talk with them. The case load in these courts was far beyond that which could be handled by the staff. It was necessary therefore, to allow most accused a "break" of sorts. Minor incidents would be bargained to lower the fines to a level below the threshold set by law in the case of a first time offender. Police officers in general did not like this, especially the young ones. The older ones who had been around the block a time or two knew that this was the way the system worked. The only way it could work given the increasing volume of regulations and laws enacted with little thought to the practicality of enforcing them. The responsibility for determining who got what kind of deal generally rested on the shoulders of Crown counsel. Most of them developed a keen ability to determine which cases were winnable, which were not, and which were best handled by a "wakeup call" bargain. They were not always right, they did not always take the advice of the investigating officers, and sometimes there was pressure from above, but in the end the system worked as well as it could, and better than any other system yet devised. Newton waited patiently for the attorneys to work their way to him. He took the time to casually scan the crowd for someone who looked like the picture of Reginald that the museum had sent over. Willy stood just inside the door of the court and kept an eye on those leaving and entering.

Gradually the line diminished and Newton had a chance to check the Crown's list. Reginald Johnson had not checked in, but someone acting on his behalf had. The prosecutor indicated that person to be a young man in an ill fitting suit seated just behind the defence council table. He had a briefcase in front of him that he was nervously fidgeting with.

Newton got Willy's attention and nodded towards the man in the suit. Willy approached to a position just behind him and then Newton walked over and sat down beside him.
"Good morning, sir," Newton began, the young man appeared startled and turned to face the detective.
"I see that you are representing Mr. Johnson this morning, perhaps I can have a word with you."
"Are you the charging officer?"
"Actually, no, I have a different interest in your client."
"My instructions are to speak only to the charging officer."
"Your instructions—from whom?"
"Why, Mr. Johnson of course."
"You're his lawyer then?"
"Oh no, just his agent, I'm not a lawyer, yes, just an articling

student."

"Are you pleading on his behalf?"

The young man adjusted his glasses, "Mr. Johnson wishes to plead guilty, but seeks a reduced fine, my instructions are to speak to the charging officer and make those arrangements."

"You got these instructions directly from Mr. Johnson then?"

"I'm not at liberty to say."

Newton looked over at Willy, "Suppose I could tell this charging officer to speak to the Crown and get the charges dropped, would you be at liberty to say then?"

"Oh, well, I don't know," the young man stammered, "I suppose I could."

"Willy, why don't you have a word with the Crown and arrange that then?" Newton said.

"Sure thing, I'll go do that now—if this young man answers your question."

After looking at both officers in turn, the young man opened his briefcase and took out some papers. "Mr. Johnson contacted legal aid this morning, about an hour ago, and gave me these instructions."

"Did he drop by in person?"

"No, by phone."

"You spoke to him then?"

"Yes."

"Did he mention where he was calling from?"

"No, but the line was very noisy, I got the impression it was long distance. Of course these days it is hard to say."

"Did he mention by chance when he would be contacting you again?"

"No, no he didn't, but," the young man said rummaging through his briefcase, "he did leave a number to call to let him know what happened, this is it here."

Newton took the number and copied it into his notebook. It was a local number.

"Thank you, counselor. You have been a great help."

"I'm not a real lawyer. As I told you, I'm just a student."

"Well, I'm sure you'll do just fine, do you have a card?"

"Not really, just the regular legal aid office card but let me write my name on it."

"Thanks," said Willy, "I'll recommend you to all my clients."

"Um, you'll speak to the Crown now, about Mr. Johnson's charges?"

"Of course," Newton said, and Willy went off to have a word with them.

The Crown agreed to drop the charges, he was already overworked and one less case to deal with was welcome. Unlike the common portrayal in the movies, the Crown attorneys were approachable and most preferred to work with an accused person on minor offences. The policy was set by each office as to the latitude available to do that.

Sometimes even the best efforts of the Crown to give an accused person a break met with stubborn resistance. There were always some folks who would not take yes for an answer. Newton remembered as a young constable a certain lawyer who always had his client sit in the gallery. The reasoning behind this was that if the officer could not identify him from within the crowd of people in court, then that would cast sufficient doubt on the case to earn an acquittal. On this occasion, the Crown had seen this happen once too many times and deliberately held off calling the case until the end of the session. When the accuser's name was called, only his counsel appeared at the bench. Newton was sworn in and asked to identify the accused from the gallery, he responded with a pin point description of the man, his clothing, his demeanour and the row he was sitting in. Counsel then responded with the expected "And how can you be so sure officer, that your identification is correct in that it has been six months since the incident?" Newton was about to answer when the judge peered over his glasses in the time honoured way and said, "I expect it is probably because the accused is the only one sitting in the gallery, and the court does not appreciate its time being wasted in such a manner."

The accused was not acquitted.

On this occasion, the young man known as the "holding tank bandit" had been persuaded by his lawyer that it was in his best interests to plead guilty and the case was dealt with in a few minutes.

Newton and Willy left immediately afterwards to trace down the local number.

CHAPTER TWENTY SIX

Newton returned to his office and sorted through the pile of papers that had grown on his desk in his absence. It seemed to him the pile reached a state of equilibrium over the years from which it neither grew larger or smaller. Must be that "the amount of paperwork grows to fill the available space" law of the universe he thought to himself.
Willy came into the office with his battered coffee mug and took a seat opposite the desk.
"Get anywhere with that phone number?" Newton asked.
"Working in it, it's a cell number so we have to go through the company, and you know how they are."
"Do I ever, you would think it was the combination to their safe the way they guard it."
"Not to worry, I have a few contacts over there and it will be resolved by the end of the day."

Newton chuckled; Willy had contacts everywhere it seemed.

Turning his thoughts to the original Jane Doe, he ran through what had happened in the last few days. He was not aware of any direct connection to her and Reggie Johnson, but it was beginning to appear that there may be. He used the whiteboard to diagram what he had developed up 'til now. On one part of the board, next to the lines of inquiry that he had marked out at the outset of the case, he began to write down what he had learned on his trip to the Charlottes.

"OK, let's review what we know on this," Newton began. He and Willy began to mark down all the facts and suppositions they had.

1. Jane Doe was seen with Alicia.
2. Alicia worked at the museum.
3. Reggie Johnson worked at the museum.
4. Alicia was in charge of the Haida exhibit that featured carvings.
5. Johnson was involved in a scheme to defraud the museum and sell the carvings.
6. Inevitably Alicia would find out and there would be a resolution, either by reporting the thefts or some other means.
7. Alicia turns up dead in a Jeep owned by a Haida carver seeking to sell his works.
8. Mel himself ends up in a coma in hospital after being discovered on an island with a stab wound to the abdomen.

Next, he marked off a fresh area and concentrated on the new questions that flowed from the previous points.

1. Did Johnson meet up with the pair on the Charlottes?
2. Was he responsible in some way for the damage to the Jeep and subsequent events?
3. Johnson's whereabouts were unaccounted for at the time, and he was missing from his job at the museum. So where was he?
4. If he was involved, was he also involved with Newton's Jane Doe?

Now the trick was develop another line of inquiry that could help in answering the new questions.
"Any results on the fingerprints yet?" Willy asked.
"No, but I'll remind the drug squad team to check any they find."
The drug boys would soon have, if they didn't already, a warrant to search his apartment or house, and he wanted to be notified on what they found.

Newton made the call to the drug squad office, asking them to check any fingerprints found at Johnson's house against both Alicia and his Jane Doe. After a pause he also included a request to have any unmatched print referred to "K" division for checking against the ones found up north. One never knew where the next break in a case would come from, but the chances were always better when you covered all the bases.

He arranged for a picture of Johnson to be circulated to the detachments on the West Coast. Johnson had to stay somewhere, eat somewhere, buy gas if he had a vehicle, or tickets to travel if he did not.

He would also ask Cpl.Taylor to ask around the village to see if Mel and Johnson had any sort of history that they knew about.

"You're thinking about something," Newton said noting the look on Willy's face.
"Just running things through my head here, making sure we covered all the bases."
"What's troubling you then?"
"This Johnson character, he seems to be a wild card in all this."
"I get your point, I sent out a request to the American National Crime Information Centre, N.C.I.C., with Johnson's picture and fingerprints. I'm thinking he may be from south of the border."
"Well, it would not be the first time someone from down south had it in their minds that the far too liberal criminal justice system of Canada

meant easy pickings compared to the United States." Willy said "I mean, look at the penalty differences, even if they were caught, the "Club Fed" philosophy of the heads of the correctional service dictated a shorter sentence and a much more pleasant stay."

The cottages on the grounds of William Head Prison just up the road from Newton's office, and the sight of the inmates fishing from the dock or playing golf were a constant reminder to Willy, of how a good idea, rehabilitation, could result in decisions utterly devoid of common sense.

As for murder, well, Canada had done away with capital punishment, willing instead to sacrifice the lives of the men women and children who had been killed by those who had escaped custody, violated parole, or otherwise been set free. In other countries these individuals would have long ago seen the justice of a rope or lethal injection. Willy kept a list in his office of the innocent victims murdered by those set free on parole or escaped custody in Canada, at last count it was over 400 in just twenty years.

"Your guess is that Johnson is from out of country then?"
"That's where my money is, at least until I see some evidence to the contrary. He had to get a driver's licence, and for that he needed some kind of identification, maybe we can dig up something there."
"A long shot, but look into it, fake I.D. isn't exactly hard to come by."
"OK, I'll make that my mission for the rest of the day. Have you heard anything from up north?"
"Nothing further, it will take time for things to travel in official channels, and perhaps something will turn up there."
"Right, well, I'm off then. Don't forget you have a visitor coming, you tend to lose track of time in this office."
Willy left heading for the coffee machine and a telephone.

Next on Newton's to-do list was to decide what to do now that Frances decided to visit. Like most detectives he had an abundance of vacation and overtime the department was forever trying to get him to use up. It accumulated from late nights and early mornings spent at the office, or some crime scene. Court time always seemed scheduled for his days off, and there was always something that seemed to require he cut short what little time he did manage to get away. The problem was where to go when she arrived. Restaurants were fine for dinner and the movies and theatres took care of the evenings, but the days required some planning. He did not own a boat like many of the other detectives did, and in any case he was not sure if Fran liked boating. He wanted to take her someplace where he would not be reminded of work, and for a detective that could pose a problem. In the end he decided on one of the foremost tourists attractions the island offered and that he had not yet visited in all the time he had been here. No reservations were required, and it was open all day long. His itinerary set, all he had to do now was wait for the lady to call and announce exactly when she would arrive.

 That call came later in the evening. She would arrive the next day, and Newton spent most of the night awake.

CHAPTER TWENTY SEVEN

The next morning found him at the office earlier than usual. Nothing had been received yet about the fingerprints found during the search of Johnson's house. He wasn't there, which was a disappointment and there was nothing new forthcoming with the local enquiries about his Jane Doe. As he usually did, he had arranged for Willy to go over the case results with the rest of the team. A second set of eyes could sometimes see things in a different light and he might have missed something. That done he cleared his calendar for the next couple of days and headed out to the airport to meet the plane.

The plane was on time, which was not unusual, but the island weather was fickle at times, even in these summer months. The airport lay on a low lying strip inland with the runway running more or less east-west. To the east lay the open waters of the Strait of Juan De Fuca. North and south were hills and the west end of the runway pointed to Saanich Inlet. Beyond that the mountains of the Malahat blocked any approach. Depending upon the water temperature and the time of day, fog could roll in and blanket the airport causing flights to either circle looking for a break, or divert to Vancouver. Today was bright and sunny, and the flight landed without any problems. The airport terminal was, as are most such complexes, in a constant state of renewal and new building. Temporary barricades seemed to be everywhere, and construction workers from several trades were engaged in what looked to be a vast symphony of noise and confusion. Each group seemingly trying to drown out the others in a clashing ballet of sound and motion.

Mixed into this scene were the constant stream of arriving and departing passengers, employees and crew, well wishers, cabbies, and bus drivers. Construction and security concerns meant Newton had to wait in a confined area for Fran to appear from behind frosted glass doors. In the old days, one could see the plane land and taxi to the terminal. Passengers would disembark from a stairway and walk to the terminal and disperse through any of a number of doors. Now all passengers had to exit from a single set of doors and those awaiting them congregated in a lounge hemmed in by baggage trucks and conveyers on one side, and freshly placed walls on the other. At least, thought Newton, no one could exist without being seen, and he need not worry about waiting for Fran at one door, while she was at another wondering where he was.

A grinding noise emanated from the baggage conveyer and it began to move, simultaneously the P.A. system announced the arrival of the flight. Newton's eyes, along with all the others in the lounge awaiting the arrival switched to the door. First off were the first class passengers, business people who paid a premium not to have to wait in line. Those whose time or nature demanded they be out of the parking lot first so they could arrive a full five minutes earlier at the city limits than the competition, and to them everyone else was the competition. Some went immediately to waiting cabs or cars, their only luggage being a carryon bag, or leaving the mundane job of baggage collection and forwarding to an underling. Next were the business class folks, those to whom economy was more important than a few minutes of time. They carried briefcases, coats, and laptop computers. Following close on were the regular travelers, adults without kids and those not requiring assistance to board or de-plane. Last would be travelers with children or those who needed a wheelchair or help of some sort. Newton expected Fran to be in the second to last group. He settled into watching the stream of people exiting the doorway, mentally assigning them to one group or another. The first through was a small man, impeccably dressed in a light suit. Hair perfectly set, a determined look on his face, already thinking about the next business meeting or task. He carried a single leather briefcase, no coat, likely engaged in a specific task for the day. He strode quickly past the baggage counter and entered the back seat of a car waiting with a driver for him at the curb. The driver gave no greeting other than a slight nod, so this was not the first time for either of them. The next group of three, two men and a woman, all in their thirties were also traveling light, they went to the curb and hailed a taxi which quickly whisked them away. The bus fare to town was currently 10 dollars, 50 by taxi. The next group was mixed, mostly business folks who were being met by relatives, or who were content to take the bus. Some studied the luggage carousel for signs of their bags, some just waited patiently at the curb.

Tourists made up the next group, cameras already out and recording the mountains and other scenery. Then amongst the last was Fran, holding the hand of a little girl of about eight years. The youngster was dressed in a tee shirt sporting the picture of one the current pop stars. Navy slacks, pink runners with bright blue laces, and a cardigan.

"Hello Alfred, this is Meagan, she was traveling all by herself from Vancouver and kept me company on the plane," said Fran. "Meagan, this is Alfred Newton, and he is a police officer."
Meagan smiled up at Newton, "Hi," she said, "I'm Meagan and I'm going to visit my daddy. I like to fly on the airplanes. I do it a lot,

every second weekend, except when it's my birthday or something, then I do it more, or sometimes my daddy comes over to visit me. But mostly I come over here and he meets me, then we spend the weekend together, unless it's a holiday, or summertime. Then I stay a week or more, like I'm doing now and we have lots of fun. This week we are going to a place called Long Beach. I've never been there but daddy says it really nice with lots of sand and waves and seashells. Have you ever been there, Mr. Newton?" The little girl continued without a pause. "Sometimes my teacher says I talk too much, but I don't think so, do you think I talk too much? Oh, there's my daddy now."

With that she ran into the arms of her father who was just exiting a cab at the curb, he scooped her up and she waved back at Fran before the cab sped away.

"Goodness," said Newton, "did she talk like that the whole way?"
"Every mile," said Fran, "and I enjoyed every minute of it."

Newton's full attention was on Fran, and he didn't notice the last passenger select a large bag from the carousel and walk to a waiting car. He and Fran drove back to Victoria in Newton's old Oldsmobile.

"Good Flight?"
"Yes, for once, not that I travel a lot, but George was kind enough to take me to Rupert, and I caught the commercial flight from there. I'll probably not be so lucky on the trip back though, the Herring season is opening and he is always busy ferrying something, or someone out to one boat or another."
"When do you have to get back?"
"I have two days, that's all, so I hope you have the same, I tried for more but one of the girls has to leave for down east and I couldn't leave the others short staffed."
"Two days is better than no time at all."
"We'll just have to make the best use of it," she smiled.

Dinner was a homemade affair. Newton was a decent cook, as long as he stuck pretty much to the basics. It was a simple meal of spaghetti, salad, and bread, with a dry red wine. He had even scrounged up a couple of candles that had lain unused in a drawer. A tablecloth and napkins from the local chain store completed an ambiance he had not created for years. After dinner, they took a long walk on the beach, the tide was just turning and the fresh, washed sand provided a canvas for their footsteps. The evening air was warm and light. To the east the moon was on the rise, its reflected light competing with the last golden rays of the sun as it set in the west. They walked slowly, her head on his shoulder, and his arm around her waist.

The morning promised another bright and sunny day. For the first time in ages, Newton did not check with his office, and for the first time in recent memory, he did not feel guilty about it. Fran had got up before him and the sounds and smells emanating from the kitchen signaled breakfast being prepared. He entered to find her rummaging around in the fridge, a pile of fresh chopped onions and cheese on the counter.

"Do you have any fresh mushrooms in here, darling?""
"Sorry, no, I do however have a rare canned vintage available that I have been hoarding for a special occasion such as this," Newton said pulling a can out of the pantry.
"Hmmm, I'm not noticing any dust on it; does that mean, Mr. Detective, that you have had other such 'special occasions' in the recent past?"
"But, of course, mon cheri," replied in his best stage accent, "I am a man of the world; women are usually lined up three deep at my door when I return each day from a hard day's work. You have much competition, or perhaps it is just that I am a good housekeeper."
"Or perhaps it is because you just bought it, the expiry date being some months into the future," she said pretending to study the can closely. "The evidence is incontrovertible."
"Coises! Foiled again!"
"And what, my love, have you planned for us today?"
"I thought I'd treat you to a visit to a world famous attraction that's close by, called Butchart's Gardens. It's only a short drive from here."
"Ah, I've heard of that, never been there though, what a wonderful plan."

"Nothing but the best, for the best," Newton started to say when the ringing phone interrupted him. He went into the living room and picked it up.

"Hello?"
"Morning, Alfred, hate to disturb what little time off you have, but I thought I'd better let you know, Mr. Johnson is back in town."
"Really? When?"
"Yesterday apparently, had a fight with one of his clients last night over on Cedar Hill Cross. It seems Mr. Johnson has taken to arming himself. There was quite a firefight, it's all over the news, haven't you seen it yet?"

"Nope, I haven't turned the damn thing on. Isn't this a little out of character for him?"

"I would have thought so, that is until yesterday morning when we got the latest results from 'K' Division, they matched his prints to one found on that aluminum boat you guys found up north, and that's not all, his prints were also on one of the carvings you dug up."

"Damn, that spells trouble, Have you located him yet?"

"Nope, he is still on the loose, but the airport detail reports that a bag with his name on it was unclaimed at the terminal. I've got a car on the way to pick it up now."

"OK, Willy, thanks for the info, if there is anything new let me know."

"I'll leave a message for your boss, don't take your beeper today, just enjoy your time off. Say hello to the lady for me." Willy clicked off.

Fran came around the corner and looked questioningly at Newton. "Anything wrong?"

"Not a thing, just the office checking in with me. Tell me, did you ever hear of Mel hanging around with a guy named Reggie Johnson?"

"Reggie the weasel?"

"You knew him?"

"All the girls knew him, he would come up every few months and ask around for anyone doing carvings, he would try to hit on all the girls, but no one ever went out with him."

"Why the 'weasel' moniker?"

"I don't know really, one of the girls gave him that name because he tried to weasel out of giving a tip, and it suited him. He did know Mel though; I remember them having coffee a few times."

"Was there ever any trouble between them?"

"Not at the start, but recently, they had a few arguments, but last I knew things were cool again, why?"

"Just a hunch."

"Does this mean you have to go into work today?"

"Nope! I'm still free to squire you about the countryside m'lady."

CHAPTER TWENTY EIGHT

They arrived at midmorning along with the usual busloads of tourists. They were mostly Japanese with their legendary love of gardens, and several from Europe, some of them Dutch, whose world famous bulbs accounted for a good portion of the spring flowers. The gardens took up several acres of land, and were divided into themes. Throughout the season focus shifted to highlight whatever was most suited to the time of year. Like most patrons, they planned to spend most of the day there. Taking a map from the information booth, they moved arm in arm, along the paths.

"These are so lovely," Fran said, indicating a bed of multi-coloured shrubs and bushes, "How did the garden start?"
"Well, in the late part of the 1800s and early 1900s Vancouver Island was as they now say, 'a happening place.' There was a lot of construction, and construction needed cement. This whole place was a giant quarry, there even used to be a smelter at one time, to heat the limestone. The roads of the time meant coming out here was a day trip, and Jennie Butchart, the wife of the owner, would entertain the wives of the leaders of the business community and so this gained a reputation for being 'the place' to be. She had an extraordinary talent for gardening, and as the quarry works moved from one part of the property to another, she planted gardens on what they left behind. Eventually the limestone was exhausted in 1916, but the gardens remained, and the family has carried on her work."

Newton led Fran down a long path on the side of a hill. To the front, a large rock, some 10 meters high, provided a lookout point that oversaw most of the 55 acres. To the south lay the pools with their coloured lights and fountains. Further south was Todd Inlet and the last remaining buildings from the old quarry. They continued on past the fountains, and through the sunken gardens. To the North a water powered bamboo chime boomed. Everywhere people marveled at the over one million plants. After two hours they ended up at the famous rose gardens, and paused to have coffee in the restaurant. Newton felt rested and at peace, a feeling he had not had for a very long time. Fran smiled over at him, "Well, you certainly look like the proverbial contented cat."
"A beautiful day, a beautiful place, and most importantly, a beautiful companion, what more could a guy want?"

What he didn't want, was to be reminded of work, unfortunately, the sight of Willy walking purposefully up to him made that a rapidly vanishing hope.

"Morning, Willy, what brings you to this land of beauty and wonder?"

"Beauty and wonder indeed! Good morning, miss."

"Fran, this is Willy, my sometimes partner, and a general pain in the ass." Newton said good naturedly with a grin. "Here no doubt to spoil the rest of our day."

"Pleased to meet you, miss. I hate to interrupt such a loquacious speech, as no doubt you have learned my esteemed comrade is apt to present. However, I need only take a scant few minutes of his time, so as to provide him with some edification in the art of being a gentleman, and how to treat so fine a lady as yourself."

"My, my, Mr., um, sorry but I don't know your last name?"

"Jackson miss, Jackson of the yard they call me when I'm around the office."

"Which is much nicer than what we call him when he isn't," Newton added, also dropping into a cockney accent.

"Well, Mr. Jackson, I see you are a student of Conan Doyle then."

"And a poor student at that," Willy replied, beating Newton to the punch. "But if you will excuse us for only a few moments, I shall detain you two for the briefest time."

"But of course, gentlemen, I shall take a stroll and study the flora of this idyllic place whilst you two converse, you may find me in the rose garden when you are done."

Fran started to rise from her chair, but Willy stopped her, "Perhaps it would be better if you remained in your seat, miss, I'd hate to think I chased you away."

With that Willy motioned Newton to come with him. They stepped off to the side, stopping at a small alcove that was out of earshot from the table where Fran was now pretending to study the array of flowers in the garden.

"What's this all about then?"

"Its Johnson, he was spotted downtown."

"Did they arrest him?"

"They tried, two officers, Wilson and Harris were shot, Wilson is dead and Harris is barely holding his own."

"That doesn't sound like the workup on Johnson; there were no signs of violence in his record."

"Not the version we got," said Willy. "But we didn't get the whole story. Turns out Mr. Johnson was in the witness protection program, his real name is Alonso D'Zaria, and before he got in the program he was a collector for one of the families in New York. He turned state's

evidence, and in return they shipped him here."
"What! He's an American felon, how did he get into Canada?"
"How else? He showed up on the ferry, went into immigration and claimed refugee status."

Newton shook his head; the overworked and understaffed members of Canadian Immigration were overwhelmed by a flood of people. A recent Supreme Court ruling, one made in the estimation of most front line police officers, in the type of vacuum that could only exist in an a completely unaccountable organization such as the Supreme Court. It ruled that anyone who managed to set foot in the country by any means, legal or not, was entitled to free legal representation, food, shelter, medical care, and to wander free about the country whilst the inevitable appeal process wound its laborious way through the courts. The most visible result of this was a sharp rise in the numbers of the legal community willing to make their living off other people's taxes. Deliberate delays, missed appearances, and the inability to locate many of the "refugees" once they had been set loose, meant it would be years before they faced a deportation order. Then the order itself could be appealed resulting in still more years before an actual deportation took place. The ones who paid the price for all this was of course those folks who were legitimately trying to escape a physically brutal regime in another country.

"That's not the whole story; they recovered a briefcase at the scene and found both your name and Fran's on a list inside."
"List, what kind of list?"
"Nothing to indicate, but I don't think it's for a Christmas card."
"Any idea where he is now?"
"Nope, there was some indication he was hit during the exchange of gunfire, but how bad, we don't know. In light of all this I thought you might want to have this."
Willy opened his briefcase and took out Newton's 40 caliber Smith & Wesson automatic in a clip on holster.
Newton slipped it into the waist band of his pants.
"Better take this too," Willy said handing over a cell phone, "I might need to call you."

"So what now, we leave?"
"Actually, here may be the safest place, there isn't any way for him to know that you two are here is there?"
"No, we didn't tell anyone."
"It's likely that Johnson or D'Azaria or whoever the hell he is will be hiding out downtown rather than showing his face in a public place like

this, especially since every cop on the island will be looking for him now."

Newton nodded "OK, then, what are your plans?"

"Funny thing about this place, I have been on the island for over ten years and I haven't even been here once. I think I'd like to stay and wander about."

"OK, then, we'll stay here and enjoy the day, I think you're right, I don't see any reason for him to come out here, and I'd just get in the way if I went back into the office."

Willy and Newton returned to Fran, and she rose to meet them. "So then, what have you two cooked up?"

"Willy is going to spend the day getting acquainted with the lovely flowers, it'll bring out the feminine side of his character," Newton quipped.

"Buried as it is under my immense masculinity it rarely sees the light of day," added Willy. "But in order to remain the well rounded and adjusted person that I am, I feel compelled to let it breathe every now and then."

"So you will be joining us then?"

"No, I thought I'd strike out on my own, sort of chat up the ladies, who knows, I may meet someone interesting."

"I'm sure you will do quite well in that regard Mr. Jackson."

"We are off then," Newton said, "I think we will head out to the Japanese gardens and then over to the inlet, back past the fountains and up the promenade. That should put us back here in about two hours. What do you say to meeting us then and having some lunch before heading back?"

"Sounds good to me, don't make any concrete plans though, I may find myself trapped in the arms of some lovely maiden by then." With a wink, Willy left the couple and headed out into the gardens.

Newton and Fran proceeded arm in arm from the dining room and headed west to the Japanese gardens. The gardens were laid out on the edge of an embankment, with groves of bamboo, bonsai gardens, and many water features. From one of these, a deep booming echoed ever few minutes.

"That's a Japanese water chime," said Newton and they made their way to the pond. There a single large bamboo stalk was fashioned like a teeter-totter. Another bamboo stalk had been hollowed out and carried water like a pipe to flow slowly into one end of the pivoting bamboo. As it slowly filled with water it would raise the other end, and in so doing, sink to a level where the water suddenly spilled out, the raised end would snap down and hit a large horizontal piece of bamboo, emitting a deep boom when it did.

"I'm sure I heard it earlier when we came up here."
"There is so much to see here; most people end up going over the same ground more than once. Just coming into a garden from a different direction gives you a new perspective. At night when the lights come on, it's an entirely new scene."

They stood and watched the process cycle through a couple of times, fascinated with the simple mechanics of it all. Other nearby ponds featured ceramic frogs and exotic lilies. Ferns and rushes framed the edges and orchids and other heavily scented flowers permeated the atmosphere. A small bonsai garden, with its elaborately bent stunted trees and raked sand surface anchored another part of the display, a simple wooden bench was placed nearby for visitors to rest and they sat on it for a few minutes to enjoy the silence.

Eventually others came by and they moved on. Further to the west the grounds gave way to a manicured grass field. A large amphitheatre with rows of benches and large outdoor speakers told of an outdoor concert or playhouse. The grass field extended all the way to the shore of Saanich Inlet, and across from that the mountains of the Malahat rose sharply from water. A few boats were plying the water, some for fishing, others sail boats and motor cruisers.

"So, when are you going to tell me?" Fran asked.
"Tell you what?"
"About them."
"Who?"
"Your family silly."
"Not much to tell, really."
"Any children?" Fran gently asked.
"One, a daughter, Ellie."
"Where is she now, obviously she doesn't live with you."
"That's the thing," Newton said quietly, "I don't know."
Fran said nothing for a few minutes, waiting for him to carry on. When he didn't she added, "And your wife?"
"I'm divorced, police work and family life don't mix very well."
"Oh, Alfred, I didn't know, I'm so sorry." Fran turned with a worried look on her face, "Please forgive me for asking. It's really none of my

business."

"It's OK," Newton responded, "As you can tell I don't talk about it much, never had anyone I could talk with, 'til now."

Fran squeezed his hand tighter, "You can tell me now if you like."

"Old story, for cops anyway, and others I expect," he began and they talked quietly as they made their way along the paths. The beauty of the gardens a stark contrast to the darkness of the past.

They made their way southward along the edge of the gardens towards Todd Inlet, where carefully manicured bushes formed an Alice in Wonderland like maze. Even though both Fran and Newton could see over the top of it, the artful crafting and clipping hid the passageways. It took them almost half an hour to negotiate it. Laughing along with the others in the same circumstances, they finally made it to the other side and continued on their way.

When they returned to the fountains, they took a seat along with many others and waited for the fountains to cycle through their programmed display. The pond that fed them was located over the deepest part of the old quarry and held several million liters of water. In addition to the fountain pipes and pumps, waterproof lights were rigged to accent the display at night. The engineers had hooked up the whole thing to work in time with several different musical numbers for special occasions. During the day the music was turned off to allow the visitors to enjoy the natural sounds of the water as it danced. Some of the floodlights were on and they competed with the natural rainbows created by the mist and sun. As with any large park, maintenance was always ongoing. It made sense thought Newton, as it couldn't be done in the dark.

As if to provide proof of that very thing, a figure appeared at the edge of the pond, dressed in a wet suit and air tanks. Around his waist hung a tool belt with a couple of underwater lights, and several brass tools. Brass doesn't rust Newton noted to himself, and if they used ordinary steel tools they would have to be regularly coated in some sort of oily preservative to protect them. Over time the residue from that would show up in the water. Everything about this place seems to be on a very professional level.

It was that fact that made the gardener working on the flower bed off to the right stand out more than he should.

The man was on his knees digging at the dirt, which in itself was not unusual. What stood out though, was that he was the only employee he had seen all day working in the gardens to be dressed in jeans, not a coverall. Also his tools were the cheap tin ones bought at a box store for home use. The clincher was that he was not wearing either the knee pads that all the other gardeners wore, nor did he have the mandatory back support belt that was required by law.

Newton changed position slightly to get a better look when the fountains came on and started their display to the appreciation of the crowd. For a moment he lost sight of the gardener behind the spray. When the column of water subsided, the figure was gone. Newton automatically went into his search pattern. What was different? What stood out because it was either missing or didn't belong? There, he had it; the tool the gardener was using was sitting with its tip embedded into the soil. The fountains cycled again and Newton began to rise from the bench, Fran looked up at him with a questioning look.

Newton reached down and pulled her up, as he did so he saw something else that should not be present. A fresh splinter of wood suddenly appeared soundlessly where she had been sitting. The fountains shot 16 columns of water skyward, forming a curtain between them and the opposite bank where the gardener had been. Newton pulled Fran close and began to make way for them to the rear of the crowd.

"What's going on?"
"It's time to go," Newton whispered. "Please don't ask questions, just do as I say."
In a few moments they had got free of the crowd, and ducked behind the concrete pump house located on the south part of the garden. Pausing there, Newton took a quick look at the crowd, the gardener was nowhere in sight. Fran sensed something was very wrong, and as if to confirm it, Newton reached under his coat and drew his pistol.
"If this is a plan to impress me, you can stop," she said.
"It's not that, somebody out there is shooting at us."
"How do you know, I didn't see anything?"
"Trust me, I know."

Fran turned to reply when the concrete wall suddenly erupted in a shower of shards accompanied with a loud "thwack." Newton grabbed her and dragged her to the ground.

Thwack!
Thwack!
Two more craters in the wall.

"Why is someone trying to kill us?" Fran said stifling a scream.

"Not sure at the moment, but we will sort it out later, keep your head down."

Newton tried to figure out where the gunman was firing from by using the bullet holes as a guide, tracing back along their flight path. There, over by the low creeping shrubbery, he thought he saw a movement. His brain detected something odd in the sound of the bullets as another flew by close to his head. Then he had it; the lack of the distinctive snap of a bullet breaking the sound barrier told him the bullets were sub sonic. Changing position they found themselves behind a large tree. Cautiously Newton peered around it. The rest of the crowd were continuing as if nothing had happened, so apparently they had not seen anything unusual, neither had they heard any gunshots. Obviously the gunman was using a silencer thought Newton, his brain never really out of detective mode, still analyzing all the data it could.

The crowd at this point was also sparse, either watching the fountain display, or gathered around one of the other gardens. No way to lose ourselves in the crowd, thought Newton. Besides, the gunman might continue shooting, and that would endanger other people present. The best thing would be to try and get to an area where the gunman would have to follow, and thus expose himself.

One shot would be all Newton needed.

In order to get that opportunity, Newton would have to draw the gunman away from the crowd. But to where? Then he had it, the old office and factory buildings! Years ago, Newton had trained there with the emergency response team. They had spent hours in the rubble and old offices, honing their building search techniques. Separated by a dirt embankment from the rest of the gardens, the site was the last part of the original holdings still not reclaimed for garden use. With its shoreline on the north side of Todd Inlet, it would provide a spectacular garden site, and plans had been made to do just that, but right now it could provide a refuge for the two of them until Newton could summon help.

"Let's go," he called, and took her by the arm.

Trusting in his direction, Fran allowed herself to be led away from the fountains. Working their way over the embankment, they headed away from the pump house and down the other side. Here they found the remains of the original cement factory. Two massive chimneys, one lying broken on its side, the other still standing, marked the smelter. A row of concrete and wood housing and offices stretched down to the shores of Todd Inlet. Bits of iron machinery lay scattered everywhere. Taking Fran's hand in his, they ran together to the remains of the largest concrete structure. No shots followed them and no craters started appearing in the walls. Ducking through an open doorway Newton found what he was looking for, a small side office, undisturbed for years. An old desk stood gathering dust against one wall. A large window, the glass long since gone, was set into the outside wall. From behind the desk you could see if anyone approached the building from either the front or the back, and if necessary, escape through the door or the window, keeping a cement wall between yourself and the intruder. The open doors had allowed the wind to scour the dust from the floor so there would be no footprints to follow, or give away their passage.

A quick scan outside showed no one in pursuit. Newton pulled out the cell phone from his pocket and crouched down beside the desk. The keypad glowed when the power was switched on and he anxiously scanned the screen. To his dismay, the words "no signal" flashed repeatedly.

"Damn," he whispered, "There must be too much steel around here for the signal to get through."

"What now," Fran asked breathing heavily from the exertion of the run and the stress of being shot at.

"I'll try to get a better position, the phone tower is on the Malahat and that is much higher than we are, the remnants of the chimney must be blocking the signal. If I can work my way around to the other side then I can perhaps get a message out."

"Well then, let's go."

"You must wait here," he told Fran. "I think I know where he may be, and I'll come back for you as soon as I can. If you see anyone except for me approach this building, go out the door or window, and make your way back into the gardens. Lose yourself in the crowd and get to the administration office and call 911."

"I'm going with you!"

Her voice was strong with only a hint of fear.

"No, you're not. Whoever he is, he is after me, not you, and he'll be looking for a couple not just me alone. Whatever happens, If I don't come back, wait at least an hour, then head for the gardens, got

that?"
"Yes, but-"
"No buts, promise me."
"I promise."
Newton gave her a long kiss, like it could be the last one, and taking a look around disappeared out the door, leaving her behind the desk.

To the front of the old offices lay the collapsed portions of one of the original two chimneys. The circumference was about eight feet at this point and gradually narrowed to a four foot space. Parts of the concrete had been broken in the fall and were flattened with no way to get through them. Newton considered his route carefully. If he could get into the old chimney, he could make his way to the other side of the site, and at that point the bulk of the concrete and steel would be behind him and no longer blocking the signal. But that meant leaving Fran alone much longer than he wanted too, and if he had to return in a hurry, he would have to negotiate a lot of rubble. The other option was to head back up the embankment, away from the building site. There was much less cover there, but it was a shorter route to cover. In the end it was one other fact that decided it. Many of the tourists had been using their cell phones when Newton and Fran had started their day, thus he reasoned, it was more likely that the shorter route would bring him into range of the towers. The quicker he got the message out, the quicker he could return to her.

On the hill side above, a gardener, adjusting the branches on a rose bush, watched his movements with more than passing interest. His cell phone worked and he made a quick call.

CHAPTER TWENTY NINE

Newton quickly headed back to the hillside, and finding a secluded spot within a grove of manicured pines, pulled out the cell phone again and turned it on. It seemed to take forever to come alive. This time the cell phone responded with a welcoming three bars indicating he was getting a strong signal. The dial tone came on as soon as he hit the talk button, and he quickly punched in Willy's number. Calling him instead of the dispatcher was a calculated risk, the dispatcher could marshal more in the way of resources, but they were a long distance away. Willy was here now, and the same person hunting Newton may also be hunting him. Newton had to warn him of the danger.

The phone rang with agonizing slowness. One ring, two rings, three rings, then Willy's voice came on the line, "I'm not available to take your call at the moment, please leave a message."

"Damn, doesn't he have his cell on?"

"Willy it's me, I think Reggie is here, someone has been taking pot shots at Fran and I. Be careful. We are in the old building complex down by the inlet, call the office and have them send the E.R.T. team our way."

Newton clicked the "end call" button and punched in some more numbers. This time the phone did not respond and a quick look at the screen showed the "low battery" symbol flashing just before it went dark. Frustrated, Newton stuffed the phone back into his pocket. He hoped his gamble paid off, that Willy would get the message and call in the cavalry. Best thing to do now was to head back and wait.

From his position on the embankment he watched the building where Fran was hiding for a full five minutes, then satisfied no one was approaching it, he began to plan his way back down to the old offices.

A quick scramble down the hill and he was once again at the base of the collapsed chimney. Pausing to scan the area ahead of him, Newton noticed something had changed. Instead of just his tracks, and Fran's smaller ones, he saw something that had not been there before, fresh dirt and bark. There was only one place it could have come from, a flower bed, and only one way for it to have got there.

The new tracks were over top of his old ones, and Newton spent a few moments to analyze them. They were the same size as his, so likely it was a man, someone of the same height and weight as himself. He could see how they followed his own, even stopping in the same places. So someone had followed Fran and himself into the old site. Could it be Willy? Did he get the message or just happen along, making the same guesses as he did? The bark and dirt were definitely from the flower beds, but that in itself did not mean it was brought to this place by anything more sinister than Willy taking the shortest route to the old buildings. Still, it could be their assailant, and that meant caution. If Fran's whereabouts were as yet undiscovered, he didn't want to lead the gunman to her. On the other hand, if she had already been found then he wanted to get there as soon as he could. Damn the cell phone anyway, all using it had done was to create another set of uncertainties.

Newton knew he had to act quickly; time was not on his side here. Although there was a chance that the tracks were Willy's, he would act as if they belonged to the assailant, and he peered ahead along his intended route checking to see were the tell-tale footprints led. As far as he could see, they matched his own earlier path, and with a quick scan of the windows and doorways ahead of him, he moved forward, keeping low to the ground and taking advantage of the cover offered by the rubble. The ruins of the old chimney and the remaining building structures allowed him to proceed at a quick pace. From his semi-upright position, he had a good view of the tracks in the dust, the pattern was changing. There were smudges in the dust, as would be made by someone kneeling and peering over the window sills of the old buildings, checking out each room and then moving on. Newton followed and at a faster pace, an unease gnawing at him now. Although there was no clear indication that this was the track of the gunman and not Willy, he could not shake the feeling of dread that was growing in his gut.

He had now reached a point only two buildings away from where he left Fran, and the tracks ahead of him had been obscured by the wind so that he could no longer tell where they led. Desperately he scanned the area past the buildings, was that a fresh set of footprints? Perhaps, maybe his mind was playing tricks on him, showing him what he wanted to see. Newton took a deep breath and forced his brain into performing the scan that had so often revealed things about a crime scene that others had missed. Near ground he saw a single footprint at the base of the window leading to the room Fran was hiding in. The defined edge in the dust told him it had been made by someone putting all his weight on that leg. He looked closer, a second foot print would indicate the person had not seen anything and moved on. No such marker appeared, instead there was the faint outline of a smudge that could have been made by a boot, or a knee.

So far the evidence was leading down both paths, then his eye caught the flash of some bright, the newness of the object made it stand out against the faded grey of the buildings. Half buried in the dust and leaves was a small shell casing.

Now Newton threw caution to the wind, holding his Smith & Wesson pistol in front of him, he advanced at a run and flew through the door way ready to fire. One word on his lips.

"Fran?"

At first he didn't see anything but the old furniture and bits of wood and paint and dust deposited by years of wind and weather. With his heart beating in his ears he made his way to the desk where he had left Fran, afraid of what he might find. Empty. The space under the desk contained nothing but marks in the dust showing where she had been. Forcing his fears to the back of his mind, Newton quickly scanned the room. What was here that shouldn't be, and what was not here that should? He checked the floor, no signs of a scuffle, no fresh damage to the old furniture and wood, and most important, no pools of blood. He began to breathe easier. Perhaps she had seen the gunman and moved to another spot. Good girl, he thought, she knows how to think on her feet. Now he checked the walls, what did that shell casing mean? Had the gunman fired into the room? Or at something, or someone in another direction, maybe he had been shooting at Willy, maybe it was from another day, some kids plinking at rabbits or another previous incident and he had missed the presence of the casing when they had first arrived. After all he wasn't looking for evidence then. Yes, that had to be it. Please God, make it so. He began to relax a bit and looked for a set of Fran's footprint leading away from the room. She must have seen the gunman coming and left the other way just like he had told her to do. Or maybe it was Willy, and he had taken her to safety and they were now looking for him. Sure, that had to be it; otherwise there would signs of a struggle, something to indicate that she had been taken away against her will. Some tell-tale sign, like—like the small spot of blood he had hoped he would not find, but which he now saw on the door post. Not much, just a drop or too, but it was fresh and sticky, and it was no doubt Fran's.

CHAPTER THIRTY

Newton's Heart skipped a beat, and he stepped over to the doorway and began to look around in the hallway. One drop of blood didn't mean much. His heart told him that it could have come from a scratch as she escaped out the door. There were shards of wood, old bits of glass, and lots of things to snag an unprotected hand or arm, but his mind didn't believe it. He quickly looked in the other rooms in the old building, nothing, no new blood spots, and no new tracks. Then he saw one, and then another small footprint leading out what had been the back door. Good! She was alive and escaping and he would find her he promised himself, no matter what, he would find her. He stepped out the door way and the door jamb exploded in a mist of paint and dust and wooden splinters. Without thinking he dropped to the ground and brought his pistol up in front, searching for the gunman. Another shower of wood and dust spurred him to take cover behind the remains of a wooden work bench. The old wood would not withstand much, but at least it would hide his movements.

Catching his breath he tried to pinpoint the origin of the shooting. He heard no gunfire, a twenty-two pistol he guessed, that fit the shell casing he had seen, and that meant a low velocity bullet. That also meant the gunman had previously fired from his position by the window. Studying the bullet holes in the wood indicated the shots came from the direction of the last standing building to the east. The tracks Newton had studied indicated Fran had left heading west, so that was the direction he intended to head also. There were three rows of buildings arranged in a line facing north to the embankment and the gardens, and south to the water's edge. To his west each row contained the remains of four buildings of different sizes. Some were just rubble now, and others still stood. Of the ones that still stood, most were in the middle row. Newton was in the north row and facing south. There were a few bits of equipment scattered about the site, none large enough to give cover to a running man. They would only shield him if he was crawling, and then he judged, only if the assailant was at ground level, and only if he had remained in the same spot. Neither was likely, Newton thought, given the actions of the gunman so far. He had every earmark of being a pro.

Two possible courses of action were open to him, run fast across the gap between the northern row and the middle, or try to scoot from cover to cover. He was too old for both choices. Just then, the sound of voices and machinery came from the embankment. Two large green six wheel drive garden vehicles with a party of five or six gardeners were moving across the top of the rise and then they stopped. Looking back in the direction that the shots had come from, he saw a figure in Jeans walk quickly away from the buildings and up the path to the south end. It then disappeared over the hill in the direction of the fountain.

Newton scrambled to his feet and looked back towards the work party; they themselves had moved on to the west end of the ridge and headed for a tool shed. Torn between finding Fran and alerting the work party, he opted to find her first. The employees were not in danger, he reasoned, they were not the target, and the gunman had deliberately left them alone. He would find Fran first, and then get her help. After that there would be time to deal with his assailant.

Heading west along the rows of buildings Newton called out her name; thankfully he saw no more blood and his search ended in the last standing office. Fran greeted him with a weak smile as he came through the door and found her curled up beside the remains of a desk. One look told him that she was in pain, her face was white and there was blood on her collar.

"Interesting day you arranged for us," she quipped. "But I think I want to go home now."
He reached her in a moment. "Where are you hurt?"
"My head is ringing," she said. "I think I must have bumped it."
Newton reached around the back of her thick hair and his hands came away covered in blood, dark red and sticky. He looked closely at her eyes, both pupils were dilated, one more than the other.

"How does it look?" She asked.
"Just a scratch, but we should probably let a doctor look at it, public healthcare and all that," he smiled back.
"OK," she said in a dreamy voice, "but I'm very tired, just let me rest a bit."
"Good idea, there are some workers just at the top of the hill with a garden cart, I'll get them to give you a ride."
"Lovely idea, I'll just wait here then," and with that she lost consciousness.

Newton turned to the doorway and saw the workers will still at the shed, he stepped there and making sure his gun was holstered yelled at them. At first no one seemed to hear him, and he started to take a few steps in their direction. His movements finally caught the eye of one them, and they looked in his direction. Two headed towards him and he ran up to meet them on the hillside.

Quickly he explained that he had an injured person who needed help and they signaled for the garden cart to come down. None of them had a radio with them.

"You shouldn't be here, this area is off limits to guests, too dangerous with all the old buildings and equipment." The oldest said.
"Yes, yes I realize that."
"What were you two doing here anyway?"

Newton was torn between telling them the truth, and not starting a panic. With the gardens filled with people a panic would likely result in more injuries, and erase any chance of catching the gunman. It was a tough decision, but until more help showed up, it was the better choice. He would get Fran to a hospital and then see about capturing the gunman, who was likely on his way out of the parking lot by now anyway.

"Do any of you have a cell phone?" he asked as the large garden tractor pulled up.

No one did.

With the help of two of the gardeners they quickly loaded Fran onto the flat rear deck and started her off towards the main office.
"I'm afraid we will have to call the police," one of the gardeners said to Newton. "You will have to explain to them what you were doing here."
"Never mind that," came a voice from the back. "We're already here." Newton looked up to see Willy who had just arrived, standing at the back of the crowd. "We'll take it from here." He had a cell phone in his hand. "There is an ambulance already coming down the driveway, they'll meet you at the front gate."

Newton and Willy rode back to the front entrance with Fran, who was lying still on the decking. Newton checked her breathing; it was shallow, but regular. Willy was talking on his cell phone. A number of uniformed and plain clothed officers had arrived and were taking up positions around the gardens. Every vehicle leaving was being searched, and the guests were being quietly directed to the exits.

They arrived at the front gate to find the ambulance waiting for them, and Fran was quickly transferred to the gurney. The attendants took various readings and hooked up monitors to her as they prepared to leave. Already her vital signs were being transmitted by radio to the hospital located a few kilometers away. On receipt of these, the emergency physician talked briefly to the ambulance crew now leaving the parking lot. Then he picked up a phone and made another call. At the airport, the large blades of the air rescue helicopter started to turn, and the neurosurgeon on call in Victoria received an urgent page.

Newton knew none of this. Despite the urging of Willy to go along with her, he knew he could not do anything that would change the situation from the back of an ambulance. It was his job now to stay here. Officers armed with Reggie's picture and description had been checking each vehicle as it left, and no one looking like that had been seen. The gunman was probably still on the scene.

He now set about the task of finding one gardener amongst many.

CHAPTER THIRTY ONE

"What now Alfred?" Willy asked.
"The last sighting I had came from the direction of the low ridge by the fountains. It's an area covered in creeping shrubs that marked the border of that garden with the next. By now the shooter would have disappeared and be hidden in the crowd."
"Right, let's count on his likely still being disguised as a worker. As that way he could go anywhere in the gardens without drawing the attention of any of the sightseers."
"So if he was careful, he could remain virtually invisible, just another gardener."
"Let the men know," Newton said, "and remind them to look for a staff member doing something out of place."

Gardeners are associated in one's mind as being in several physical positions, kneeling, bending, pruning and planting. Lying flat out with a gun in their hands would register as being somewhat odd, even in the mind of the most jaded tourist.

Willy made a call to the command post, which had been set up in one of the offices close to the staff radio link. All across the expanse of the gardens, police and staff alike were being alerted as to what to watch for.
"The fountains are to the south, right?" Willy asked, pointing his cell phone in the direction of Todd Inlet.
"Right," Newton said in a dark voice.

It was in this direction they headed now. Newton was intent on trying to look as if he was simply enjoying the scenery, with one eye on the crowd, and the other searching for a bona fide employee, preferably female. In the hope that she would have a two way radio that could be used to alert any other workers who had not yet got the news. Even though the office had radioed to all its workers to return immediately to the office, reception was not universal due to the topography of the grounds. Like most organizations, the terrorist actions on 9/11 had caused a rethink of day to day operations. A general disaster and recall plan had been implemented. A code word would be broadcast over the pocket radios some of the staff carried. There would be no specifics of course, no one wanted a panic. Upon receipt, the employees would simply gather at a prearranged spot. Regular drills had been done to test the effectiveness of the system, and the last time the code word had been broadcast it was to gather the employees for a surprise birthday celebration for one of the younger members. All over the gardens, employees who had received the word were gathering their tools and preparing to head back to the main complex.

"Take the north side Willy, and come back along the ridge towards the east, I'll head over and start from the tree line east of the fountains and we'll work our way to the center. He will be expecting a line of police from the north, so watch for someone heading down towards the old buildings."

Splitting up from Willy, Newton headed over to the area of the fountain gardens again. The gunman would not know the code word, nor would he wish to mingle with the staff, where his identity would be questioned. Newton was counting on that. As the patrons and employees gradually got the word and headed back, they would leave the outlying areas clear. The gunman would be forced to head to the outskirts of the gardens, or attempt to escape the grounds as a member of the public. He had to know the police were on the scene now, and that they would be checking every one as they left. His only escape route would be via a boat on the Todd Inlet side.
That would be the easiest way in and out for him. That's why he had been in the area of the fountains in the first place and that's how he found Fran. Newton was sure he would head back there where he must have a boat. Newton looked around for Willy, making sure he had traveled far enough to begin the sweep before continuing himself.
Questions flooded his mind, as they always did when running an operation. Did the possibility of escape via water occur to the

commanders overseeing the deployment of the officers around the gardens? As if to answer his question an R.C.M.P. helicopter flew in low over the West end of the complex and headed out to the middle of the inlet where its occupants could observe the shoreline.

Ahead of Newton, a gardener, with a shovel on his shoulder, was also observing the position of the helicopter. He put the shovel down, and headed back to the pathways.

Newton was not in a position to see that he was still on his way to the fountain area. He didn't want to risk scaring the remaining crowd of tourists; their numbers were still too great to risk a panic. To lessen the danger of any of them being hit by stray bullets, he tried to keep to the edge of the crowd, where any shots directed at him would strike the hillsides or trees. Like that large dogwood beside him, and if it did, then he would expect to see a hole or splintering of bark, like the one that just appeared at his side. Of course in this case, the fact that someone was shooting at him was quite apparent from the stinging blow to his arm, and if that was not enough then the blood now dripping out his jacket sleeve would. This, thought Newton, is what we policemen call "a clue."

Dropping to the ground, he sought the concealment of whatever shrubbery was planted there. Concealment of course did not mean cover. It only meant that your adversary could not see you clearly, if at all. Bushes could hide you, they could not stop bullets. Trees, on the other hand, could do both. A copse of large fir trees was a few yards to his left. Newton began to crawl towards them, keeping the bushes between him and where he thought the gunman was.

Whoever was firing at him didn't have to obey the same rules of concealment. They knew where he was and they had a much larger range of movement open to them. Dressed as a gardener, he was free to move on any of the pathways as well as through the various displays without rousing suspicion, appearing to anyone looking to be just another employee carrying tools heading out to do a job.

Newton's progress was slow but steady and he finally made it to the trees. Safe for the moment, he paused to scan the area. Now hidden within the trunks and low creeping shrubs that provided the concealment he needed, he paused and tried to control his breathing and heart rate. Stripping off his jacket, he found the wound on his arm. Luckily it was in the fleshy area of the bicep. Whilst bleeding and painful, it missed the bone and he still had limited use of his limb. No arteries appeared to have been hit and already the bleeding was slowing down. A few tugs at his shirt sleeve ripped the material free from the cuff and gave him a bandage of sorts. Tying it around his arm was impossible, so he simply wrapped it as tight as he could with his free hand, and tucked in the ends. It would not take much to work it loose, especially if he had to use his arm much, but he hoped that by then the clotting blood would have soaked the cloth and bound the fabric together. As long as his body didn't go into shock, he should be OK.

That chore done, he turned his full attention once again to finding his assailant.

The fir trees ran for only a few yards, and the hollow he was in, less than that, before giving way to another flower display. Not a lot of protection for him there he judged. A few rocks had been retained to accent the beds and provide natural focal points. Only a couple of these were big enough to provide cover, however. Newton raised his head above the ground cover and peered carefully out around the base of a tree. The plants ahead of him blurred his vision but would also distort the outline of his head, making it almost impossible for anyone to pinpoint his position.

Below, the path was again filling with visitors, moving from the fountains, whose display cycle had concluded, along to the next attraction. Some of them had gotten the word that something was amiss. Friends with cell phones at the main gate were calling those still in the gardens. Along the path, more and more people were receiving these calls, stopping to make sure everyone in their party was present and looking around with increasing anxiousness. Across the path, a flower bed was in the process of being weeded and here Newton found what he was looking for. Three gardeners were working with rakes and hoes. Two of them were female and chatting lightly amongst themselves. One of them wore a radio strapped to her belt, she must not have it turned on, or perhaps the reception was poor here. If he chose his route carefully, Newton judged he could make it to their area in no more than three minutes. But first he had to get out of the woods, so to speak.

He began by setting his route like a "connect the dots" puzzle from one feature to the next, mapping his next movements carefully. He needed to go down the ridge to his left, there a large rock provided cover if needed; that was objective number one. After that a few yards took him to a small stand of trees near the path; objective number two. Once there he could head for a drinking fountain made of concrete; that made it three. From there he would cross the path and head up to the flower beds by means of a set of wooden steps. Three metal lampposts with hanging baskets of flowers spaced along the steps, each with a bench at their base, would be the last possible places of refuge. Once there he could summons one of the working party to radio for help.

Taking a deep breath he scrambled to the rock. Breathing heavier than exertion demanded, he knew the next legs of the route were the hardest, he would have to walk upright, seemingly just another visitor, and that would make him a target. A target the gunman had already identified. That also meant avoiding the presence of others; he didn't want the gunman to hit anyone else. Moving out from the side of the rock, Newton began a journey that seemed to stretch further with every step. Keeping his pace steady he reached the drinking fountain. Sudden thirst overcame him and he took a long drink, his eyes scanning for anything out of the ordinary. The working party was making its way to the edge of the flower bed furthest from him. Straightening up, he left the fountain and made it across the path, the first lamppost a few yards in from of him. A glance at the workers told him he needed to hurry; one of them was already gathering the rakes and hoes. He tried to increase his pace up the stairs to the second lamppost, but the loss of blood was making him dizzy, and he had to stop to catch his breath. The worker with the radio was pulling it out from its protective case on her belt, and starting to talk into it. Were they leaving?

No, one of them was still pulling weeds, using a small hand tool to loosen the roots and placing the offending plant into a large green bag. The other two stood and dusted off their clothes, shaking loose the clods of dirt from the moist soil where they had been kneeling.

Newton reached the second post. His head was reeling now, and his body cried out for him to stop and rest on the bench. Something tugged at the corner of his brain, something here was strange, what was it? If he could only shake the cobwebs from his head. Passing the bench, he headed slowly up the stairs towards the third lamppost. The workers had noticed him now, the two girls looking with growing unease in his direction. The man rose from his position with a weed in his hand, dirt on his sleeves and dark moist patches on his knees. Newton could hear snatches of their conversation.

They turned to go over the hill.

NO! Newton tried to cry out but his throat was dry and no words came.

Tired now, he sat on the last bench to catch his breath. Were they leaving? It was difficult to see, for some reason his eyes would not focus and his breath came in short spurts. He looked at his arm, blood once again dripped from his hand. One of the figures turned and studied him as he sat on the bench. He tried again to call out, but his voice was weak and barely above a whisper. They seemed to be having a conversation, looking his way then talking again.

"It's OK; I'll see what he wants."
"He looks hurt." Said one of the girls.
"Drunk probably," said the man. "I'll look after him; you two can head back now."
The girls, one with the radio, turned and slinging their tools over their shoulders headed away.

Newton felt himself drifting now, it was getting harder and harder to focus his eyes, and the fountains must have started up again, for a roaring filled his ears. He thought he made out the shape of two of the gardeners going over the hill, but one was coming his way, the taller one, and he was carrying what appeared to be a small trowel. Newton slowly got to his feet and swaying slightly, waited for the dizziness to abate.

The trowel must have been used to work with the flowers his brain told him, because it blossomed into an orange colour. Then he felt a blow to his arm.

It spun him around on his unsteady feet. He reached for the bench with his good hand and regained his balance. Then came the pain, short sharp waves that sharpened his senses and gave a sense of focus, if only momentarily. His eyes found the gardener standing about 40 feet away. In response to his training more than a deliberate act of consciousness, Newton felt his arm extend in a pointing motion, the police issue Smith & Wesson pistol in his hand. Time compressed and extended all at the same time. Everything moved with deliberate slowness. Like a movie in his mind, his brain registered the scene in absolute clarity. The sunshine on the flowers and trees, the gently moving foliage exhibiting colours brighter and clearer than any he had ever seen before. Shades of yellow, green, and red accented by the bright shiny brass cartridge cases as they gently arced up and to the right from his gun. The second following on the heels of the first so that both were in the air at the same time. He felt the familiar push of recoil against the palm of his hand and saw the slide move smoothly to the rear and forward again. Strangely there was no sound, at least not at first, and then the distant booming of the gun's report echoed in his ears. All this came as a side show, for his eyes were fixed on the figure in front of him. He watched as first one, and then another hole appeared in the chest of the coveralls. Funny, he thought, there should be a spray of blood, just like in the movies, but nothing, only the orange yellow and noiseless flash from the trowel coming back at him.

Of course, he thought, he has a silencer! That explains it! And body armour too!

Another blow to Newton's chest caused him to stumble. He was tired, very tired, and having great difficulty keeping his eyes open. Funny, he thought, I expected there would be more pain than this. Head spinning began to twist to his left and he fell back onto the bench. With blurry vision he recorded the advance of the gardener who was now standing in front of him. How odd, thought Newton, as the figure disappeared from his view, where did he go? With the sound of the fountains roaring in his ears, he struggled to keep his eyes open,

Someone appeared at the periphery of his diminishing vision, a young man, dressed in street clothes, not gardener's overalls.

"Are you OK?" The figure asked.
Newton tried to respond but the words wouldn't come, no breath to speak with.

The figure sat beside him and helped him sit up. He bent closer to his ear and whispered something but Newton couldn't quite hear him.
"Tell me....."
The voice got louder.
"Tell me where it is."

The young man grabbed Newton's arm and squeezed, the pain shocked him into a higher level of consciousness.
"Tell me where it is!"

Newton forced his voice to reply, and the words came out dry and slow and stretched. "Where what is? I don't know what you're talking about."
"The carving, where is it?"

"What carving?"
"She must have told you where it was, tell me now and I'll make the pain go away."
"I don't understand, what carving?"
"Liar! You must know!"

Newton was drifting again now, his breathing shallower, the figure kept talking, kept asking, asking for what? A carving? What carving? Why did he think he had it? So many thoughts—so hard to think, so tired now, maybe if he just had a little sleep it would be clearer, yes that's it, a little sleep, just a little sleep. Not long, just a moment, wouldn't that be OK? A small moment in this endless time.

He never heard the final shot.

CHAPTER THIRTY TWO

The world was swimming around in a kaleidoscope of colours and sound. If this was heaven, then heaven was a very noisy place. That can't be right—heaven is quiet, nothing but clouds and cream cheese, all the commercials say so, and commercials are never wrong, are they? "Who's to say," said a voice on his left. "Heaven is what you believe it to be. You can always change your mind, change the picture like you do in a dream. After all, you have eternity to get it right."

"What happened?" chimed in another voice.

How could they not know what happened? Thought Newton, why would they ask me? I don't know, angels are supposed to be all knowing, and answer your questions. Didn't they have any fairy tales up here? Angels always knew the answers in the fairy tales. What kind of outfit were they running anyway?

More noise, and lights, lots of lights, pretty colours, red and blue and white. Is it night? Did the fountain lights come on? Then the noise grew louder, and Newton recognized it, it was his own song, one he had played so many times over the years.

The wailing of a siren.

Newton began to doubt that he was in heaven at all. No he thought, I can't be, too much confusion, heaven would be a place of structure and order, this was bedlam and chaos. So if that's true, then I simply……… can't………. be in heaven.

193

The next thing Newton saw provided absolute proof of it.

He opened his eyes and saw Willy's face looking down at him.

Well, he thought, maybe next time, and the blackness returned.

The next time he awoke, it was in much different circumstances. The room was quieter, the lighting was a monochromatic white, and the face bending over him was not Willy's. It was a much older man. He wore a white coat accented with a rubber tube connected to earphones on one end and a flat chunk of metal on the other. He also wore glasses; that was good, Newton thought, doctors should always wear glasses, makes people believe they studied a lot. The expression on his face was of concern, but not too much of it. Also good, thought Newton, doctors should always look like they think a lot, people expect them to think, especially their patients. The man was also sporting grey hair and balding. An excellent sign Newton agreed with himself, who wants a doctor who spends all his time dying his hair and wearing a wig or hair piece, besides looking ridiculous what if it should happen to fall off during an operation or something, would the doctor grab for it and drop the scalpel? What then? What if they didn't find it, would I have to go through life with a scalpel lost somewhere in me? I'd never be able to get on an airplane again, I couldn't pass security.
"Ah ha!" they would say. "We've caught a terrorist, he is trying to smuggle a sharp instrument onto a plane!" They would never understand that it wasn't his fault, he never wanted it in the first place. Maybe the hairpiece wouldn't be so bad.

Oh look, the doctor is speaking now, slowly and using small words, at least I think they're small words, his lips aren't moving that much, so they must be small. Doctors should always use small words when talking to their patients, so they could be understood, then they could use large words when they teach the new doctors, that way they wouldn't forget how to use them, large words can be useful you know.

This is all so hard, Newton thought, trying to listen to a doctor use small words and not wear a hair piece, maybe I'll sort it out later, I'm so tired, it must be bedtime, good night, mummy.

Angel hair.

I remember that, Newton thought, we put it on the tree, around the lights so it would soften them and look like a street lamp in the fog.

Nice lights, all bumpy with glass beads and things, but nice. When you put them up that meant Christmas was the next day, lots of family, lots of presents, such a nice time, Newton relaxed, and slept again.

Silence.

The trouble with silence, thought Newton, was it was so damn hard to tell if you're awake, I mean you can't really tell, can you? Oh sure, you can hear your heart beat, but you also hear that when you sleep, don't you?

Silence really does have a sound of its own.

Pain.

Pain can be considered a good thing, he thought, in some circumstances. Pain keeps you from doing silly things, like falling off your bike, or putting out a fire with your face. Yes, all things considered, pain is probably a good thing. Like everything else in life though, too much of it is not so good.

Smell.

Of all the senses, smell is the one most linked with memory. Newton sat at the back of the class, listening to the teacher try to explain the sense of smell. How could one do that? You smell what you smell. But he was right about it triggering memories though. Baking bread was a house on the beach with a wood stove. Pans of dough rising, crusty surfaces, and the warm welcoming comfort of home, and so it would always be.

Newton awoke with a start, and to a numbing sensation in his chest. Slowly his eyes adjusted to the dim light in the room, he was confused for a moment, his brain trying to create order from the strange environment his body found itself in. He listened to the sounds in the room. A beeping sound, regular and somehow reassuring came from a machine in a rack on his left. Like a metronome, it kept time with his heart. He turned his head and watched the screen; the numbers were increasing as he became more fully awake. He tried next to move his hands, but they were held by straps to the side rails of his bed. Looking down he saw tubes and wires leading out of the blankets and they disappeared out of his view. He could see his toes, when he tried to wiggle them the blanket moved in response. He didn't know why, but that gave a solid feeling of comfort, that he was going to be all right. His bed was surrounded by curtains and outside of them lights were coming on and shadows moved with purpose and direction. His head sank back on the pillow and he studied the ceiling, the same multi-holed sound absorbent board that decorated the ceilings of almost every hospital in the western world.

Well, he thought, I guess that means I'm not dead and this isn't heaven after all.

He closed his eyes and took a deep breath, OUCH, bad move, "not ready for that yet," he announced out loud and took comfort in the sound of his own voice.

"Not ready for what?"
Newton opened his eyes again and turned to the sound of the question. Willy was there, sitting in a chair where he had obviously been camping out for some time. Empty coffee cups and sandwich wrappers littered the nearby table, and the stubble on his chin was longer than the overnight growth he had witnessed on the occasional stakeout they had pulled together.

"Not ready for that ugly face of yours," said Newton. "How long have I been here?"
"Three nights, two days," Willy replied, rising and coming over to stand by the bedside. The curtains were drawn back with a snap as a nurse came in with a tray, summonsed by the monitoring equipment connected to Newton's arm and chest.

"You stand back now," she said to Willy, "and don't get him all excited and upset." With a glance at the beeping monitor, she recorded some figures on a clipboard and lifted Newton's good arm to take his pulse. Looking down at his left arm, Newton was thankful to see it all there and apparently in one piece.

"Now then, Mr. Newton, if you promise to be good and not thrash around like you were doing, I'll not strap this arm down, but the other stays as it is 'til the doctor says different, understand?"
"Works for me" he replied.
"All right then, you be good and the doctor will be round in an hour or so." She turned to leave, stopped and looked directly at Willy, "Remember what I said—no getting him excited."
Willy nodded and she left, the squeaking of her rubber soled shoes receding beyond the curtained horizons of his room.
"What the hell happened, Willy, and where is Fran, is she OK?"

"Hey, boss, I got my orders, we can talk about this later." Willy said glancing down at the floor.

An icy hand gripped Newton's heart and the monitor began a sharp rise.

The look of helplessness on Willy's face said it all and Newton slumped back onto the bed. He took several deep breaths and fixed him with a stare.

"Tell me now Willy, and don't leave anything out."

"She's still with us Al."

"And?"

"She's a fighter. She'll pull through," Willy's voice said weakly.

But his eyes said different.

CHAPTER THIRTY THREE

Daylight

It filled the room from large double paned glass at the end of the room. The bright rays playing over the now disconnected machinery of life that stood on wheeled racks against the wall. Dust particles rose and fell, caught in the currents of air warmed by those rays reflected tiny glints of colour around the room, a brief celebration of motion and the laws of physics. The light stretched across the bed, now made up and tidy, with a small suitcase placed on top of it. Newton sat in a wheelchair, waiting. A nurse was with him, to ensure that he didn't violate the mysterious policy that patients were wheeled to the property line in a chair. Once they had crossed over onto public property again, they were turfed from that same chair and forced to make their own ambulatory arrangements. It made no sense, but nothing made sense now, and Newton knew it would be some time before anything made sense again. His wounds, whilst critical at the time, were treatable. His punctured lung had been repaired, in the immediate by surgeons, and in the long term by nature and ability of the human body to heal itself, to grow new tissue and scar over the wounds of the flesh. The wounds of the mind did not heal so quickly, if at all. In that province, scars never healed, new tissue was rarely formed and some wounds would bleed forever.

Willy showed up, along with half the squad, as many as the hospital would allow. They all spoke in voices full of happy sounds and hollow laughter. Awkward and loud in the only way men know how to deal with loss, their eyes, though full of unshed tears, held an empathy that was instantly understood, in a way that words could never convey.

They drove him home and toasted his recovery, wished him luck and spoke of the good times, and the bad, of how in this job somehow you always wound up with the short end of the stick. They prayed with the police chaplain when he arrived, and shook his hand as they left. Willy stayed behind after all the rest had left, tidying up and putting the dishes away. In the end, he left too, with a promise to return if needed and added his "If you need anything, just call" to all the rest.

One of the wives or girlfriends had been around while he was in hospital and collected all her things. They had tidied up the apartment and vacuumed and done all the other small touches men seem oblivious to doing. The fridge was full of homemade this and that, labels on the Tupperware with phone numbers and best wishes.

Martha had dropped off a number of vouchers good for a cab ride anywhere he needed to go. The guys had all left a plentiful supply of liquor behind, and Newton appreciated their genuine attempts at providing comfort. He settled uncomfortably into his chair and began reading the police reports.

They were written in the official third person, one from the ambulance crew, one from the local police, and the most important one was from Willy.

After alerting Newton to Johnson's return to the island Willy had stayed on in the gardens. There wasn't any specific information he could point to that would lead him to believe that Johnson was there, and certainly nothing pointing to the violence that ensued. But he had a feeling, and good cops assign a certain amount of weight to such feelings. It was those feelings that caused him to bring Newton's gun out to him in the first place. Johnson had returned from the Charlottes, where he had gone for a specific reason. While Willy didn't know the reason, he knew it had to be significant for such a journey. An accident/murder had taken place up there in which Johnson was somehow involved. The only persons Willy knew of who came from there, were Newton and Fran. In the absence of anything else more concrete, it was the best lead he had to work with.

So he kept an eye out without being conspicuous. But the crowds were big and he didn't want to intrude on Newton's day out with Fran. The result being he lost sight of them until he noticed Newton returning alone from the abandoned buildings of the cement plant. He noticed something else, Newton had his gun out. Not that he could see the gun itself, but the way he held his hands made it plain. Willy had paused long enough to put through a phone call to the dispatcher, letting them know the situation and asking for backup, which would come from the local forces. With the shootings earlier in the day, all available resources were committed, and it took a few moments to free up a team of plain clothes officers. Uniformed members were dispatched immediately, but their orders were to wait for the arrival of the detectives, who could then melt in with the crowd.

With that done, Willy had tried to locate Newton, who seemed to have disappeared again. He made his way to the last known location, and looked around. From his standpoint he could see both the abandoned buildings and the edge of the gardens. Looking in the directions of the old cement plant he noticed a shadowy figure moving in the doorway of one of the buildings, and went to investigate. In the dust he saw footprints. The first set being composed of one large and one small set of tracks that would be Newton and Fran he surmised. The second was a distinctive set of boot tracks that he had seen earlier that day, and he instantly knew two things, the first was that these were Johnson's and the second was that Johnson was hunting the couple. He made his way carefully through the worksite, following the trail. At times he thought he felt, more than saw, Johnson searching the buildings ahead of him. The offshore breeze stirred the dust about, making tracking difficult, and masking any sounds.

Willy picked up the pace.

 Two buildings were left to search, one, an all concrete structure, that looked like a main office was just ahead of him and to his right. This time he definitely saw a shadow. With gun in hand he entered, trying to keep his eye on all the doorways and possible hiding places. He knew Newton had left the area, but where was Fran? And why was Johnson still here? He heard voices from one of the rooms on the other side of the building, but he couldn't tell which. The voices ceased, and Willy caught a glimpse of Johnson's back as he left one office and exited the building in a flash.

 Not wanting to give away his position, Willy moved carefully to crouch by the door. He peered around it, nothing in the room but an old desk. Who had Johnson been talking to? Then he saw the blood, just a small patch, just enough to reflect the sunlight from the windows. It was coming from somewhere on the other side of the desk and Willy's heart sank as he approached the desk and looked over to the other side. There crumpled on the dusty floor was Fran, her hands clutching a shoe with a broken heel, and a wound on the side of her head. Willy made another call on the cell phone, and this time the officers heading to the entrance flipped on the siren and lights.

They would not be waiting for any detectives to arrive.

Fran, lying beneath the desk, looked up with a confused smile. Willy checked the wound and found a little blood, it didn't look too serious, but her long hair prevented a clear examination.
"What happened?" She asked.
"You got a little bang on the head," said Willy, "just lay back; I've got help on the way."

Peering out the side of the doorway, Willy attempted to get a fix on Johnson's position. Nothing was moving, and then out of the corner of his eye he saw a shadow. Johnson had moved to the end of the row of buildings. There stood the remnants of what had been workers quarters. Old rusted beds, a stove, and bits of furniture still lay scattered around. One of the pieces held what had been a full length mirror, now broken in half. In the reflection of the remaining half, Willy clearly saw Johnson crouching, his gun drawn. Good, he thought, as long as he stays like that, maybe I get closer and take him out.

Willy began to crawl towards the old bunkhouse while keeping an eye on the mirror, and himself between Johnson and Fran. Twice the gunman's reflection disappeared from view, and Willy froze until it reappeared. After what seemed like an eternity, he had reached a position of cover behind a chunk of concrete, no more than a dozen yards away.

You're mine now, he thought, as he lined up the sights on his Smith & Wesson and prepared to call out a challenge.

A sudden movement to his left caused Willy to pause, who was that, another gunman? Could there be two? Maybe it was a worker, or a lost tourist. Willy took his eyes off the mirror for a second to check. Damn, it was Newton, headed back this way. Looking back at the mirror, he saw nothing. Johnson had also seen Newton and was gone.

Shit!

Willy broke cover and headed into the west side of the building, intending to take Johnson in a rush before he could get a shot off at Newton. Arriving on the east side of the building he prepared to challenge the gunman, but found nothing. By now Newton had reached the middle row of buildings. Willy waited a few minutes to make sure the gunman was not trying to set an ambush, or sneak through the piles of rubble. Then he saw a group of workers with a garden tractor crest the hillside. As quickly as he could, he made his way back to Newton, who had now found Fran, and was preparing to load her onto the tractor bed.

After seeing to it that Fran was loaded into the ambulance, Willy and Newton headed back for the last place they had seen Johnson. They split with Willy taking the east path past the fountains. There he found a couple of young ladies who were working as gardeners. They had no radio with them and were not aware of what had been happening. Willy quickly told them to gather their tools and leave, and he accompanied them towards a shed where they kept their shovels and trowels. A figure left the shed as they came up. It was Johnson, now dressed in coveralls, and as Willy got close he saw him topping the ridge, and disappearing into the crowd. Willy used his cell phone to alert the incoming officers to his description. The gunman's wearing coveralls, which while it allowed him to blend into the staff, also made him stand out from the crowds. Using less caution than before, Willy made his way to the ridge and stopped to scan the area. Only a few members of the crowd were in sight, most were still watching the fountain display. Willy moved in that direction, pausing every few minutes to scan the crowd and the surroundings. Looking back, he observed three gardeners begin work on a flower bed. Two of them were female; he headed back that way intending to ask them if they had seen any other gardeners who looked perhaps out of place, and to warn them. The crowds got suddenly bigger, the fountain show was over, and the numbers of visitors slowed Willy down. They also blocked his view from time to time so that he had to get off the trail and seek higher ground to observe the working party ahead. He saw them talking in a group. Damn, he had to get to them before they split up. The crowd closed and thinned in a last wave before Willy caught sight of them again. When he did, he also observed Newton struggling up the path to their position. He was weaving and appeared hurt. One of the workers, holding a tool or something in his hand, approached Newton, and Newton staggered again and sat heavily on the last bench. The worker removed his coveralls and sat down beside him. Willy began to run towards them, he was below and behind the bench and out of their line of sight. Keep talking, he whispered to himself, keep talking I'm almost there.

They kept talking, at least for a while, then the gardener, his right hand holding, what? A pistol? Yes, a pistol with a silencer. Next he brought it up behind the bench and pointed it at the base of Newton's skull. Willy drew his own gun and steadying his arm against the side of a lamp post took aim. The gunman on the bench tilted the barrel up, now only millimeters from Newton's head; he took a last look around to check for possible witnesses.

Willy fired.

CHAPTER THIRTY FOUR

The sound of the shot was swallowed up in the roar of the crowd. Gathered around the fountains as the first jets of water arched skyward, they heard only the rush of water. Still, some, in other parts of the garden, heard it and looked skyward for the presence of a plane. For others it was dismissed as a car noise, coming from some nearby highway. Johnson never heard it at all. The 40 caliber soft nosed slug was traveling at 2,350 feet per second when it left the muzzle of Willy's pistol. The command to squeeze the trigger of Johnson's pistol left his brain at the same time. It was a tie. If the pistol had been fitted with a hair trigger, Newton would have died. But it was a stock factory piece. The pistol's trigger required a force of eight pounds of pressure to be applied. Only then would the sear in the firing mechanism be moved enough to release the pent up pressure behind the hammer spring. In the end, Johnson was a pro, and that worked against him. He had practiced for hours on the range to perfect a smooth pull on the trigger. To accomplish this, the gunman's finger muscles depended upon a continuing stream of instructions from his brain. A stream that was interrupted by Willy's bullet with a full two pounds of trigger pull left to go. Had he simply jerked on the trigger like a novice shooter Newtown would be dead. But all those hours of practice took over, and that's what saved the detective. The bullet from Willy's pistol had struck at the base of gunman's skull. In its passage it destroyed the bundle of nerves at the top of the spinal column. If death was not instantaneous, the cessation of nerve impulses was. The main part of the bullet continued, exiting through Johnson's mouth in a spray of blood and coming to rest in the flower beds, where it was later recovered by the forensic team. Both bodies tumbled off the bench.

During this time those guests at the rear of the gardens were wondering about the sudden arrival of the police cars, and an ambulance. Probably a heart attack, some of them thought, the younger ones guessed an accident of some sort. To their dismay, the garden staff and the police were asking them to leave. Many had traveled from different parts of the world and their vacation schedules would not allow them to return at the later date being offered. Some began to argue, but the look on the officers' faces told them this was not the time to press the point. The tour buses filled up and left, and the huge parking lots began to empty.

The gardens were closed for the rest of the day whilst the official investigations took place, but everything they were going to know, they knew within 15 minutes. Still, there was a job to do, another police officer shot, a civilian wounded. This time they said amongst themselves, the bastard who did it got popped himself. No chance of his getting off on a technicality now. So they went about their jobs. Taking pictures of the tracks in the dust, collecting shell casings, blood samples, and footprint impressions. All the minutiae of forensic police work. Remember, they were told, we don't know that there was only one shooter, not yet.

CHAPTER THIRTY FIVE

In the hospital, Newton had told Willy about the questions that Johnson asked. Obviously he was looking for a carving, but which one, and why did he think Newton had that knowledge? It had to have something to do with Alicia and her trip to the Charlottes. Johnson must have known that he had been up there. Did he also know Fran? Why had she been killed? Had this anything to do with his Jane Doe, could she be a significant link between all these events? Or was her death just a coincidental occurrence?

For the next three days Newton rested at home, Fran's body had been shipped home to her parents in Vancouver before he got out of the hospital. He had spoken to them on the phone and promised to visit as soon as he was able. He had indefinite leave from work; his physical wounds were healing fast. His arm was recovering nicely, no bone damage, just some torn muscles. The bullet to his chest had collapsed one lung and penetrated his diaphragm, which accounted for his difficulty in breathing. He had of course lost a lot blood, but every day he felt stronger and already was anxious to get out of his apartment. The office crew had been very attentive, so much so that he had Willy spread the word that he had enough flowers, liquor, and doughnuts to last a lifetime. The fridge was full; he feared he would forget how to cook before he worked his way through it all.

On the morning of the fourth day, he awoke feeling refreshed and for the first time, without pain, unless he tried to overtax his arm. Going to the kitchen, he found his coffee can empty and headed to the pantry for another he knew he had purchased prior to leaving for the Charlottes. All he had to do was find it. Like most bachelors, his method of storage was last bought, first off the shelf. But the good intentions of his well wishers had extended to organizing the pantry by type of goods, canned or boxed, meal type and so forth. He was now hopelessly lost, and had only one good arm to search with to boot.

Newton sighed, went to the kitchen and got a chair to stand on and a flashlight to illuminate the furthest reaches of the shelves. Normally he didn't store much on the top shelf, but his well meaning visitors had piled it with objects that didn't fit their method of organization. Luckily the coffee cans were brightly marked in red and taller than their surrounding containers and he readily saw it at the back. Now the trick was to reach the damn thing without falling off the chair and breaking his good arm. The only way to that, he thought after a moment, was to take all the other stuff blocking the way out, then he would have a clear path, and be able to "reorganize" the pantry the way it should be, with everything in plain sight. It took several trips to cart the odds and ends to kitchen table, but finally there was only a brown paper package between him and the now much needed coffee. Reaching in as far as he could he worked the package with his finger tips until he could grab it and push it to the side. Then he tipped the coffee can over and coaxed it to the front of the shelf where he could grab it. That done, he took it to the kitchen and started up his ancient percolator. The appliance was almost as old as he was, but nothing made better coffee as far as he was concerned. Its only drawback was the time it took to do it. Filling it with water and the normal amount of grounds he set it on the boil and turned to the task of replacing the many items he had pulled out.

Alfred's normal method of organization called for the things he used most to be in the front, and everything else in the back of the shelf. Stuff used in the first part of the week went on the left, and everything else progressed in order to the right. If something was not used at its allotted time, then it stayed there and he would quickly notice it prior to shopping. That way, he avoided buying something he used little of, and could actually plan out a week or two in a few minutes of observation. After all, he was a trained investigator, and used to looking for things that seemed to be out of place, or missing. Setting about arranging the items on the table in the order that he would put them on the shelf, he made adjustments to his mental notebook about things that he needed to get. First though, he decided, he better see if they were already "organized" onto another shelf.

This was going to take some time, he thought, as he scanned the pantry shelves. Obviously everyone had a different idea of what he would need, and so covered all the bases by bringing everything they could think of. The first thing he needed to do, he thought, was to get a box to put the things he would never use into. These he would give to Martha down at the taxi company, and she would see they ended up with someone who needed it. Martha had for years been supplying selected folks with goods donated by her crew of cabbies. Some of it bought new, most of it scavenged from back alleys at night. Once she learned that so and so needed a crib, or working lawn mower, or extra chair, the item would be marked on a board outside her office, and the item would sooner or later appear in the trunk of a taxi. The mechanics had a small workshop set up where simple repairs and painting brought an item to life and it would find its way to a needy family. The network extended to local moving companies who let their clients know that anything they didn't want to haul to the next place of residence would be given a good home and taken away at no cost, reaped a surprising amount of goods. In addition, most folks who were moving were happy to have someone take away any groceries that cluttered their cupboards and were not worth the cost of moving.

Newton remembered the box or package that was unfamiliar on the top shelf. More donated food, he expected, as good a place to start as any. Balancing on the chair he pulled it towards him, it was heavy, probably canned goods, and he put it in the growing pile on the kitchen table. An hour or so later, after stopping for coffee, he had the pantry arranged the way he wanted it, and he had quite a pile of donated goods filling a couple of boxes in the kitchen. He would rest a bit, and then phone Martha and let her know it was ready for pickup. First though, it was best if made sure none of the stuff he was donating originated with her! He inventoried the items in the boxes, which as expected were mostly canned goods from the local supermarkets. Some homemade stuff, like canned carrots and beets, a couple of home canned salmon, maybe he'd reconsider those, and the usual boxed goods like crackers and cookies. Thankfully there was nothing that appeared perishable or in imminent danger of going bad.

That's when he picked up the wrapped package.

It was just a brown paper wrapping, nothing special, no writing on it to indicate its contents. It felt like a heavy box of chocolates or candy. Newton liked chocolate of course, but he never bought any for himself, only as gifts, and he suspected this was an unused gift someone had laying around waiting for a suitable circumstance to present itself. Generally, these would be birthdays and anniversaries, not shootings. He carefully undid the wrapping.

The first thing he noticed was it was not candy, but a black velvet presentation box wrapped with a ribbon and bow, and sealed with tape. Good tape too, it would not yield to his fingernails. Damn, he thought, I must be in worse shape than I imagined, and got a knife from the drawer. Another cup of coffee demanded his attention, and he managed to refill his cup without spilling it all over the counter. Well, he said aloud, at least some things are going right today. Sitting back at the table he used the knife blade to cut the tape around the perimeter of the box and then lifted the lid. As he did, a note fell out and fluttered to the floor, in the box was a scarf and a black Argillite carving, and the scent of a familiar perfume.

Newton snatched the note from the floor and began to read.

My Darling

If you are reading this and I am still here, then shame on you! You peeked! This is something I picked up at the hotel just before leaving. It was in our stock of tourist goods and by far the best one there, at least to me. I don't know who carved it, but it looks old, maybe Elijah will know, we'll ask him together. I sense there is some history behind it from its age and workmanship. Something that stands the test of time. So it's perfect for us, don't you think?

When you look at it, think of me, think of us, and think of our future. I want you to know how happy I have been since we met, and how much I look forward to our being together. I know that you have been alone a long time, so have I, too long for both of us. I made you the scarf to keep you warm on chilly nights 'til I can wrap you in my arms again. I'll only be gone a short while and I miss you already!

'Til Then
All My love
Frances

Newton sat, silent in the chair and stared unseeingly at the paper. The he laid his head in his arms, and let the tears flow.

CHAPTER THIRTY SIX

Evening arrived with the soft glow of the setting sun, its last rays reflecting off the bottom of the clouds that were making their way north across the horizon. It found Newton sitting in an easy chair, his eyes were red and he was tired, very tired. A cold cup sat in a dried ring of coffee on the table. In front of him, the open box held the scarf and the note; he placed the lid on the box and moved it to one side. In front of him the carving lay flat and he picked it up. All of the carvings he had seen up 'til now were like etchings, lines scribed in the soft stone to create the image, but this one was different. This carving was in bas-relief. The stone had been removed to form a sculpture of two eagles in flight over the sea. One was higher than the other, standing guard while the lower one hunted. Each feather was exquisitely carved in detail. As Newton studied it further it knew it was the work of a master. Fran was right; it was not like any other he had seen. He ran his fingers over the relief, feeling each cutting stroke. Even sitting on the table they caught the suns dying rays and refracted them into tiny rainbows. He watched, fascinated, as the rays marched across the face of the carving revealing more detail as it went, until it reached the top and, wait, more rainbows appeared. Newton tipped the carving up and sighted down the edge, he thought he could make out a pair of faint lines.

The lines were very hard to see, and he would have missed them completely had it not been for the oblique angle of the sun's rays. When he tried to study them with the lights on, they seemed to disappear. It took the assistance of a magnifying glass along with a polarized filter borrowed from his camera kit to reveal them again. He could see now that they ran all along the edge of the carving, as if it was made in two pieces. On the back two screws were set into the stone, with a wire strung between them, obviously there to allow the piece to be hung on the wall. Newton thought for a minute. The old Sesame Street tune playing in his head, "One of these things is not like the other, one of these things doesn't belong." Then he had it, a piece of art of this quality would never be hung on a wall, it would be matted and framed, or displayed in a case. The part that didn't belong was the cheap wire and he rummaged through a kitchen drawer to locate a small screw driver.

Sliding a sheet of paper under the carving lest anything fall away and be lost, he gently undid the screws, first one then the other till they lay, with the wire, on top of the paper. Taking the magnifying glass, he carefully examined the screw holes and the wire. Nothing, nada, zip, just your regular, everyday wall mounting system. Well, he thought, maybe I got it wrong; Lord knows it's not the first time. He returned his attention to the carving. Thank you my love, he whispered to himself, thank you for this, we did not have a long time together, and I'd happily change places with you, but you were the best thing in my life for a very long time and I'll see you in my dreams. As he thought of her, his shoulders trembled with the weight of his grief, and the carving slipped from his hands and fell with a loud clunk onto the table.

Newton stumbled from the chair to his bedroom, turning out the lights on the way, 'til the darkness of the apartment matched the feeling in his heart.

The next morning he awoke to an insistent pounding on his door, Willy's voice calling from the hallway. Newton opened it to find him standing there with two cups of coffee and bag of bagels.

"Let's go, boss, times a-wasting."
"Let's go where."
"Work, golf, shopping, fishing, doesn't matter, as long as you're out of this place, you need to be doing something."
"I AM doing something Willy, I'm recuperating."
"You'll do that better when you're not doing it."
"Says who?"
"My mom, and she's never wrong, unless it's to think I did something I wasn't supposed to, when it was really my sister getting me in trouble again."
Newton began to smile in spite of all that had happened.
"That's the ticket, boss, Fran wouldn't want you to mope around I'm sure, she struck me as the type who lived life as best as she could."

The mention of her name caused the memories to flood back, and Newton felt the tears surface again.

"Damn it Alfred, I'm sorry, I guess I stuck my foot in my mouth again."
"No, no actually you're right Willy, that's exactly the way she was, come in and sit down, I'll get dressed."

Newton headed off to the bathroom and started his morning routine, "Make some more coffee if you like," he called to Willy, "and there's better stuff than those bagels in the fridge."
"Ha!" said Willy. "Nothing's better than Timmy's bagels."

A short time later, shaved, showered, and feeling the better for it, he returned to the kitchen to find Willy sitting at the table examining the carving. "Where did this come from?" He asked, "Did you pick it up from the Charlottes?"
"It was a gift," Newton replied. "Fran brought it with her, I found it yesterday."
"It's really a beautiful piece," Willy said. "How did it get broken?"
"Broken?"
"Yeah, or maybe it's supposed to be in two pieces."

Newton strode quickly to the table and took it from Willy. The lines on the edges, so well masked the day before were now well defined, and on one corner a space between them had appeared. Willy was right— the carving was actually two pieces. Newton studied it closely. Of course! The screws that he thought were for mounting were just a disguise, they actually held the back on, and when he dropped it, that must have jarred it loose. He searched for and found the screwdriver he had used last night. The blade was just the right size to slip between the pieces and perhaps pry them apart.

"Ah, I wouldn't do that boss."
"Why not?"
"Argillite is very soft and that metal will mark it, you need a piece of wood, something softer than the stone."
"Of course, you're right Willy, I knew that."

A search of the kitchen brought forth a wooden spoon and a sharp knife. Shaping the end of the handle down to a narrow strip, Newton fashioned a wedge and tapped it into the gap. Working his way around the perimeter, the two halves separated with a slight pop. They lifted the back off the carving and found it was hollow. A small leather bag was inside.

CHAPTER THIRTY SEVEN

The bag was not heavy, and Newton opened it and spread the contents on the paper.

Diamonds!

They counted 51 stones. Each finished stone was ready for setting, and although they varied in size and weight, none appeared to be under one and a half carats.

"Whew," whispered Willy. "That's a lot rocks there, must be worth a bundle."

"More than a month's pay, that's for sure."

"So that's what Johnson was after, but how did he know that Fran had it?"

Newton thought for a minute, "My guess is he was using the carvings for smuggling, probably getting the stones from off shore, hiding them in the carvings and then using Alicia to bring them down to the museum where he picked them up and dropped them off to someone in town."

"Somehow I'm thinking this is a little out of Johnson's league," Willy mused. "I wonder who his partners were?"

"Good question, assuming the story about his being in the witness program is true, then it has to be one of two things. Either someone inside the program hatched this scheme, or he was a plant all along."

"A plant?"

"Sure, think about it for a minute, the guy most likely to be overlooked is the one you already processed, whom no one supposed to know about, whose whereabouts are already a guarded secret. The local cops know nothing about him, and according to the rules, they will never be told the truth. It's a perfect plant. Once settled into the program, he keeps his nose clean for a couple of years then quietly goes about letting his former pals know where he is. They set up an operation and he is the perfect go between."

"So, you figure he set this up with Alicia?"

"Probably not, I think he just recognized the opportunity when it came. As a museum guard he would be free to wander around and chat with all the learned folks there. I'm betting he found out from them that some of the carvings were hollow and with his knowledge of Alicia's trips back and forth, he made a few calls to his pals."

"So when did the wheels come off?"

"Since he was in the witness program, he couldn't be seen with a suddenly new and expensive lifestyle, that would have raised all sorts of suspicions and he would have been found out quickly. So, I'm betting he took some of his rewards in the form of drugs, and that was fatal when he got hooked and ran out of cash. He had to peddle something—the carvings—to pay his debts, and that's when things fell apart."

"OK, I'm with you so far, but how did Fran get hold of this?"
"Just as she said, the hotel tourist shop was a perfect drop for the carvings. Alicia would always stay at the hotel, and with her contacts amongst the carvers, like Mel, they would be after her to look at their work every time she was there. The quality of the pieces—and I'm sure there are more like this one—would do the rest. A scheme like this would not require a regular schedule of pickups. Part of the value of the diamonds is their scarcity, uniqueness, and the uncertainty in their availability. I'll bet regular deliveries would even be discouraged."
"So it was just blind luck she happened to pick this carving up?"
"Yes, the worst kind of luck, if she hadn't, then..."

Newton's voice trailed off to silence.

CHAPTER THIRTY EIGHT

A week later Newton returned to work over the objections of his doctor.

"Physically speaking, Alfred," she said, "I don't think you have given it enough time to heal."

"My shoulder or my lung?" He questioned.

"Your heart," she answered.

He went to work anyway.

"Hello, boss," Willy announced when he showed up. "I've managed to keep most of the garbage off your desk, but there are a few things there for you."

Newton sat down behind his desk, uncluttered for the first time in recent memory. A few interdepartmental memos noted changes in this organization or that, different responsibilities or duties, the normal rotation of personnel here and there. Newspaper clippings someone had cut out and stuck into a scrapbook along with a copy of a commendation he received whilst still in the hospital. But the world had moved on, and already new cases were competing for resources.

Newton found a couple of envelopes buried in the pile. A card from the R.C.M.P. detachment signed by all the staff wished him a speedy recovery. Elijah even sent along a bear claw as a good luck talisman. To his surprise, there was an envelope bearing the return address of the Salvation Army in Calgary. The note was written in neat penmanship from Rusty, along with a money order for $50. So, maybe out of all this some good would eventually sprout forth Newton mused. The note said Rusty had found work in the building trades. He had gained ten pounds and was saving for a place of his own, and he had met a girl and they had hit it off together. She worked as a waitress in a little place a few blocks from the Sally-Ann, the kind of place the homeless and lost come through on their way to where ever it was they went. I was talking to her one night about the girl you found on the beach, Rusty wrote, and then I showed her the pictures you gave me. She didn't know her though, nor the girl from the museum. Sorry to hear about her dying up in the islands and all. But here's the strange thing, you know the picture of the other girl, the one from Bellingham? Rosy thinks she saw her a few months back, before the snow last fall. She was traveling alone, headed for the east coast of the States, some big city out there, New York or maybe it was Boston. Anyway, got to go to work now, some days are a drudge, but it sure beats getting beat up! Thanks for your help and all.

Newton froze for a moment at his desk. Just a year ago, Rusty had said, no wait, last fall it was, before the snow, that's less than nine months. Newton read the letter again.

"Get anything interesting in that pile of stuff?"
Newton looked up at Willy who had arrived, coffee cup in hand, and took a seat across from him, like he always did.
"Some, but where are we on present day cases?"
"I called the Mounties in the Charlottes and we went over your theory. Turns out you were correct, they found another carving at the hotel with a false bottom. It was empty though, no diamonds."
"And Mr. Johnson?"
"An audit of Johnson's phone records had revealed calls between him and one of his old bosses from New York. Funny thing about that when the New York cops ran that number. It turns out they had been calling the museum too, but not Reggie. They had been to a guy called Homer Baker."
"So Johnson had a partner after all."
"Probably. Mr. Baker has left the employ of the museum. We're looking for him at present."
"Good work, Willy."
"Oh, it gets better. We had the curator produce all the carvings they had in stock, even the ones from the back rooms that hadn't been put on display yet. Turns out there was one other hollowed out piece, found empty of course.
Taylor interviewed Mel after he had regained consciousness, and got more facts about the operation. He had been approached by Johnson over a year earlier when Alicia had brought back one of Mel's pieces. Her intent had been to display works at various stages of completion and talent to round out the exhibit. The museum had other ideas, they only wanted the best they could get, so the carving sat around in storage until Johnson spotted it. Once he got Mel's name he went up and made him a deal."
"What kind of a deal?"
"He would market Mel's art if Mel would in turn steer Alicia to certain pieces of Johnson's choosing. On the night Alicia died, Johnson had been pressuring Mel to get him some better quality pieces to sell, and Mel had refused since the money for the previous pieces had never reached him."
"They had a fight?" Newton asked.
"Yep, Johnson lost it and forced Mel's Jeep onto the sand where it got stuck. Panic set in when Mel couldn't get Alicia's seatbelt to unlock and

he went for help. Instead he found Johnson headed his way in the aluminum boat. Johnson had finally realized that without Mel and Alicia, he had no operation at all, no carvings, no diamonds, nothing but trouble. They returned to the jeep and when Mel attempted to cut Alicia Free in the rapidly rising tide, he missed and stabbed himself."
"But Johnson knew he couldn't let the both of them be found together so he set up the boat to head out to sea and swam for shore. Somehow the boat made it to the eisland where we found it and Mel." Newton filled in. "Then Fran found the carving and brought it down here."
"Right. The carving Alicia was supposed to pick up had been left at the hotel, by who was still a mystery because Johnson was with them."

"Lots of questions still unanswered yet, Willy, like the identity of our Jane Doe."

"Sometimes that's way it works out, boss, sometimes you never get all the answers."
"And sometimes they just come around later, Willy," Newton said, fingering Rusty's letter. "It's all just a matter of time before you find out why."

As he spent the next week going over the evidence and leads, Newton came to several conclusions. One being he would probably never find out the true identity of the girl, another being he would never stop trying. The next was that he had been in this job too long, it was time to retire.

CHAPTER THIRTY NINE

Later that week, the coroner's inquest for the unidentified young girl from the beach was held. The inquest was like a trial. There was a jury, a tired old coroner acting as a judge, and provisions for evidence to be given by witnesses and even a lawyer representing the family of the deceased. In this case, the evidence was scant and unchallenged. The jury hardly needed to retire to confirm the verdict, death by drowning. The how then was established, the why was still a mystery.

By the end of the week, no one had come to claim the girl. She still lay on the metal slab in the dark room at the end of the long corridor. Arrangements were made for a plot in a cemetery. Usually the government set aside a "potters field" for those who were unclaimed. It was located in a small corner of the public cemetery. Newton had a word with those in charge of such plans and a change was made.

The cemetery had grown in stages over the years as the city had grown. The city authorities, recognizing the economies of centralized services, had quietly purchased land on the borders of the field as it became available. Thus, areas that were once at the edge of the field became centralized as the field itself grew. Within such areas, an empty plot could still be found.

The same hearse that brought her there waited at the morgue for her last trip. Usually there was no funeral service in such cases, only a burial. Nevertheless, she was brought to a funeral home whose staff were known to Newton. Officially, the purpose of the service was to see who came. A small announcement was made in the obituary column; the hope was that someone would come. That someone would perhaps be able to shed some light on who she was and what had happened to her. Newton would also be there, observing from the side rooms.

She arrived at the rear of the funeral home. Once again the gurney was unfolded and bore her to another table. A beautician arrived. As she washed the young girl's hair, she wondered who had done that before.

Her mother?
A friend?

Did she have it done at a local parlor?
Where did she apply her makeup on that final day?

And why?
Was she meeting someone?
Going to work?
What were her thoughts?
Where was she going?

In the end no one came.

At the appointed time, a minister arrived at the gravesite to read from the book. Since there was no way to tell the girl's religion, the task of officiating fell to a rotating cycle of clergy. Such duties often fell into a schedule that was eclectic at best. The rites were read, the passages from the book alluding to a new life, a life beyond that of this earth. The promise of resurrection, and a place where there were no mysteries. The staff at the funeral home attended, though none had been asked to. The procession from the home to cemetery was short when it left. As it continued several cabs joined in, their lights on. By the time it arrived an observer from the streets might have guessed it was a funeral for a cabbie.

CHAPTER FORTY

Newton sat at the table, a bottle was open in front of him with a glass. Both were half full. Also on the table was a box, the kind you store evidence in, a common item in police work. The top was dusty and the sides creased with the strain of many moves over the years.

The date on the side was from this day many years ago.

Newton took a sip from the glass and waited for the dawn. The black of night had not yet surrendered to the first rays of the sun, and the low clouds reflected the streetlights. It was a time to reflect on ones' life, the meanderings and strides along a path that we are all destined to walk. The streetlights were of the plans that were manmade, eventually overwhelmed by the much brighter and inexorable light of nature. The path of the one, bright pools in a sea of darkness, each a target to reach, a milestone on the journey, was replaced by a much wider and sharper view, where the possibilities were endless, but the direction less sure.

Newton's life had been that way.

He had not planned to be a police officer. He had planned a life full of adventure on a different front. He had planned on being a pilot; someone whose journeys led to far off lands and interesting people. He had wanted to see the good in the world, to take others to complete their journeys, to meet loved ones and fulfill dreams that had been born of good feelings and happy times.

But the light of a day long ago revealed that that path would be forever closed to him, what God had given him to dream of, he had not provided for in crafting his body. And so he became a policeman by accident, a turn in his path born of circumstance rather than conviction or desire.

Karma

Being a police officer was at first not a bad job, there were many opportunities to use his intellect and natural logic. This despite belonging to an organization that sought out the best and the brightest and then immersed them in a strait jacket like system that seemed to hamstring their efforts and individuality at every turn.

He had married, had a family, and established himself in the community as a whole and in the brotherhood of police.

You couldn't join the brotherhood by whim or wish, it had to accept you first, it allowed you in or it did not.

Membership in the community came about from simply living there and taking part in its activities, coaching a local team, playing hockey in a community league, attending school meetings, and helping out where you could.

The brotherhood was different, another world at times, and the cost of membership was steep.

There were no membership cards, but there were meetings. Those who were members knew their brothers and sisters just by looking at them. Their eyes held the passkeys. A single glance told you if they were in or out.

A moment's conversation told you if they understood.

The world is not always what it seems on the surface, it has many levels. For those of the brotherhood its days were not marked by the normal crises and troubles of life. A car that won't start, a dripping faucet, grass that needs mowing, these are the day to day concerns of others.

For Newton they represented a world that had once been, and to which he had long wished to return. It was a world to which he was now allowed to visit; he could live there for a short time 'til other realities pulled him back. It was like being on vacation for a week or two and then having to return to what he called the "real" world.

The "real" world was a much different place.

The "real" world, his world, the world of the brotherhood was not marked by the same events that the rest of the community saw. Where they looked forward to holidays as a time to relax and be with friends and relatives, for the brotherhood it was a time of battle. They knew these times would be punctuated not by toasts of cheer and the greetings of friends, but by the shattering of glass and metal and lives, by gunshots and angry cries of hate, by brutality dealt with clubs and knives and words.

Their days and nights would likely be spent trying to breath live back into the still warm body of some accident victim, if they could find one with all the pieces.

Eventually life "on the job" superseded life at home. It's not that fixing a squeaky door didn't count, it just that it would never reach a level where it would be noticed.

The gap would widen over time and eventually the world became what it was now, those who understand and those who had never been there, and so could never understand.

Newton sighed softly, took another sip and watched the first rays of the sun as they crept over the horizon. Slowly he reached for the box in front and lifted the lid.

From inside he lifted out a picture. It was of a young girl, a woman really, caught unprepared as she leaned against the railing of a hotel balcony. The picture caught her in transition, no longer a girl, and not yet a woman. She was not smiling, but looking pensively at the sea below, as if she was struggling with that which she was and that which she was becoming.

Newton set the picture up on the table where it would remain for the day. Reaching into the box again he removed a gift wrapped box with a ribbon, and a card. The envelope was old and stained. He removed the card and placed it on top of the unopened present.

"Happy 18th Birthday," it read.

Inside, "With love From Dad."

Newton walked over to the phone and moved it from its place beside the couch to the table. He lifted the receiver to check that it was still working.

His mind knew it would be.

He would wait for the whole day, past sunset until the clock struck 12:00, for the phone to ring.

His mind knew it would not, his heart had to believe it would.

The next day, Newton returned to the patch of earth that marked her final resting place. He removed the small marker that read "Jane Doe."

Un-wrapping a package he took from his coat, he placed it at the head of the grave.

"Someone's Child."
"Age 18."

The End

www.ingramcontent.com/pod-product-compliance
Lightning Source LLC
Chambersburg PA
CBHW022141050726

47590CB00002B/535